CONDOR DREAMS

Western Literature Series

OTHER BOOKS BY GERALD W. HASLAM

Fiction

Okies: Selected Stories

Masks: A Novel

The Wages of Sin: Collected Stories

Hawk Flights: Visions of the West

Snapshots: Glimpses of the Other California

The Man Who Cultivated Fire and Other Stories

That Constant Coyote: California Stories

Many Californias: Literature from the Golden State (*editor*)

Nonfiction

Forgotten Pages of American Literature (*editor*)

The Language of the Oil Fields

Western Writing (*editor*)

California Heartland: Writing from the Great Central Valley (*coeditor*)

A Literary History of the American West (*coeditor*)

Voices of a Place: Social and Literary Essays from the Other California

The Other California: The Great Central Valley in Life and Letters

Coming of Age in California: Personal Essays

The Great Central Valley: California's Heartland

Gerald W. Haslam

Afterword by Gary Soto

UNIVERSITY OF NEVADA PRESS ▲▲ *Reno Las Vegas London*

Condor Dreams

& Other Fictions

Western Literature Series Editor:
John H. Irsfeld

A list of books in the series appears at
the end of the book.

The paper used in this book meets the
requirements of American National
Standard for Information Sciences –
Permanence of Paper for Printed
Library Materials, ANSI Z39.48-1984.
Binding materials were selected for
strength and durability.

Library of Congress
Cataloging-in-Publication Data

Haslam, Gerald W.
Condor dreams and other fictions /
Gerald W. Haslam ; afterword by
Gary Soto.
p.   cm. — (Western literature series)
ISBN 0-87417-227-6 (alk. paper)
ISBN 0-87417-232-2 (pbk. : alk. paper)
1. Working class – California – Central
Valley (Valley) – Fiction.   2. Men –
California – Central Valley (Valley) –
Fiction.   3. Central Valley (Calif. :
Valley) – Fiction.   I. Title.
II. Series.
PS3558.A724C66   1994
813'.54 – dc20   93-33531
                                      CIP

University of Nevada Press
Reno, Nevada 89557 USA
Copyright © 1994 University of
Nevada Press
All rights reserved
Design by Richard Hendel
Printed in the United States
of America
9 8 7 6 5 4 3 2 1

To the memory of my grandparents . . .

Ramona Silva and Jack Johnson,

Marie Martin and Fred Haslam

CONTENTS

CONDOR DREAMS

Standing with his nearly empty coffee cup in one hand, Dan gazed into tule fog dense as oatmeal. It obscured the boundary between sky and earth, between breath and wind, and he was momentarily uncertain where or what he was. He could see nothing. He could not be seen. This must be what nothingness is, he thought, what extinction is . . . like what's happened to the condors. Then he chuckled at himself: Don't lose it, pal. Don't lose it. Stress will do that to you.

He rubbed his chest where it was again tightening. This field is real and those critters are gone, as defunct as family farmers soon will be. As I'll be, Dan thought. His chuckle turned grim.

Nearly fifty years before, on a morning as sunny and clear as this one was foggy and obscure, he had stood next to his father in this same field and seen for the first time a wonder soaring high above – a vast black shape like death itself. Frightened, he moved closer to his father. Then he noticed the bird's bare head and its vast wings. Those dark sails were cored with white, their farthest feathers spread like fingers grasping sky. It appeared to belong to another, sterner time.

"Look, Daniel," his father said, "that's a California condor. See, its wings, they never move. It rides the wind."

"It rides the wind? How, Papa?"

"Ahhh . . . it is just a wind rider, I guess."

"Can I be one?"

"Only in your dreams, Daniel."

"Where did he come from, Papa?" Dan asked.

His father pointed southeast, where the Tehachapi Mountains loomed, where mysterious canyons slashed into them. "There," he explained. "They live where men can't. Years ago, when I come here from the old country, those condors they'd fly out here over the valley every spring to eat winter kills. Sometimes fifty or sixty of 'em. Sometimes maybe a hundred. You could hear their beaks clicking. Now, only four or five ever come."

"Why, Papa?"

"Why?" His father had migrated here from the Azores and worked for other people until he could buy a patch of worn-out range, which he'd then turned into this farm. "I don't know," he finally replied. "Things they changed, eh? Maybe some ranchers they shoot 'em 'cause they think those condors take calves . . . or for the fun of it. Maybe there's not so much for 'em to eat no more. All I ever seen 'em eat is winter kills. I don't know . . ." His voice trailed off, and he seemed genuinely puzzled. A few years later, the boy's father had been a winter kill, drowned by a freak flood pouring from one of those mountain canyons.

Just a few days before his father's death, the two of them had stood on the edge of this very field and spied a dot high against the mountains. They leaned on their shovels and watched it grow larger, closer, since by then appearances of condors over the valley had become rare indeed. A young heifer had died and, as was his habit, his father had left the carcass next to the reservoir, and a cluster of buzzards busied themselves cleaning it up.

Neither man said anything and they stood waiting: Perhaps the great condor might strip this heifer's bones. As though tantalizing them, it approached slowly, so slowly, its white-splotched wings tipping, never pumping, as it sailed far above, then began to swing lower, its great shadow sliding over these acres. Finally, the antique flier swooped down from the wind, and the smaller, squabbling birds quickly bounced away and scrambled into the sky. As the condor began to feed, father and son turned and smiled at one another; they were gazing at a California older than memory.

Dan stood now on the land his family had reclaimed, and he could not see the sky because of the fog that had risen, as it so often did following rains, obscuring nearly everything. If the condors were out there anymore, they were as hidden as other people's dreams. If they were there. Crazy thoughts.

He walked up one long row, grapevines staked on both sides of him, their bare branches trained on wires. Normally the campesinos would be pruning them now, but not this year. Not any year, perhaps. Dan had grown up working these fields that his father and uncle had originally cleared and plowed, that his brothers and sisters and he had irrigated and cultivated and reaped. Now a bank would take it all, the land and the memories. It was grinding to accept. One part of him wanted to weep, another wanted vengeance. He wandered the field now because he could not bring himself to tell Mary everything he had heard the day before at the bank. It was the first significant thing he had ever withheld from her, and that too compounded his tension. Thank God the kids were grown.

He stopped, far from house or road, surrounded by the gray-velvet haze, and listened closely. He had heard a voice. Then he realized it was his own, arguing with himself. That's what this was doing to him, driving him nuts. It would take nearly $300,000 to convert his fields to profitable crops now that table grapes with seeds no longer sold well, but five consecutive losing years had so eroded his credit that he could not raise that kind of backing. His note was due and the once friendly banker demanded payment.

Dan tilted his face skyward and stared into the colorless miasma surrounding him, wanting to scream like a dying animal. Were there condors left up there? Would they come clean his bones? He trudged back toward the house to give his wife the bad news.

The next morning, they sat at the dinette table sipping coffee and gazing out the window at fog as soft as kittens' fur. "Another cold one," he sighed, meaningless talk to fill the silence.

"Why don't you start the pruning?" his wife asked. "It's not like you to give up."

"What's the point?" His voice edged toward anger, for he'd sensed reproach even before she spoke. She didn't understand. This land was his body, and now it would be torn from him. Her way was to stay busy; when her mother'd died, Mary had cooked for three days. But you can't stay busy when your land, your flesh, is being devoured like so much carrion. She didn't understand that.

No, Dan simply wanted revenge. But on whom? The banker who had urged him to expand and had staked him for so many years? The public that ate only Thompson seedless grapes and Perlettes? The county agriculture agent who hadn't warned him about changing tastes? Who?

There was the sharp sound of a car door slamming, then a light knock at the kitchen door. It was 6:45 A.M., and the two glanced at each other across the table before Dan stood and strode to the door.

"Buenos días, Señor Silva," said the old man who stood there, battered five-gallon hat in hand. "Estoy aquí para trabajar." His chin was not quite half shaven, and his faded jeans were only partly buttoned.

"Come on in, Don Felipe," Dan smiled. "You want coffee?"

"Sí, por favor."

"Como? Americano o Mexicano?" It was an old joke between them.

"Solo Mexicano, por favor." The grin was nearly toothless.

Despite the gentle humor, here was one more problem. Felipe Ramirez had been working on this land as long as Dan could remember. His father had originally employed the old man years before. Despite his name and fluent Spanish, he was more than half Yokuts – local Indian. In his prime he had been a vaquero in those far away condor mountains. Dan had always liked him, with his strange but amusing yarns, his unabashed belief in the supernatural – which he said *was* natural.

The old man now lived with a niece in Bakersfield, and Dan annually hired him to help prune grapevines, then kept him on over the summer as a general helper. He was a link to the past, to Dan's own father. Don Felipe remained a strong worker, but his peculiar tales – amusing during good times – would be a burden now.

At the table, Don Felipe bowed to Mary, who smiled and greeted him. He seated himself and accepted a steaming mug of coffee into which he spooned a great mound of sugar. Their conversation was, as always, conducted in two languages, a comfortable weaving of Spanish and English. "Where are the others?" asked the old man.

Dan was suddenly embarrassed. "We haven't begun pruning yet."

"It is too wet?"

"No."

There was a long silence, for the old man would not ask why. It was not his way to probe. "It will be a fine growing year," he finally observed, "all this rain. In my dream, the great green gods were touching you."

"It could be a good year," Dan responded.

"Tell him," said Mary. Her husband briefly glared at her. This was difficult enough without being rushed. She had never understood how men speak to one another . . . or don't speak to one another about some things.

Again there was silence. The old man did not appear anxious. "Would you like some tobacco?" he asked, extending his pouch of Bull Durham.

"No thanks."

Don Felipe knew Mary did not smoke, so no tobacco was offered her. Instead, he rolled a drooping cigarette, carefully twisting both ends. "Do you no longer wish to employ me, Daniel?" He pronounced the name "Don-yale."

"We are losing our ranch, Don Felipe. A bank will take it. But I want you to work with me because there are still some things to be done."

"I am your servant."

"Just take it easy today. Tomorrow I'll have a list of jobs."

"As you wish, Daniel."

Two hours later, a brisk wind broke from the mountains and cleared the fog. Dan emerged from the barn when he heard its swift whine, and walked into cold sunlight, then noted on what they called the old section a lone figure among the vines. What the hell? He strode to the place where Don Felipe pruned grapes.

"Why are you doing this?" he asked, almost demanded, for this land would soon no longer be his, and to work it was suddenly a personal offense. He had not even told Mary that it was rumored the bank would subdivide ranchettes here, a prospect too painful for words.

"It must be done."

"Don't you understand, I won't own this land much longer. I won't harvest grapes this year."

"Daniel," the old man said in a tone Dan had heard before, "no one owns the land. The earth must be nurtured, never owned. Your father knew that and you, deep within, you know that too. It is like a woman, to be loved but never owned. It is not an empty thing but full of life. And these vines are our children."

"Tell the bank that," Dan spat.

"They will build no houses here."

"Houses? Who won't?"

"The bank will build no houses here."

"Of course not. Who said they would?" How had the old man guessed that?

A smile lit the leathery face and the eyes rolled skyward. "Your father started here with only eighty acres, true?"

"Yes."

"How many do you plant now?"

"About thirteen hundred. Why?"

"I am pruning the old eighty acres. You must save them. No houses here, Daniel."

This conversation was crazy. He didn't need it; he had problems enough. "I'm saving all of it or none of it," he snapped. His chest began tightening as he fought rage. Why didn't the old man sense the trouble he was causing? Dan was tempted to call Don Felipe's niece and have her come back for him.

Wind was picking up, blowing north from the distant mountains, and dust was beginning to pepper them. The old man removed a thong from one pocket, wrapped it over his sombrero, and tied it under his chin. "It is the dust of the condors," he said, squinting toward the peaks and canyons to the south. "They will protect this land."

"The condors are dead."

The old man's eyes seemed to crackle for a second, then he smiled. "No, not all of them."

"I'll need some condors, or buzzards maybe, when the bank is through with me."

"The condors, my son, are not mere carrion birds. They bring life from death. They renew, that is why their dust is a good sign. It will be a good year."

"For the bank," Dan said, and he turned toward the house.

That night he could not relax. In the cusp between sleep and wakefulness near dawn, he saw the earth rupture and a gray flatus ooze out, then a great inky bird seemed to swim from it while he struggled to find light . . . find light. He awoke, his breast tight, and immediately stared out the window: Heavy fog pressed against the glass, the world rendered low-contrast and colorless. He couldn't even see the land he was about to lose, and the compression in his chest and jaw were edging toward pain.

He rose quietly, but Mary stirred. "Getting up?" she asked drowsily.

"Yeah." He headed for the bathroom, where he gulped two antacid tablets, then pulled on his jeans and boots, shrugged on a shirt, and finally washed up. In the kitchen, he started coffee, one hand holding his aching breast, then put on his hat and walked out the back door to smell the morning fog.

As he stood in that near-darkness, he heard – or thought he heard – an irregular clicking. Condors? Condors' beaks? For a moment he was puzzled, rubbing his chest, then realized what it had to be: Someone was pruning grapes.

On the old field, he confronted Don Felipe. "Why are you doing this? I'm going to lose the ranch, don't you understand?"

The leathery face smiled, and the old man, still bent with pruning shears in one hand, replied, "When I was a young man, I worked with an old Indian named Castro on the Tejon Ranch in those mountains. He was what you call it? a . . . a wizard, maybe, or a . . . a medicine man. He could do many strange things. He could turn a snake by looking at it. One time I saw him touch a wolf that had killed some sheep and the wolf understood; it never came back. No horse ever bucked him.

"That guy, one time he told me that this life we think is real isn't real at all. He said we live only in the dreams of condors. He said that us Indians

were condors' good dreams, and you pale people were their nightmares."
The old man smiled, then he continued, "He said we can live only if
those birds dream of us."

Dan didn't need this nonsense. "Condors are extinct," he pointed out.
He was sure he'd read that in the newspaper.

The old man only grinned. "Then how are we talking? We are still
here, Daniel, so the condors cannot be gone. You are still here." The old
man paused, then added, "I think that guy he *was* a condor."

Too much, this was just too damned much. He would have to call
Don Felipe's niece as soon as he returned to the house. He just didn't
need this mumbo jumbo on top of the distress he was already suffering.
"Why do you think that?" the younger man snapped.

"Because one day he flew away up a canyon into the heart of the
mountains, and we never saw him again. He said that if the condors
disappeared, so would their dreams. That's what that old Indian told me."

"*Right*," said the despondent farmer, turning away. Why couldn't this
old man understand? Why couldn't he deal with reality? Dan was becoming agitated enough to fire Don Felipe on the spot.

Before he could speak, though, the pain surged from his chest into his
arm and jaw. "Listen . . . ," he began, but did not finish, for breath left
him. "Listen . . . ," he croaked just before he swayed to the damp soil.

"Daniel!" Don Felipe cried. He knelt, and his hard old hands, like
talons, touched the fallen man's face. Dan was straining to speak when
he sensed the fog beginning to swirl and vaguely saw the old man's body
begin to deepen and darken and oscillate. A shadowy shape suddenly
surged and a liquid wing swelled beneath Dan, lofting him from his pain.

A startled moment later, he hovered above a great gray organism that
sent misty tendrils into nearby canyons and arroyos, that moved within
itself and stretched as far north into the great valley as his vision could
reach. It was . . . all . . . so . . . beautiful, and his anxiety drained as he
skimmed wind far above the fog, far beyond it, as he rode his own returning breath, and below the mist began clearing. His fields focused as the
earth-cloud thinned. The land too was breathing, he suddenly realized,
its colors as iridescent as sunlight on the wings of condors. It was all so
alluring that he stretched a hand to touch . . . touch . . . it.

"Dan," Mary's voice startled him, "are you all right?" She cradled his head in her hands and her own face was tight with fear.

It was like waking from his deepest dream but, after a second of confusion, he managed a smile. "I'm okay." An edge of breathlessness remained, that and pain's shadow, so he hesitated before, with her help, climbing to his feet. Past his wife's shoulder he saw the old man, whose dark eyes merged momentarily with his. "I just let tension get to me," he explained. Rising, he brushed wet earth from his jeans. "I'll drive into town and see the doc just in case."

The easy tone of his voice seemed to reassure his wife. "Let's go have our coffee," she urged.

"Sure," he replied, putting an arm around her waist, his relief at being able to touch her as tangible as breath itself, then turning toward the old man. "Don Felipe, are you coming in?"

"I must finish the field."

"Okay," Dan replied, "I'll bring something out, and I'll give you a hand when I get back from the doctor's." This place, even eighty acres of it, was worth saving. There had to be a way.

"I will be grateful," the old man nodded.

After Dan and Mary turned, they could hear Don Felipe's shears clicking like a condor's beak. Arm in arm, they walked toward home. The fog had dissipated enough so that their house shone sharp and white across the field of dormant vines. Behind it, bordering the hazy valley, those mountains, the Tehachapis, bulked like the land's surging muscles: creased and burnished and darkened with bursts of oaks and pines, flexing into silent summits and deep canyons where valley winds were born, into the hidden heart of the range where Dan now knew a secret condor still dreamed.

COWBOYS

This old boy named Shorty Moore used to haul mud out to the rig, see. Shorty he could whup a man and he never ducked a fight, so not many guys in the oil fields ever give him much trouble.

One time old Shorty he was sittin' around the doghouse at quittin' time discussin' this new pistol he'd just bought while us guys changed to go home, and a engineer looked at Shorty's duds, then asked real smart alecky if he was a cowboy. All of us on the crew just set back to watch Shorty stomp the bastard, see, but old Shorty he fooled us. He looked around, kind of grinned, and said real quiet: Naw, I ain't no cowboy. Never have been. But I wear these boots and this belt and shirt because they're western, see, workin' men's clothes. And I feel western. I ain't no college sissy with a necktie and pink hands. I'm a man and that's what my clothes say. Any old boy that doubts it ain't got but to jump and I'll kick his ass for him.

That was that. The engineer never said nothin' more, so old Shorty just let things slide and I guess everyone was happy to get out of the doghouse that afternoon.

But, you know, every time a guy turns around in Bakersfield nowadays, seems like, some pasty-faced bastard's eyein' your belt buckle or boots, and you just know he's a-thinkin' *cowboy* and laughin' at you to hisself. They all think they're high powers. I ain't like old Shorty; things like that just eat on me. I work as hard as any man does for my wages, a-buckin' pig iron on a drillin' rig, and I can't take some pencil-necked fairy that works in a office looking down his nose at me. I'll break his nose for him, by God.

Last summer, whenever the college kids come out to replace guys goin' on vacation, wouldn't you know we'd get us a hippie. And it was comical as hell whenever this kid first drove up to the rig. We'd just spudded in, see, a-hopin' to hit gas on Suisun Bay up near Fairfield. It was tower change and my crew was workin' daylights. About the time we walked out of the doghouse, and old Turk Brown's crew was comin' off, see, up sputters a little red sports car with this great big long-haired kid a-drivin' it. Well, he gets out of the car, all the guys kinda standing back watchin' him, and he commences talkin' to the pusher. That kid was so huge, and his car was so small, he looked like a big old snake coming out of a little basket: more and more of him kept coming after you just knew the car couldn't hold all of him.

Old Arkie Williams he made a kissin' sound with his mouth and the kid looked at him. I seen cold eyes before, but that kid looked like he could put a fire out starin' at it. And I could see that even though Arkie kept on bullshittin', he knew he'd made a mistake. Is it a boy or a girl? Arkie said. He never did have enough sense to admit he was wrong after he started spoutin' off. The pusher told us to get up on the rig and pull them slips, and the kid he was still just a-lookin' at Arkie, not sayin' nothin'; I figured Arkie was into it. Too bad for him too. He never could fight a lick.

The kid he went to work that mornin' and spent the whole tower helping Buford Kileen clean out the pumps. Come quittin' time, we all headed for the doghouse hot to get changed and go drink us some beer. Just about the time Arkie walked up to the doorway from between pipe racks, the new kid he stepped in front of him and bam! one-punch-cold-

cocked him. Jesus, could that big old kid hit! And that ain't all; Arkie
hadn't but hit the ground and the hippie had him kicked three or four
times. We grabbed the kid and had one hell of a time holdin' him while
two boys from the crew that was just comin' to work helped Arkie. The
pusher he took the kid into his office and told him, I guess, any more
fightin' and he'd be canned. And the pusher took Arkie aside and told
him he'd got just what he deserved.

What really disturbed me though was that the new kid never said nothing. After it was over he just climbed out of his work clothes and into them
suede drawers with fringes on 'em, and high cowboy boots, and a western
belt with a big turquoise buckle. He put on some little colored beads and
a leather sombrero and out he walked, no shirt a-tall. He climbed into
his little red car, see, and drove off without saying good-bye or kiss my ass
or nothin'.

After he was gone some of the guys commenced kidding about the
highfalutin cowboy clothes the kid wore. I'll bet he never rode nothing
but that little red car, old Buford said, 'cept maybe a few of them college
coeds. Everyone laughed. Yeah, Easy Ed Davis said, he's a real cowpoke,
that one, must think he's Buffalo Bill with that long hair. Reckon we
ought to buy him some ribbons to go with them beads? I asked. Arkie
never laughed, then pretty soon he ups and says that if the kid ever messed
with him again, by God, there'd be one more cowboy on Boot Hill.
Shorty Moore showed up a little later at this beer joint where we usually
went, and he said he didn't have no use for hippies period. No use a-tall.

The kid turned out to be one hell of a worker; he give a honest jump for
his wages, I'll say that much. He never let none of the boys on the job get
real friendly with him, but he seemed to like it when they commenced
callin' him Cowboy. He didn't know that most of the guys wanted to call
him Dude, but they thought better of it. He was a big old boy.

I could tell he really didn't give a damn for none of us. Whenever he
did talk to us it was to show off all of his book learnin' and to hint at how
ignorant he figured we was. You know, one of us might say he thought
the Dodgers would go all the way this year, and young Cowboy he'd kind
of sneer: It all depends on whether they can exploit more blacks than
the other teams, he'd say – shit like that. Hell, he couldn't stand to see
us enjoy nothin'; he liked to wreck things for everyone, it seemed like.

Cowboy he was studying to be a college pro-fessor and he had about that much sense.

A couple of months after he first come to work, we finally lifted the kid. He was tougher than most summer hires to trick because he didn't talk much, and he didn't seem to give a damn about what we thought of him. But old Easy Ed, our derrick man, he finally bullshitted the kid into it. Easy Ed could talk a coon white if you give him half a chance. He just kept a-gabbin' at Cowboy all the time, see, telling him he didn't know what a strong man was. Hell, old Ed would say, a young buck like you ain't seen a stout man till you seen a old-timer like me hot after it. There ain't many old boys in this oil patch can lift as much weight as me, by God. I can pick up three guys at one time. Easy Ed's just a little bitty fart, and the kid would kind of look at him funny but not say nothin'. It was comical, really. Cowboy would bring all these books with him to read when he ate, but he'd no more than get his dinner bucket open than Easy Ed would be a-chewing on his ear. I believe that kid finally give in just to shut Ed up.

We was circulatin' mud and waitin' for the engineers to give us the go-ahead on making more hole that day; everyone was pretty bored. We'd just finished unloading sacks of chemicals off Shorty's truck, and we was kind of layin' around on the mud rack chewin' tobacco and tellin' lies. Pretty soon up comes Easy Ed and he right away starts in on Cowboy. Before long the kid said okay, let's see you lift three guys.

So everybody trooped around behind the rig, and old Ed he laid down a length of rope on the ground. Then he said: three of you boys lay down on her. Heavy, he said to me, you take one side. Shorty, you take the other. Cowboy, you crawl in the middle. I want you to know there ain't no trick to it. We three got down on our backs while the other guys stood around us. Ed just kept a-jabbering, see. I swear, that guy should of been a preacher; he damn sure coulda talked some sisters into the bushes.

Well, anyways, old Ed he tells us three to wrap our arms and legs around each other (me and Shorty knowin' this stuff from way back but not lettin' on, so the kid won't suspect nothin'). Now make her real tight, Ed tells us, I don't want nobody slippin' whenever I pick y'all up. Me and Shorty really cinched up on the kid's arms and legs, see. We had him pinned to the ground, and I could tell he was catchin' on.

Ed, a-yackin' all the time, commenced unbuttonin' Cowboy's fly and Buford handed Ed the dope brush. The kid tensed up, then kind of chuckled and relaxed. Ah, shit, he said, laughin' a little. I figured then it was gonna be a easy liftin', and that the kid wasn't half bad after all. But just about the time Easy Ed started painting the kid's balls with dope, old Arkie couldn't keep his mouth shut. He kind of spit at the kid: In the position you let us get you in, weevil, just thinka all the things we *could* do to you. Then he made that kissin' sound.

Oh Jesus! The kid just exploded! I'm a pretty stout old boy myownself, see, but Cowboy just sort of shook me loose, then kicked Ed in the slats with his free foot. I've helped lift maybe a hundred weevils in my day, and nobody never just shook me off before. Old Shorty hung on and in a minute the two of them was rollin' around in the dust and puncture vines. Shorty don't know how to give up in a fight, and he held on to that big old boy like a dog on a bull.

We knew the pusher would can the kid if he seen him fightin', so we all jumped in and broke her up. When we managed to get 'em apart, the kid's eyes locked on Shorty, and Shorty he stuck his finger in the kid's face and said: Name the place, Cowboy. We'll finish her where there ain't nobody gonna get in the way. The kid just kept starin' and said anyplace was fine with him.

There was this little beer joint at a eucalyptus grove between where we was drillin' and Rio Vista. That's where Shorty and the kid decided to meet after work. The whole crew drove right over there and drank beer while they waited for Shorty to get back from Lodi where he left his truck in the chemical company's yard every evenin'. The kid he stayed out-side a-leanin' on his little red car, see, his sombrero tilted back, his long hair a-blowin' in the wind. Them frozen blue eyes of his just glowed. Damned if he don't look like some old-time gunfighter, Buford said, lookin' out the window. I told him that was one cowboy I didn't want to tangle with. You notice he never messes with me no more, Arkie bragged, and all the guys laughed, but old Arkie was serious and he didn't see nothin' funny. Naturally, Easy Ed took to laying bets: I taken old Shorty, he said, and I'll put five bucks on him. Buford covered him right away. Arkie bet on Shorty too, and Buford covered him. Ain't you a-bettin',

Heavy? Ed asked me, but I said no. I never felt too good about the whole thing.

Shorty he drove up directly and crawled out of his Chevy. It was near sundown and the light it'd turned all funny like in a movie. For a minute him and Cowboy just stood there starin' at each other, then Cowboy he bent over and reached into his car and pulled out a gunbelt, the old kind with ammunition loops and long thongs danglin' from the holster. He slipped her on and tied the thongs around his right thigh. Hey! I heard Buford say and when I looked away from the kid, I seen old Shorty he was doin' the same thing.

All of us guys froze. Cowboy and Shorty they pulled their six-guns from the holsters, spun the cylinders and kinda blew on the sights. Then they slid the revolvers back into leather and commenced walkin' toward each other. What the hell is this? Easy Ed whispered, but I couldn't answer, my heart was a-stompin' inside my chest and I couldn't even swallow. I wanted to holler, but I just stood there.

When they was about twenty-five or thirty foot apart – real close – Cowboy and Shorty stopped, then spread their legs like they was gonna pick up somethin' heavy. It's yer play, dude, Shorty said, his eyes pointed straight at Cowboy's. Cowboy he kinda rocked back on his heels: You've been alive too long, he croaked. You've outlived yourself.

Then a roar! For what seemed like forever, they dipped their right shoulders and threw their right hands straight down. There wasn't no fancy grabbin' and wingin', movie-style, just two short, efficient moves, like when a good worker shovels.

And Shorty busted backwards, almost up in the air, then fell, a puppet without no strings, empty, his gun in the dirt. A cloud of blue smoke hung where he'd stood.

Oh sweet lovin' Jesus! I cried out, and I run over to Shorty, but he'd had it. He was all sprawled out, his eyes lookin' like egg-whites. Little frothy bubbles was comin' from his brisket, but not much blood. He coughed, choked maybe, and a gusher shot up from his mouth and from the hole in his middle, then the bubbles quit.

Get your ass away from him, I heard Cowboy say. I looked at the kid. He still held his six-gun, and some of the blue smoke still hung there in front of him; there wasn't no wind. I looked back down at Shorty and seen a great big puddle of blood was growing underneath him, peekin' out, not red but maroon, almost black. Get! Cowboy hollered again, so I walked back to where the other boys stood. I couldn't do old Shorty no good.

Cowboy he holstered his pistol, untied the thong, then slipped the gunbelt off and dropped it into his car. You guys gonna buy me a beer? he asked. None of us said nothin'. I didn't figure so, he said. He climbed into his car, backed up – me afraid he was a-gonna run over Shorty but he was real careful not to – then started out onto the road. Then he done something real funny; he slowed down, almost stopped, and flashed us one of them V-peace signs hippies are always makin'. He drove away toward Fairfield, up over a low hill into the fadin' sun.

Jesus, Buford said, what're we gonna do?

Easy Ed he just kept lookin' from where Shorty lay with a big old blow-fly already doin' business on his bloody lower lip, then back toward the hill where Cowboy'd disappeared. We might could form a posse, he said.

IT'S OVER . . .

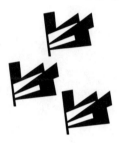

Over Wynonna's shoulder, I see Elaine chatting with friends, then I grin at the attractive woman standing directly in front of me and reply, "Sure, why not?"

"For old times' sake," she adds. "Right, old-timer?"

"Right, old-timer," I chuckle, and we join other couples on the floor.

The first time I ever danced with Wynonna was in this same high school multipurpose room nearly thirty years ago. We were fourteen-year-old freshmen at an afternoon sock hop. There was a girls'-choice dance, and her cronies dared her to ask a boy. Saucy, she bounced to the stag line and without hesitation pulled me onto the floor.

We went steady for the next four years until she departed for college and a much larger world than Bakersfield promised, leaving me devastated by the certain knowledge that my plans – my assumptions – had been wrong and would never be realized. Shortly thereafter, I was drafted into the army and began the odyssey that would lead me from a dead-end job at a gas station to college, then graduate school. Nearly thirty years ago it had started in this very room . . .

> *It's over.*
> *All over,*
> *And soon somebody else*
> *will make a fuss over you*
> *but how about me?*

As a singer purrs, my high school love and I move together, facing one another, bodies still familiar. Despite my casual smile, I am breathless. "Your wife is lovely, Nicky," Wynonna smiles. "She really is. I'd heard that, but she's even nicer and prettier than I expected."

"Elaine's a great gal."

"You've been lucky."

"Yeah, I have . . . we have. And you?" It is an unintentionally thought-less question. She's been married three times, I know.

Without hesitation, she grins. "Mixed bag. All big shots, dot the o's, if you get my meaning." Her legal practice in Santa Barbara is elite, mutual friends have told me. Little wonder she encounters big shots, dotted o's or not.

"I'm sorry."

"*You're* sorry"; she raises her eyebrows. Her voice is thick with wine, and mine is too, I guess. We're well into the evening.

From the moment Wynonna entered the reunion – our class's twenty-fifth – I had fought not to stare at her: It had been so long and she looked so trim, so youthful, so . . . yes . . . so expensive. While she hugged old chums and laughed with them, I managed to exchange a quick hand-shake with her, a moment of eye contact, while I sensed the gaze of others on us, then drifted away to those old friends with whom Elaine and I remained close.

So many years ago, Wynonna and I had explored life's currents and channels, learned together some mysterious lessons that have not left me. We had, of course, invented sex – secret and overwhelming – and it be-came deliciously central to our relationship. But there had been another, less understandable, less escapable bonding: not sister and brother, something deeper and more enduring. It can still swoop my stomach at odd times.

"Do you remember our first dance, Nicky?" she asks. My wife – everyone else, in fact – calls me Nick.

"Yeah." She should ask if I remember breathing.

"You asked me right in this room when we were freshmen."

"No, it was girls' choice. You asked me."

"No, I didn't. *You* asked me," she giggles.

There had been hints late in our senior year – she had less time for dates, we had no more noon rendezvous, my phone calls increasingly went unanswered – signs that her interests were turning from me, and the plans we'd made, toward the universities that beckoned a top student. Although my job at the service station paid little, I had simply and naively assumed that we'd graduate, marry, and live happily ever after, as the popular songs promised.

One terrible Saturday afternoon Wynonna had emerged with an icy face from her house to greet me. She looked delicious in pink shorts and a white blouse while I stood on her porch, fresh from work, wearing an oil-stained shirt with "Nick" sewn on one pocket. I don't think I'd ever wanted to hold her more, but she curtly informed me that she would leave the following August to attend the University of California in Los Angeles. Our marriage would have to wait until after she graduated. Her tone told me far more, and that evening I'd picked a fistfight with a guy I didn't know.

"You have four kids now?" she asks.

"Two boys, Dan and Nick; two girls, Kelly and Kit."

"Do you worry about your girls? You sure made my folks worry about me – for good reason, as it turned out." Her laugh is deep and intimate.

"No, I really don't, not about *that* anyway. Or about my boys either. What we did all seems pretty innocent today . . . so – what's the word? – so *sincere*, so *earnest*."

"Yes," she replies, and her eyes leave mine. Her voice has suddenly lost its happy edge.

"And your family?" I ask, changing the subject.

"I have the one boy, Bradley, from my first marriage. He's at Dartmouth."

"Danny and Kelly are both attending Cal Poly."

"Oh," she says with – or do I merely imagine – the tiniest hint of condescension.

If we had actually married immediately after high school, I wouldn't have been drafted, wouldn't have qualified for the GI Bill and wouldn't have been able to attend college; I certainly wouldn't have become principal of the local junior high school. What either of us would be doing now is anyone's guess. Whether I'd have been the first of a string of husbands, whether she'd be another frustrated housewife or ex-wife struggling through college in her forties, whether we'd be mired in debt and hopelessness and mutual disdain or be one of those rare and enchanting couples who somehow have managed to keep it all together – it's anybody's guess.

While the music sweeps, she says, "My folks were relieved to be rid of you." Her eyes still look away, her voice remains deep.

"Your folks? I thought they liked me."

"They said you were going nowhere, that you were irresponsible and didn't have any ambition. They even said you'd probably get tired of me and leave me."

"Your folks? They said that? I *really* thought they liked me." I have never heard this before and am both shocked and pained by it.

"Oh, they did. But they *loved* me, and they were ambitious for me. They wanted me to have chances they didn't have. You were an obstacle."

Still uncomfortable about what she has revealed, I reply, "Not much of one, as it turned out."

"They said you weren't dumb but that you weren't motivated."

"I was young and in love," I point out, having to clear my thickening throat.

"Yes," she says, her own voice softer. We fall silent once more, and her head is suddenly on my shoulder, her cheek next to mine. "Do you remember when we broke up, Nicky?" she breathes into my ear.

"I remember that we unraveled like a bad braid."

"No. I mean what happened at Don and Donna's party?"

We had been at Don Smith and Donna Pasquinni's wedding reception, just before Wynonna left for UCLA. We had danced – the last time until tonight – then sipped champagne at a corner table while she delicately explained that, after talking with her mother, she had decided that each of us should date others while she was away at school. "Is that all?" I asked. "Do we do anything besides 'date'?"

"I wouldn't do *that* with anyone else." Her eyes glistened, and one hand reached across the table and took mine, but I was receiving another, darker message, the final shredding of my dream.

"Do you really want someone else's babies?" I demanded in a cracking voice. Irrational as it seems now, it was my soundless heart's most honest cry. I'd sensed even before this conversation that other forces now determined her life and that I was powerless, but at least I could speak what I felt.

Her eyes flashed. "I didn't say *breed*, I said *date*," she snapped, her rationality and resolve negating my plea.

A moment later, I stood and said, "I've gotta go."

"I want to stay till Donna throws her bouquet." Wynonna remained seated. My eyes were imploring, hers implacable.

"Fine," I said. "I'll see you." I turned and walked away, my heart crumpling, my pride intact. Yearning immediately dislodged my innards as I drove away, a desolation I would not fully escape for years, and I kept glancing at the rearview mirror hoping that she'd emerge from the increasingly distant doorway to join me, but she didn't. For the first time since childhood, I wept.

Wynonna's voice grows even softer, her breath warmer on my ear where her lips brush. "I wanted your baby, Nicky, I really did, but my folks put so much pressure on me . . ." I feel that odd-but-not-unfamiliar sensation of her warm tears wetting my cheek. There is a sigh so deep that I seem to feel her lighten, then she adds, "I still want it."

Our bodies are moving together, her breath lurching into my ear and that distant, familiar passion again dislodges my heart. I cannot breathe. I cannot move my head to reply. And I cannot allow the music to stop.

But it does.

SCARS

. . . on left calf. Unobtrusive. No surgery recommended.

No. 16 (age 11): Chicken pox. Pitting on forehead and both cheeks. Cosmetic surgery recommended but declined.

No. 17 (age 12): Bicycle accident. Severe contusion and laceration of lower jaw. Large cicatrixive seam on chin. Cosmetic surgery successful.

No. 18 (age 12): The smell of alcohol and perfume awakened him, those and her touch. "What?" he asked groggily. No reply, but he felt her hands moving, caressing him there. "Momma?" he said. "What're you doing?" The hands moving, then the mouth on him. "Momma? What're . . . *ohhhh!*" Psychotherapy continues.

No. 19 (age 14): Football. Fractured nose. Slightly askew after healing. Adds character. No surgery recommended.

No. 20 (age 16): "Hey, pretty boy! You look like a queen to me. Come 'ere. I wanna feed you through this tube. Come 'ere sweetness, I got a tube steak for you." Psychotherapy continues.

No. 21 (age 17): Fistfight. Lacerated right upper lip. Cracked right incisor. Tooth later capped. Cicatrix on lip. Adds character. No surgery recommended.

No. 22 (age 17): He flipped on the light and a nude stranger jerked upright from the couch, blinking. Then he heard his mother's mushy voice – "Who'sh there?" – and she sat up. Also naked. Psychotherapy continues.

No. 23 (age 17): Basketball. Severe laceration of left ocular region. Disfiguring keloid extending from mid-eyebrow, around outer portion of ocular depression onto upper cheek. Cosmetic surgery only partially successful.

No. 24 (age 17): "Hey, Paul, look at this guy's picture in the paper that got sentenced to prison in L.A. He looks just like you, and he's even got the same name. He's not your *dad*, is he? Ha-ha!" Psychotherapy continues.

No. 25 (age 17): "I mean it, man. She wants to have you. Nobody at school knows she screws but me. I been tappin' her since sophomore year. Now she wants to try you. Hey, I can share. Pussies don't wear out. Come on, man. Come on." Psychotherapy continues.

No. 26 (age 18): Football. Major disruption of collateral ligaments of right knee. Surgically repaired. Further participation in contact sports barred. Keloid on knee obtrusive. Psychotherapy continues.

No. 27 (*age 20*): "Do you really, Paul? Do you really love me? Do you. . . . Uhhh! Uhhh! Uhhh! Ohhh! Dooo! Youuu?" Psychotherapy continues.

No. 28 (*age 21*): Second-degree burn on palm of right hand. Keloid in unobtrusive location. Surgery postponed pending further evaluation.

No. 29 (*age 22*): "Listen, you're a good-lookin' kid. I can use you for the part. Now sit down, relax, have a drink with me. Unbutton your shirt, why don't you? No one's gonna interrupt us here in my office." Psychotherapy continues.

No. 30 (*age 23*): Laceration of left elbow. Patient shows increasing tendency to produce keloids. Further evaluation pending.

No. 31 . . .

MAL DE OJO

My grandmother really didn't want me hanging around Mr. Samuelian's yard, but I did anyways. He was the old poet who lived next door to Abuelita and me, and for some reason she didn't like him; she said he was crazy, but us guys all loved him. He was the only grown-up in the neighborhood who treated us like friends, not kids. That week me and Flaco Perez and Mando Padilla we were working with him on a big birdhouse – "a hotel for our little friends," he called it.

"Friends!" huffed Grandma when I told her. "Those birds eat my garden. They leave the nasty white spots! First that mad Armenian *feeds* them, and now he *houses* them. He is *loco!*" She sounded genuinely agitated.

"They're just birds, Abuelita," I pointed out.

"You have no idea the damage they do. Like that crazy Armenian, they are a menace."

What could I say? "Okay."

"I warn you, *mijito*. Avoid that Armenian. He is *peligroso*."

"Dangerous?"

"He reads all those books."

"Oh," I said.

Abuelita prided herself in being plainspoken. My father had once said to me, "Your grandmother not only calls a spade a spade, she calls a lot of other things spades too."

She had not liked the poet much since that first day when he'd moved into the neighborhood and she'd asked if he wasn't an Armenian. He said no, his parents had been Armenians but he was an American, born and raised in Fresno. That answer displeased Abuelita, who always identified people by nationalities . . . or her version of nationalities, anyways.

Mr. Samuelian, in response, asked what nationality she was and, like always, my grandma said, "Spanish."

"Spanish," he grinned, "what part of Spain are you from?"

Abuelita really didn't like that – the words or the grin – since she, like me, had been born in Bakersfield. "My *people* were from Spain," she spat. What's funny is that my Mom told me our family came from Mexico, not Spain.

"*Voy a pagarlo en la misma moneda*," Abuelita had mumbled after that encounter, but I didn't understand what she meant, something about paying him the same money. My father was a gringo and he hadn't let my momma use much Spanish around me – before they got divorced, I mean – and I had come to live with my grandma so Momma could go to L.A. and find a good job.

Anyways, me and Flaco and Mando were working on the hotel that next afternoon while Mr. Samuelian was at the library. We were finishing it up, really, when a big shiny car swooped into the dirt driveway of the yard. Since our neighbor owned only a bicycle, I had rarely seen an automobile here.

A husky man who favored Mr. Samuelian, but real suntanned like he worked outside all the time, he swung from the door. He had the same burst of white hair, the same hook of a nose; his eyebrows were black and he had a ferocious black mustache. One of his eyes was covered by a dark patch. "Hello, my lads!" he called. "Where is Sarkis Samuelian?"

"He went to the library," I answered.

"Always reading. He will destroy his vision yet. And who are you young men?"

"I'm Gilbert. I live next door. This is Flaco and Mando."

"Well, young gentlemen, I am Haig Samuelian, brother of Sarkis Samuelian. And what do you work on?"

"It's just this birdhouse," Mando answered.

"Be careful with those tools, my lads. See this?" he tugged at the patch that covered his eye. "A stray screwdriver can put your eye out!"

"Oh!" I said involuntarily. I'd heard all my life about the variety of implements that might put an eye out, but this was my first contact with someone to whom it had actually happened.

Before I could inquire further, the poet returned toting a load of books. "Ahhh!" he called. "My little brother visits! Why aren't you in Fresno counting your raisins?"

"Only a fool counts his raisins and ignores his grapes!" responded the one-eyed man, and he hugged Mr. Samuelian. "I've just been commiserating with your associates here."

"Oh," grinned our neighbor, "these young scamps. They're doing a fine job on the new birdhouse, though. Come in, Haig, we must have coffee. How's Aram? Where is Malik's son now? And Dorothy, still a dancer?" They disappeared into the house.

As soon as they were gone, Flaco said, "That guy I think he got his you-know-what poked out."

We enlivened the remainder of the afternoon discussing his poked eye. "I wonder what's left. I wonder is it just a hole there," said Mando.

"Maybe it's all dried up like Mrs. Lopez's dried-up old hand," Flaco suggested.

"Grossisimo!" It was a word we'd invented, so we giggled together.

"Maybe it's like that place where there use to be a boil on your brother Bruno's neck," I told Mando.

"Grossisimo!" he said.

Before we went home that night, Haig Samuelian handed each of us a small bag of pomegranates. "Those are from Fresno, my lads. They are the finest in the world."

"Gee, thanks."

I took mine to Grandma, but she would not touch them. "You got these from that Armenian *pirata*? Him with his *mal de ojo?*"

"Bad of eye?" A lot of the stuff she said in Spanish wasn't clear to me.

"The *evil* eye, *mijito,* the *evil* eye."

"Evil eye? Abuelita, that's just Mr. Samuelian's brother . . ."

"Another of those Armenians!" she hissed.

". . . and he got that eye poked out by a screwdriver."

"You are young," she told me. "You haven't seen behind that mask. You do not understand the realm of evil."

"The realm of evil?"

She stopped then and gazed directly at me. "If you ever look deeply into *un mal de ojo* you will see Hell itself."

"Hell itself?" I didn't have a clue what she was talking about.

"Pray your rosary," she cautioned.

"Okay."

"And don't be working outside in the sun with those two *malcriados*," she added.

"Why?"

"It will make you dark like a *cholo*. You must wear a hat, *mijito*."

Like a *cholo*? That's the name the guys at school called all the kids – mostly Indians – who'd just come from Mexico. Hey, I *wanted* to be dark like them so I wouldn't look different from the other kids in my class. At Our Lady of Guadalupe School, I was the only Ryan amidst Martinezes and Gonzalezes and Jiminezes. I'll tell you a secret: One day, when Abuelita wasn't home, I even put black shoe polish on my hair, but it looked real dopey. I had a heck of a time washing it out before she got back.

Anyway, the morning after our *cholo* talk I couldn't wait to dash outside into the sunlight and slip over to our neighbor's yard, maybe steal a glance behind that patch. The large car was still there, but its owner wasn't in sight, so I helped Mr. Samuelian water his weeds. Then he busied himself reciting his latest verse – "Great unconquered wilderness is calling, calling me! Its crystal peaks and wooded glens all yearn to set me free!" – while staking up peas. Before long, the man with a hole in his face emerged from the small house and began picking and sampling ripe plums from a tree in the overgrown yard. "These are wonderful," he said, "almost as good as the ones in Fresno."

After a moment, his tone deepened: "You see those sharp stakes Sarkis carves. Beware of them! My eye . . ." he said heavily, pulling at his patch.

I gulped.

Later that day, me and Mando and Flaco we were erecting the bird hotel when this big mean kid named David Avila, who had chased us home from school more than once, he swaggered up and stood on the dirt border between the yard and the pitted street. A week before he'd caught me and given me a Dutch rub and a pink belly too; he especially liked to pound my pale skin because it turned red so easily. Avila he looked like a large brown toad and he was almost that smart, but he had real biceps and the beginnings of a mustache. Only a year ahead of us at Our Lady of Guadalupe School, he was already a teenager.

Anyways, the big toad he kind of studied us, sneered, then hollered, "Hey, leettle *pendejos*, I can't wait for them birds. I got me a BB gun and I'll keell 'em all. Maybe I'll shoot you three leettle *pendejos* too. You just wait!"

"No, *you* just wait, young criminal!" I heard a shout, and Mr. Samuelian's brother dashed from the plum tree's foliage – I don't think Avila had noticed him there. In a moment, he had the bully by the neck and was shaking him with one hand while he thrust an open wallet into his face with the other. "Do you see this badge?" he demanded. "I'll have you in jail for *years* if you bring a BB gun around here! Do you understand? Do you see this patch? A BB gun!" He shook Avila again.

The bully had wilted quickly under Haig Samuelian's storm, and once released, he scurried away.

"Scalawag!" the one-eyed man shouted after him. "Scoundrel," he continued fuming as he returned, his fierce mustache twitching. "I can have him jailed!" He thrust his wallet toward us and displayed a small badge that said, "Friend of the Fresno County Sheriff's Department."

"Ah, Haig! Haig!" called Mr. Samuelian, emerging from his pea patch to pound his brother's back. "Ever the crusader!"

"BB guns!" said Haig Samuelian, and he spat vehemently on the ground and jerked his patch momentarily.

"Come," urged Mr. Samuelian, "let me give you a glass of tea, Haig," and they entered the small house.

"I bet it's a glass eye under that patch is what," said Mando. "I tried to look under when he was pickin' plums, but I couldn't see nothin'."

"I think it's a big ol' bloody hole," suggested Flaco.

"With worms, maybe," I added. "I'll bet there's big worms in it."

"Grossisimo!" chorused my pals.

I joined my grandma talking to our other neighbor, Mrs. Alcala, when I arrived home for dinner. "Esperanza, you didn't actually *eat* the pomegranates that *brujo* gave you?" Abuelita demanded.

"Of course," smiled old Mrs. Alcala, who was Flaco's grandmother. "They were delicious. And he's not a *brujo*, Lupe, he's just another Samuelian, a gentleman but . . . ah . . . *very* enthusiastic."

"Enthusiastic?"

"And very friendly," added Mrs. Alcala.

"*Two* of those Armenians now," my grandma said. "Both of them *loco*."

Mrs. Alcala was smirking when she added, "The Samuelians aren't the only *locos* in this neighborhood."

"And what is *that* supposed to mean, Esperanza?"

"Oh nothing," replied the old woman, grinning as she hobbled away on two canes. "Hasta la vista, Lupe."

That long, warm evening the Samuelian brothers sat in wooden lawn chairs talking, and after Grandma freed me from chores I wandered over to listen. "That was the day I fought Dikran Nizibian, the terror. Remember, Sarkis? I fought him for an hour and fifteen minutes nonstop, the longest and fiercest battle in the history of Fresno. We fought all the way up Van Ness Avenue to Blackstone, and then we fought for a mile down Blackstone. Our sweat flowed through the gutters. The police stood back in awe to watch such a battle. Businesses closed. Priests held crosses to their hearts. Doctors averted their eyes. Strong women prayed. Strong men fainted."

"Who won? Who won?" I asked, breathless.

"Who won?" he paused. Mr. Samuelian's brother twitched his mustache and tugged his patch. "I'll tell you who won. Do you see this eye?" he pointed at the cloth covering his empty socket. "The evil Dikran Nizibian tried to *gouge* it out in the middle of Blackstone Avenue in

Fresno forty years ago, but . . ." another pause, another twitch, another tug . . . "he regrets it to this day because I knew a secret: Never use more when less will do! Never use two when one will do! I had saved my final strength. With it, I threw the ruthless Nizibian from me and broke everything on him that could be broken. I broke several things that *couldn't* be broken. He never fought again, did he, Sarkis?"

"Not that I remember," replied Mr. Samuelian.

"He never bullied anyone again."

"Not that I remember."

"Nizibian the terror was finished," Haig Samuelian nodded with finality, pulling absently at his patch.

"*Gouged* his eye out," I mumbled as I wandered home.

I told my pals the story of the great Fresno fight the next day at school. We were all eager to hurry back that afternoon and hear more from Mr. Samuelian's brother. On our way, however, while discussing the vast pit that had been gouged in Haig Samuelian's face by the evil Nizibian, and hoping at last to catch a glimpse of its depths, we spied David Avila striding toward us. Oh, no! We immediately began sprinting, each in a different direction, in the hope the bully might be confused.

Unfortunately for me, he wasn't. I was the only blond at Guadalupe School, so when Avila selected a target, I was usually his first choice. I didn't feel honored by that. I didn't have time to feel anything but scared because I was too busy sprinting. The bully was after me at a dead run. Although I was carrying my slingshot, it never occurred to me to use it because I was too busy trying to escape.

I was pretty fast for a little kid, and I got even faster with David Avila on my tail, so at first I kept him way behind me. I was sprinting and glancing back, sprinting and glancing back, juggling my book bag. Before long, though, I realized that Avila the terror was closing the gap between us, his toad eyes slits of rage. I worked even harder to escape, but my breath was growing hot and shallow and my thighs were beginning to tighten and burn.

I shot another look behind me, and he was so close that I saw the shadow of a mustache on his upper lip and the pink pimples decorating his bronze chin. My breath was searing me and my knees couldn't seem to lift anymore; my book bag swung wildly from side to side.

Just as I turned the corner of my block, I lost control of my book bag and it dropped, spilling its contents. I was nearly safe, but if I didn't pick up my things I'd never see them again – and I knew the evil Avila had to be reaching for me.

Hesitating over my books and papers, I glanced back despondently, ready for the twisted arm, the Dutch rub, or the pink belly that was certain, and to my astonishment I realized that Avila had halted. He thrust his hands into his pockets and turned away. When I spun around, I saw the one-eyed Samuelian standing in front of his brother's yard, hands on hips, glaring at David Avila. When I peered once more at the bully, he was retreating rapidly.

I was so relieved that I almost forgot to pick up my books and papers. When I finally did, though, I hurried to our neighbor's house. The large car was being loaded with a suitcase, and Haig Samuelian said to me, "Remember, never use more when less will do, and that young hoodlum will soon learn to leave you alone."

Then the two older men returned to what seemed to be a conversation in progress. "No matter, Sarkis," the younger brother said. "I'll pass the message on to Aram. He will understand." The men hugged, then Haig Samuelian noticed what I carried and said, "Don't let this young man play with that slingshot. You remember my eye, don't you?" He pointed toward his empty socket as he swung into the driver's seat.

His brother smiled, "I remember."

"Well, I must be on my way. I have grapes to tend in Fresno." The two brothers shook hands. The larger man tugged his patch and smiled out the window as he started the engine. "Farewell, young man," he said to me.

I didn't reply because I'd noticed something a moment before when Haig Samuelian had tugged at his small mask while sitting there, his face level with mine. I noticed that there was no fair, untanned skin beneath the patch or the string that tied it.

No fair skin.

Beneath the wristwatch Abuelita had given me last Christmas my own surface was pale as a baby's. Then I realized what that had to mean: "You been changin' eyes!" I thought aloud.

"What is that?" the driver inquired.

"Your patch, it's on the other eye. You been changin' eyes," I spoke as I began to realize what had to have been happening: "You been changin' every day."

Haig Samuelian lifted his patch and winked with a twinkling eye I thought I'd never seen before, and said to his brother, "Beware of *this* one, Sarkis. He will go places."

Then he drove north toward Fresno.

MEDICINE

       First time I ever seen Lonnie he was drunker 'n hell, and a mite ornery. It was a Saturday night right after I'd took that job at Bob Manhart's ranch, and I was at the Buckhorn just outside Springville, me and other boys that worked ranches 'round there, givin' them town gals a twirl and drinkin' a little tonsil varnish just to stay loose.

Anyways, a bunch of us boys had went outside to watch two fellers have a pissin' contest, when up roars this old Ford with one door open; it throwed gravel all over us whenever it stopped. Well, I started to go whip the driver after I seen he wasn't nothin but a wrinkled old Indi'n, but Johnny Johns, this wrangler, he grabbed me. "Wes," he hissed in my ear, "don't tangle with old Lonnie less'n your insurance is up to date."

That old Indi'n climbed out of his Ford, then swayed there, his eyes little and red like a boar's, mean-lookin', him watching them two boys try to pee farther than one another. Finally he whipped out his own pecker and shot a stream clean over the hood of his car, scatterin' spectators right smart. I never seen nothin' like it before. Then he grunted: "I win. Who buys beer?"

Well, Johnny Johns he was laughin' to beat hell, and he sang out that he was buyin'. When Lonnie walked up to him, Johnny asked: "Where's Dorothy?"

Lonnie rocked on his heels for a minute, looked around, then staggered back to his car. He walked slowly around it, stoppin' next to the open door on the passenger side. "God damn," he said, "Dorothy he fall out." I laughed. Dorothy was a old gal, but Lonnie never got the "he" versus "she" stuff in English too good. Then Lonnie walked into the Buckhorn for his beer.

We was all standin' at the bar next to the door, listenin' to Johnny tell stories about Lonnie, the dancers still cuttin' a purty mean rug on the floor, when the front door busted open and in wandered the damndest specimen of a Indi'n woman, all beat up, scraped and scratched, dirty like she rolled in a ditch. She walked right up to Lonnie, and he said: "God damn, Dorothy. Where you been?"

"Fall out," Dorothy answered.

Lonnie pushed a cowpoke aside at the bar to make room for Dorothy. "God damn," he said.

It got to where I seen Lonnie regular after that, him ridin' with us at spring roundup, workin at Manhart's sugar beet spread down in the valley when he wasn't up at the ranch. He was one hell of a worker, I'll tell you; I never seen nothin' like it before. He'd work any three hands into the ground. And tough too. Whenever the Mexicans come north to thin the sugar beets, Lonnie took to whippin' them one by one till he worked his way through the whole crew. And, hell, he must've been sixty years old then.

Him and Dorothy they had 'em three boys: Elmer, he was about my age; Charley, he was around twenty; and Millard, he was just a kid, maybe fourteen. They was top hands, hard workers, and the young one was doing real good at the county high school.

Well, Elmer he taken sick. Lonnie and Dorothy they tried doctorin'

him, but he just got weaker and weaker. I recollect how Elmer kept sayin'
his head hurt, then he finally just passed out. Finally, old Bob Manhart
got wind of what was happenin', and he had Doc come out from Springville to check Elmer, but Doc said he couldn't tell right off what was
wrong with him. They carried Elmer clean up to San Francisco to the
big hospital so's they could run some tests, but before they could get him
started, he died. I never did hear what killed him.

One day not long after they buried Elmer, I was drinkin' Ripple after
work with Lonnie and Dorothy in their Ford; we was parked in front of
the Springville store just in case we needed to buy us some more. Anyways, this queer-lookin' Indi'n come walkin' up the street. He seen the
Ford settin' there, so's he made for it. Lonnie seen him comin', and he
said somethin' real fast in Yokuts to Dorothy. I couldn't savvy it, but he
sounded hot.

This Indi'n walked right up to Lonnie, and I seen he had what the boys
call flat eyes – the kind that don't show no white, all darkness – so his face
looked like a mask with an animal lurkin' behind it. He barked somethin'
in the window at Lonnie, him talkin' Yokuts, of course. Dorothy tensed
right up, and I seen Lonnie's face turn all chalky. Lonnie looked away
from the queer-lookin' Indi'n, shakin' his head no, then that other Indi'n
he turned around and walked away.

Soon as he's gone, I asked Lonnie who that was. He never answered
for a long time, pullin' long and hard on the Ripple. Finally, he told me:
"Name Coyote. Medicine man."

I waited, but that's all he said. "What did he want?" I asked.

"Money."

"Money?"

"Money."

"For what?"

"You nosey bastard," Lonnie said, so I took the hint and climbed out
of his car. I walked into the store and bought my own damn Ripple, then
walked back to where my pickup was parked. Lonnie stood there waitin'
for me, and I was afraid I'd have to fight him.

Soon as I got close, though, Lonnie said: "When Elmer sick, Dorothy
he call medicine man. Medicine man he say give five hundred dollars
and Elmer get well. I told him go hell."

"Is he still tryin' to get the five hundred for Elmer?"

Lonnie shook his head. "Naw. He say give five hundred dollars or Charley get sick."

"And you told him no?"

Lonnie nodded.

"Well, old Charley's healthy as a fresh-serviced mare," I said, but Lonnie's eyes was uncertain.

And sure enough, not more than a week later Charley took sick. It was the same thing that got Elmer, headaches and feelin' weak, so Bob Manhart he had Doc rush right out and they got Charley to the hospital before he lost consciousness. But it didn't do no good. He died anyways.

Lonnie slowed down some after that. He never hit the Buckhorn no more, and didn't talk hardly at all. He still worked like a whole crew, but he was gettin' darker, lookin' more and more like he didn't give a damn for nothin'. I never seen nothin' like it before. It was just my luck that I was to their cabin when things come to a head.

Dorothy she used to make buckskin gloves and shirts that all the boys at the ranch bought; they was twice as good as you could buy in a store and cheaper. So one afternoon I drove out to their cabin to buy me some new gloves and maybe swap tales. When I got there, I walked right in the kitchen door like always. Lonnie he set at the little table drinkin' whiskey. "What hell you want?" he asked, and I could tell he was gettin' mean drunk. I told him what I wanted, and he just grunted, his eyes little and red.

"What's wrong, Lonnie?"

He glared at me. "Go hell," he said.

"I ain't takin' no shit off you, Lonnie," I told him, knowin' good and well he could whip me.

He stood up, reached for the bottle like he was gonna belt me with it, then handed it to me. "Drink," he ordered. I drank and it was awful stuff, Thrifty Drugstore special. He finally said: "Millard he sick like Elmer, Charley." Then I savvied why Lonnie was sore.

"Oh, Jesus," I said. "I'll go get Doc."

But Lonnie shook his head. "Doc he no good," he told me. "Medicine man come."

Dorothy come shufflin' into the kitchen, lookin' all shriveled and sad.

She touched my shoulder. "Come," she said. Dorothy led me into the little room where the boys all had slept, and there was Millard on his bunk, pale, his breath shallow and ragged. I figured him for a goner. I never seen nothin' like it before, all three of them boys took sick the same way. "He's gotta see Doc," I told Dorothy.

She just shook her head. "My boys good boys," she said as much to the room as me.

"I 'preciate that, Dorothy," I answered, "but Millard's lookin' bad. He better see Doc."

She sighed and, without lookin' toward me, said: "No. Lonnie call Coyote. Lonnie make medicine with Coyote."

"You mean Lonnie's got five hundred dollars?" I asked, remembering what Lonnie'd said about the medicine man before, and knowing his fortune hadn't changed much between then and now. I couldn't figure how Lonnie could pay. Me, I had three hundred, maybe three-fifty, stashed away; I was saving for a Mexican saddle. But lookin' at that kid laying there on his bunk more dead than alive, it seemed like I didn't need a new saddle too bad. It wouldn't be much to pay for a kid's life. "Let me drive back to the ranch," I told Dorothy. "I'll scare up a little cash."

I run out the front door to my pickup, and I'd just opened the truck's door when I heard a scream, pullin' and suckin' at my brain like a wild animal's cry, but it was a guy's voice all right, and he sounded desperate. I stood froze for a minute tryin' to figure where the sound come from; when the scream cut loose one more time, I knew. I busted to the kitchen door and flew in.

Lonnie knelt on that medicine man's chest, hands white around his throat; Coyote's flat eyes wide and dark, he gurgled a little, that's all; his legs jerked and his arms flailed in slow motion. Then they stopped flailin' at all. Lonnie held on for another long minute, my heart poundin' like crazy; key-rist, I just seen him kill a man.

When he let go, Lonnie done somethin' I'll never forget: he reached down and, one at a time, pulled both the medicine man's eyes out, them murky in Lonnie's hands, and he called Dorothy in Yokuts. She come scuttlin' in, steppin' over Coyote's body like it was a sleepin' dog, and took the lid off a pot that held boiling water. Lonnie dropped the eyes in.

Then he turned to me, and I noticed he was breathin' heavy, but his own eyes was clear and untroubled. He sounded relaxed when he told me to grab Coyote's feet. For some silly reason I done just that, and we toted him out and tossed him in the bed of *my* pickup. "Drive up canyon," Lonnie said, and I did, my belly tight, my eyes wanderin' to the rearview mirror.

Lonnie set like a statue next to me as we wound up the dirt track alongside the creek, his eyes readin' the land. Right after we forded the second time, he pointed up the stream; "Stop!" he grunted. I eased up the pickup to a wide spot off the dirt road, not wanting it clobbered by some drunk hunter buzzin' back toward town. Don't ask me why, but I slipped the .30-.30 from the rack behind the seat, and slung it over my shoulder before me and Lonnie commenced to totin' Coyote. Lonnie led the way. We huffed up a side canyon, then a draw – a place I'd never even saw before – then all of a sudden the draw just opened up into the damndest meadow. Lonnie stopped and dropped Coyote, the medicine man stiffenin' up a little so it was like droppin' lumber. "You stop," Lonnie ordered. Since he'd already dropped his end, I could either stop or plow a row with Coyote's nose. I stopped.

"Now go," he ordered.

"Why?"

"You go!"

"Why?" I asked again, comfortable with that loaded .30-.30 on my shoulder.

Lonnie's eyes narrowed. "I shove rifle up ass," he said.

Well, I'd just saw old Lonnie kill a man with his bare hands, and that .30-.30 didn't look like it'd fit real comfortable, so I walked back down the draw and waited at the pickup.

After a spell – it was dark by then – down come Lonnie, his face hid but his eyes just glowin'. He climbed into the cab and said: "Go." We went.

When we got back to the cabin, I naturally let Lonnie lead the way, and lead he did. We hurried right through the kitchen door, steamed right through the kitchen to Millard's room. Dorothy was next to the bunk, spoonin' broth into Millard's mouth, and Millard he was awake, his cheeks already colorin' up. By damn! He'd been most dead when we left.

"Millard drink eyes?" Lonnie asked, and I liked to shit.

Dorothy nodded.

"Drink eyes?" I asked. I didn't mind killin' some bastard, and totin' his body off, but drinkin' his eyes? Jesus, it was uncivilized. I stood stunned for a minute. Then my own fears busted out; I couldn't stop 'em. "Jesus, Lonnie," I said, "what if the sheriff finds the body?"

"Coyote in tribal earth," he said.

"I'm hungry," said Millard.

Dorothy laughed.

Me, I just went for the kitchen door, but when I got there Lonnie was with me. He grabbed my sleeve. "Stop," he ordered. He picked up a spoon from the boilin' pot, raised it up in front of his face with both hands like I seen a preacher do in meetin' one time; he blowed on the steamin' broth, and sipped. Then he nodded.

Just as I was fixin' to turn and leave, he stuck that spoon in my face, and ordered: "Drink."

"Drink?"

"Drink," he repeated, lookin' straight at me.

Well what the hell, I'd did damn near ever' other crazy thing a man could that night, so I took me a sip. Lonnie he grinned and I had to grin back. It tasted a damn sight better'n that Thrifty Drugstore whiskey.

THAT BLACKBERRY WILDERNESS

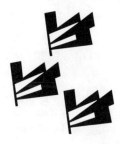

Their hands brushed not quite accidentally, then snapped back. For both it was an electric instant. A moment later, embarrassed not by the touch but by their mutual quick withdrawal, they smiled at one another. "Like a couple a kids," he remarked, and her deep chuckle moved him nearly as much as the fleeting touch had. Seeing those bright eyes smiling at him through the campfire's orange glow, he reached for her hand and grasped it firmly, intertwining his fingers with hers. "Ma'am," he said, "I hope you don't mind."

"Honored," she responded, and her hand squeezed his. She noticed that several other campers had been watching them, so she basked them with a smile, then leaned into his shoulder. As their hands warmed together, an oddly soothing excitement invaded their bodies and they were immediately alone in spite of the other fourteen people who surrounded the fire, howling camp songs with aggressive atonality.

Later the group tripped through darkened woods to a granite slab along the creek where they might lie and gaze into a sky so salted with stars that it appeared hoary, the man and woman side by side, eyes turned upward, vision turned inward, toward one another. Their hands clasped lightly, comfortably. They spoke little – no one in the group said much – the stream's gentle chuckle filling their ears. Alone there amidst the party, they allowed something as old as the stars to innocently work between them.

When the two finally wandered back toward camp, leaving the group stargazing, they still held hands and their continued silence posed questions that neither would ask. With each step, both the man and the woman felt the urgency of their attraction rising in the dark woods like the wind that now urged primordial music from swaying treetops.

At her tent, he squeezed her hand and tapped her cheek with a kiss. "Thanks, Ardith, for a wonderful evening," he said, his voice tight with desire.

"Cal?" she said, those bright eyes wide and visible even in the antique darkness.

His arms were around her before thought could interfere: She was another man's wife, he was another woman's husband, but at that moment, as their lips touched, their mouths opened, and their bodies folded together, memory and convention failed them. Later, a moment or an hour later, in their final breathless words before passion overwhelmed them, they said almost simultaneously, "I wish these damned mummy bags would zip together." The bags didn't.

Ardith awoke startled in the pale glow of pre-dawn, a lone mosquito practicing viola in her ear. For a moment she was disoriented, then her eyes focused and she searched for Cal. He was gone. The bastard. How could he just kiss and run like some high school kid? What was wrong with her, anyway, allowing circumstances and ingenuous passion to sweep her?

Then she noticed him fifty yards away, kneeling near the campfire circle, his tan, bald head wrapped in that crazy red bandana. He was mixing some concoction or other, probably pancake batter. Of course, he was on kitchen duty that morning. No wonder he was gone. At that moment he looked up, noticed her, and waved, a crooked grin on his face. Darn, she was just beginning to enjoy regret, and was contemplating hating him . . . as well as herself. Instead, she sat up and waved, having to scramble to avoid baring a breast in the process. She wished immediately that he was in the bag with her.

So much for remorse.

She finally arose a catnap later, dressed, and began rolling her sleeping pad and stuffing her down bag. Just as she was attaching them to her backpack, one of the younger girls, Lisa, slipped next to her and whispered, "I think it was so *cute*, you two holding hands last night."

Ardith smiled. "You think it's cute?"

"I think it's *darling*."

"Darling?"

"I mean," the girl explained, "you two're like *grand*parents."

"Yes, we are," the older woman smiled, but her voice was unkind. "Hasn't it occurred to you that without a little handholding between people like Cal and me there wouldn't be any grandchildren?"

Lisa giggled.

Six days before, when the group had gathered, such candid conversation had been rare. It was an assemblage of strangers drawn together as volunteers to clean a section of wilderness for the National Park Service, and everyone seemed uncertain how to act. Most were college-age singles like Lisa, although there were supposed to be older volunteers as well, people like Cal and herself, both married to nonbackpackers and grateful for the trip. All had initially been on their best behavior.

In fact, Ardith had been downright uncomfortable that first day because – as was usual for her – she was the first arrival at the assembly point, and as the group gathered, it increasingly appeared that Jed, the group's youthful leader, had failed in his stated attempt to muster a gang reflecting a range of ages. She had felt as though she was the token representative of "over forty" until, quite late that evening, a battered Chevrolet pickup swerved into the parking area. Jed had seemed relieved: "It's gotta be Cal."

A moment later a lean, bald man approached Jed and extended his right hand. "Hi," he smiled, "I'm Cal Chandler. Sorry I'm late, but I had a premature baby to deliver."

So he was the trip doctor, she mused during those first few moments while he was introduced to his fellow campers. Even then she had been riveted by his slate eyes. He sounded pleasant and smiled easily, but there was a tempered core in him. Still, she would not have picked him out of a crowd as anyone special, she knew; he looked like an aging rancher. Well, at least he was a peer. Two weeks of listening to college students' prattle did not appeal to her.

He, on the other hand, would have noticed her in any throng. While he experienced immediate relief that he wasn't the only mature participant, he observed even more intensely the woman's youthful figure and glowing smile. She was one of those rare beauties who had aged well, obviously content to be an attractive middle-aged woman rather than becoming a cosmeticized caricature of a twenty-year-old.

A few minutes of conversation had revealed differences to her. Oh, he was a physician, a Berkeley graduate no less; still, their backgrounds could scarcely have been less similar. She had been born into, raised with, and remained a part of San Francisco society; her family had been among the founders of the Sierra Club. His parents, on the other hand, had been migrant farm laborers from Oklahoma, and he had attended college thanks to the GI Bill. While she and her attorney husband championed liberal causes in the Bay Area, he ran a rural health clinic outside Fresno. When she wondered innocently why he hadn't selected a more lucrative practice, his response had stung her: "I had a responsibility to people like my folks, and I see my responsibilities through. Somebody's gotta work the front lines." Those slate eyes had hardened and she'd known better than to pursue the subject.

Aside from age and being married to nonbackpackers, they did find other areas of common interest. Both were addicted to fly-fishing and were avid readers of fiction. Both had recently become grandparents for the first time. It wasn't much, each had noted, but enough perhaps to allow them to spend two pleasant – or less unpleasant – weeks in one another's company. They certainly hoped so, since no alternatives presented themselves. They agreed on that too, each laughing at their mutual candor.

As the trip progressed, however, she found that she sought Cal's companionship not because he was the least-onerous choice but because he was a man whose vitality and humor resonated with something deep within her. And she had noticed at a stream fording when he had stripped to his shorts in order to swim a safety line across that his body retained lean, hard contours unmatched by most of the younger men. That had interested her too. What she didn't know, couldn't know from his friendly but decidedly unseductive behavior, was that he had coveted her from the moment they had first shaken hands, and that his own desire frightened him.

As the initial week wore on, they increasingly walked, worked, and ate together. One morning while they rested during a trail restoration project, he remarked, "These youngsters jumpin' from sleeping bag to sleepin' bag seem to confuse proximity with intimacy. We're only up here fourteen days. Nothin's gonna atrophy in that time."

Although she laughed, she also wondered if he wasn't covertly explaining his reserve to her. "Let them have fun," she responded. "That excitement wears off soon enough."

He flashed that crooked grin at her. "That's a fact," he said. "I'm probably just jealous."

Luckily there were no medical emergencies among the campers, but Ardith nonetheless saw enough of her new friend in action to admire the way he did business. One morning the group had set out cross country to clear away old fire rings from the shore of a small lake located off the trail. Somehow Jed became disoriented and led them too far west. As soon as it became clear to him that there was a problem, yet without giving anyone else any indication of what was wrong, Cal directed Jed back toward their proper course, then unobtrusively melted back into the group. She liked that performance. Her husband, a successful corporate attorney, would have appointed a committee.

By week's end they had discussed not only most abstract issues of mutual interest but also personal histories, leading Ardith to remark as they sat by the campfire that night, "You probably know more about my family than any living human being."

"I'll be billin' you at fifty bucks an hour," he answered, "my usual fee for psychiatric consultation."

"Where do I send *my* bill? I seem to be hearing a lot about Nell and your daughters and that little grandson of yours."

"Oops," he winced in exaggerated guilt.

"It's funny, isn't it," she continued, "fourteen days isn't such a short period when you're together constantly. A lot of us will see more of one another, under a wider range of circumstances, than we have people we call best friends at home. It'll be hard to keep our masks on for two complete weeks."

He nodded. "Yeah, that girl who fell at the ford yesterday was an inch away from having to be sedated. She was just plain terrified. And so was I before we fished her out, and I told her so. And when the momma bear chased Jed and me the other afternoon, all our college degrees and male boldness just flat disappeared. This old experienced mountaineer nearly wet his britches."

"You move pretty well for an old codger."

"I was just warmin' up. If she'd a got a step closer, I'd've hit the after-burner! I'm sure glad you and Lisa distracted that sow or I might still be runnin'," he laughed.

"You see what I mean? How many people have seen a tough hombre like you scared?"

"Not many. Course, I don't run across momma bears all that often."

"Is that the only thing that scares you?"

"No," he responded, his voice softening, "you do."

She knew immediately what he meant because he frightened her too. A moment later their hands touched.

When he finished his kitchen duty that next morning, washing the last of the pots and pans, she asked what he planned to do that day. The group was splitting, one segment building a bridge over a nearby creek deemed too dangerous to ford, while the other would troop to a distant lake and clean up a mess left by packers. "Well," he hesitated, "I thought I might go to the lake. I've worked on bridges before, but I've never seen that lake."

She guessed from his tone that he didn't want her along, so she smiled and said, "I'm working on the bridge."

Throughout that long day her emotions swerved between sorrow and outrage. After that wonderful night, why had he abandoned her? Perhaps she had been right, he *was* a bastard. But, of course, that couldn't be true, not of the man she had come to know. What was wrong? She had dreamed of a day of hidden smiles and secret touches. Instead she felt as alone as she could ever remember.

When the lake group finally returned just before supper, she did not walk out to greet them with the others, his voluntary absence having finally festered into a pocket of pain. She would not force herself on him or anyone else. Instead, she knelt, busying herself with her pack. Soon she heard the crunch of boots approaching behind her, then his voice: "Howdy, Blackberry. I missed you today."

Blackberry. She wore a purple T-shirt with "Blackberry" printed across the back. In spite of herself, her eyes glistened when she stood and turned to face him and he, without hesitation, leaned forward and kissed her, then hugged her in his wiry arms.

"I had to think some things out," he explained softly, "but mostly I just thought about you and wished you were with me."

"I know," she said. But she hadn't known; she'd only hoped.

That night their bodies blended with less awkwardness. His hands were knowledgeable yet pleasantly tentative on her firm flesh. He was so used to Nell's ample, comforting terrain that he felt a little like an excited explorer. To her, his body seemed almost boyish, so tight was it in contrast to the harbor seal alongside whom she regularly slept. Together they ventured into an urgent wilderness, a region beyond reticence and self.

He awakened before dawn, the sky lightening, the sun a pink promise behind an eastern ridge. Turning his head, he saw only her tousled gray hair protruding from the sleeping bag next to him, so he reached over and delicately pulled the material down until her face was exposed. For long moments he gazed at her – small nose, cleft chin, large eyes now closed, large lower lip. Her right eyelid twitched, so he inclined toward her and kissed it softly. The green eyes fluttered open, and Ardith yawned, then smiled.

"Mornin', Blackberry," he smiled back.

She grinned. Blackberry, she really liked that name.

"Shall I move my bag before everyone notices we slept together?" he asked.

For a moment she thought he was teasing, but his slate eyes revealed that he wasn't. "No," she assured him. "I don't think this sack-hopping group will be very judgmental." His eyes remained uncertain, so she patted his hand, then kissed its open palm. "What'll we do today?" she asked.

It was a rest day, with everyone free to make their own plans. When asked by Jed during breakfast what he'd devised, Cal smiled. "Well, Ardith and I are gonna find us a nice pond, take a dip, eat our lunch, read our books, maybe pick berries, and take a nap," which was exactly what they did. It was a day as free and happy as either could ever remember. Both felt as though they had always held hands and shared secrets, that they always would. "My God," Ardith mused aloud, "I finally know what it's all about, and I'm living it. Don't pinch me."

Two nights later, while they sat talking at the campfire, time began to tumble. He observed, innocently but insensitively, "It's almost over." He was correct, of course. In just three days they would emerge at the trailhead and head back toward those distant lives they had so comfortably forgotten.

"We've still got two nights," she pointed out.

"We've got that," he agreed, patting her hand, but his touch betrayed something deeper than doubt. What it betrayed, if only to him, was the sweep of his passion, his wonder at the need for her that had ripened so swiftly. He was in love, and the most shocking aspect of that realization was that it was a new sensation. He had never loved, at least not this way, before – never so suddenly, so deeply, so completely.

That night, multitudes of stars clouding the blackness above, they once more journeyed toward their mutual wilderness. Afterwards, as they cuddled side by side, her forefinger traced a path around his eyes, his nose, then stroked his lips until he smiled. "You feel guilty, don't you?" she asked.

The smile left him. "Don't *you?*"

"No," she answered honestly. "I feel grateful. This . . . this love" – it was the first time either of them had used that word – "has brought me so much. I feel more alive than I ever have."

In the darkness, she felt his eyes leave hers, gaze beyond her for a moment, then return. "No, I don't feel guilty about what we've done either. It's been spontaneous and innocent and, well, wonderful. I feel like a kid who's finally old enough for somethin' – a watch or long britches, maybe. I'm finally old enough for what we feel." He kissed the hand she had extended to rub his rough cheek. "But I do feel guilty because I love you in a way I've never been able to love Nell, and because of what I'm gonna want to do when this trip's over: the schemin' to see you, the lies I'll be willin' to tell, all the dishonesty that'll destroy the innocence and turn us into cheaters cuckoldin' two good people."

"Oh, Cal," she murmured, caressing him, "the burden you carry."

The next night – their last – they once more traveled that wild and secret region they had discovered, desperate energy driving them. "God, Blackberry," he sighed as they lay spent in one another's arms, "how can I live without you?"

"You don't have to," she whispered. "Whatever else happens, we've got to stay in touch, we've got to stay friends. We can't let all this go." She felt his body tighten as he only grunted. Frightened, she asked, "We can, can't we?"

"I can't," he replied in a choked voice sounding like a man about to weep. "I just can't, Blackberry."

"But *why?*"

"Because it's all gone too far. I want to walk with you, talk to you, touch you, breathe you. If we never make love again, I'll still be crazy to be with you. The only choices I've got are to leave Nell and the family and the clinic and follow you to San Francisco, or just accept the pain of stoppin' now."

As pleased as she was by his declaration of love, she was even more confused. "But I love you, Cal. We love one another. We've got to at least stay in touch." The alternatives he'd mentioned were not the only ones, she knew, but the power of his statement made arguing difficult.

His answer stunned her: "I've been readin' in books all my life that word 'bittersweet.' I think I finally know what it means."

"So because we really care, we can't stay in touch?" She fought the desperate tone that had crept into her voice.

"We just can't."

She rolled away from him, burying her face in her sleeping bag, then pulling the drawstring until she was alone in a soft cave to weep quietly over what she already knew would be the sweetest and saddest of memories. She felt Cal's arm circle her bag, but her own silent sobs masked his grief from her.

They hiked the final miles to the trailhead together the next day, not discussing the previous night's dispute but instead carrying on a civil, uncomfortable conversation ranging over impersonal topics. Good-bye, however, was not so easily contrived.

After making the rounds of other trip members, they wandered to her car and faced one another. He said exactly the wrong thing, or the right one: "Good-bye, Blackberry. This has been the greatest two weeks of my life. I finally know what it means to be alive, thanks to you. I'll miss you so much . . ." His voice trailed into that tone of controlled tears she had heard once before, his hard slate eyes glistened. He cleared his throat, then added, "We've gotta say good-bye and it won't get any easier, so let's not drag it out. You know how I feel, how I'll always feel, about you."

"I know, Cal," she whispered, as his arms circled her, yearning to reason with him – why couldn't they at least write to one another? – but sensing not only the futility of asking, sensing also the damage it might do to so beautiful a memory, she merely held him.

When he stepped back and she started the car's engine, he raised his right hand. "Good-bye, Blackberry," he sighed, then he blew her a kiss. His lips said silently, "I'll always love you." She felt as though a vital organ had been wrenched from her, and that sensation intensified as she motored across the state toward San Francisco, the four-hour trip accomplished in a kind of trance so that she almost missed the contrast between the country she was leaving and the urban web she entered. Only the great wound of loneliness seemed real by the time she traveled the Bay Bridge; Cal had grown as remote and uncapturable as the mountains themselves. In fact, when she wheeled into her driveway, turned off the car, and sat behind the wheel, she could no longer tell who or what was real, other than that terrible wound.

She was better in the morning, although her thoughts were occupied by events of the backpack trip, unsystematically reliving every word, every touch as she walked from room to room, then out into the garden. As days passed into weeks, she began healing that wound within herself with carefully arranged and coveted memories, each seeming more precious than the last.

Ardith realized that she and Cal had been together a very long time, but not long enough, and that he had brought something absolutely new to her, something that only maturity made possible. Cal's integrity, his honor, the very characteristic that now caused her such pain, was the deepest reason for loving him.

Bittersweet, indeed. As much as she hated their separation, she loved that wilderness within themselves they had discovered – or, perhaps, re-discovered – that blackberry wilderness of touched hands and touched hearts and touched lives, and she would never lose it.

Never.

CHINA GRADE

What a wife that ol' boy had! One time me and him we come screechin' down China Grade from this bar up on the bluffs, not more'n two tires on the pavement till we hit bottom and the road it straightened out, us whizzin' past steam plumes and oil creeks, past pumps and derricks, the whole place smellin' a sulfur and crude. Course we never paid it no mind. I mean, we had higher octane in us than the car did, and we's havin' a hell of a time.

Me and Cleophus we done that a lot, flew down China Grade full a giggle juice, I mean. Me, I wasn't married in them days and Cle' wished to hell he wasn't, so we hit this bar up on the bluffs real reg'lar. It's a nice place with country music and the cutest little barmaids. You could look down from this big huge picture window at oil fields spread as far as you could see. Directly under us was the refinery where me and Cle' worked and there was usually steam and this thick black smoke churnin' up from burnin' oil sumps, smoke so heavy it looked about like that greenish sky was a tore octopus a-leakin' ink. Me, I's always glad to be on top a China Grade. Somehow even the beer tasted better when us guys was up there lookin' down. The joint it had a happy hour and me and Cle' we got happy pretty steady.

Anyways, whenever we pulled up to his place in Oildale that evenin' and climbed outta my car, we's plannin' on stayin' happy, but no sir. Here come that witch steamin' out from the house. "You drunks!" she screeched.

I figured I'd kid her a little, so I said real fancy, "We just quaffed a few medicinal spirits so's we could clear obstructions from our throats." Me, I graduated high school and I can come up with them big words.

She never laughed. She grabbed big Cle' and snapped as nasty as could be, "Cleophus Titsworth, you get in that house this minute!" He give me a sick grin and done what she said. Soon as he's gone, she turned to me. "If I's your wife, I'd slit your throat," she spit.

"Hey, if you's my wife, lady, I'd slice my damn wrists!" I spit right back at her. Hell, a little tonsil varnish never hurt nobody.

Well, maybe it hurt Cleophus some, special after he took to seein' things, but that was two, three years later, just before he died. If you never knowed Cle', you missed a good ol' boy. He's might popular with all us guys 'cause we could always count on him to be there if we needed him.

Not only that, he's about as stout as they come. I seen him whup a few fellers that claimed couldn't nobody give 'em a battle, and I seen him win one hell of a lotta contests to see who's strongest. Seems like there's always somebody wanted to test a big man in a oil-field town. One of the funniest, though, happened the time that chubby slicker moseyed into the Tejon Club trailin' this big long-haired kid that was wearin' a vest without no shirt underneath; the kid had giant tattooed arms that looked like long road maps.

Ol' chubby he announced he's the kid's manager. He talked real quick and high like someone was a-playin' his record too fast. After we got to where we could understand him, we figured out that he claimed he's a big wrist-wrestlin' promoter from upstate in Petaluma and his boy, ol' what's-his-name, he could pin anybody in Kern County without even breakin' a sweat.

"You reckon?" asked Cleophus real pleasant.

"Damn right," snapped the slicker.

"Well, we might could have a little contest if you'll show me how."

"Oh, I'll show you," rattled Chubby. "But first let's see if any of your friends are willing to wager."

I couldn't resist. "I'd bet on Cleophus even if it's pecker wrestlin'," I said. "Let's see your green."

Well, once all the bets was laid, Cleophus broke that big kid's arm and shut Chubby's big mouth at the same time. Popped like a shotgun – the arm, I mean. I never noticed if the kid sweated, but ol' chubby sure as hell did whenever he had to pay off.

Don't get me wrong, Cle' wasn't never no troublemaker. In all the years I knowed him – I mean, ever since we's kids – I never seen him go out a his way to start trouble. I also never seen him swerve too hard to avoid it, but he saved a lotta ol' boys' skins by not bein' too damn rough, like the time that Marine sergeant got tight in Trout's Bar and commenced sayin' what a bunch a saps us civilians was. Cleophus picked him up and carried him out to his car, endin' the ruckus.

Miz Titsworth, though, she had his number. He couldn't handle her a-tall. It's like she had some kind a hex on him, and she's a rough customer. We's all at this dance out to the fairgrounds a few years back, and she seen Cle' sneak a little sip from this bottle a Four Roses I'd brung with me. She socked him hard, twice, right on the face, then she tried to give her purse to another woman, sayin' for all the world to hear, "Hold this so's I can clobber the bastard!" She cussed like a trooper whenever she forgot herself. Cleophus coulda eat her without burpin', but he just stood there and took it, lookin' like a man facin' the gallows. It was somethin' strange about her.

I mean, if a gal treated me or you thataway, we'd get shed of her, right? But Cleophus never. He just went about his life with that thorn in the big middle of it. He never even talked about it much, but one day I recollect his ol' lady she'd called Trout's and demanded he come home directly. He just shrugged and mumbled somethin' about birth control, so ol' Arkie Harris that was workin' behind the bar he asked Cle' if it's family night. The big man rolled his eyes and asked, "Are you shittin'? Hell no!" He went on, "I's just wishin' her folks'd used some."

Worst of it is that she's always claimin' he's up to somethin'. If it'd been me, I'd a damn sure been out tomcattin' but Cle' wasn't me. I mean, he never messed with no gals. Then word got around to the Tejon Club that Miz Titsworth had went and called the sheriff's office and claimed her husband had tried to choke her in her sleep, but the cops ignored her, sayin' there wasn't no marks on her neck. Cleophus was real hurt. He said the first thing he knowed about it was when a deputy woke him outta a sound sleep. "Shit," he spit, "if I'uz a killer she'd a been dead a long time ago."

He hit the bottle real hard after that, and it showed. He could whup any man thereabouts, but he had a hell of a time fightin' that whiskey. Wasn't too long before word got out that his wife had went and called the cops again, same ol' story, sayin' he choked her. And he was sound asleep. But it got to him. Not only was folks lookin' at him strange, but he begun to wonder about hisself: Was he crazy? Was he doin' that stuff and not rememberin'?

"Hell, Cle'," I told him, "if you's chokin' her there'd damn sure be finger marks on her neck, and the sheriffs never found none. She's just screwy."

He only grunted.

His wife, though, did one hell of a lot more than grunt. She talked to ever'one, spreadin' lies about Cle', and him takin' it just like he done that time she socked him, not fightin' back, gettin' sadder 'n' sadder.

Then one night, after he'd been a-workin' purty hard on the booze, he busted into my place, just a-blabberin' and a-carryin' on. I figgered he's naturally drunk. "Calm down," I urged. "Calm right down!" I started to offer him a drink, but I thought better. "What's wrong?"

"Oh, Jesus, Buck," he said, "I *am* goin' crazy!"

"No, you're not. What's wrong?" I patted his big ol' back.

"Jesus," he gasped, "I cain't stop shakin'."

"It's okay. What happened?"

"Leona, she sleeps like a damn rock," he told me, all the time lookin' around like he's real scared, "so I been stayin' up the last couple nights watchin' her. I wanted to see if it's somethin' really chokin' her. There I sets in the doorway of the bedroom so's I could watch this movie on the TV in the other room, whenever I hear her start to gag. I turn to look and – Jesus! – she's turnin' to a monster with two heads, her face is crawlin'!"

"What?"

"Just crawlin'. God! Two awful ugly heads!" He raised up his hands and squeezed his temples, tears in his eyes. "I just cain't . . ." he mumbled. "I just cain't . . ." He jumped up and, before I could stop him, he run out the door and jumped into his pickup and off he roared. By the time I got dressed and run outside, he's nowheres to be seen, so I made me a pot of coffee – it's 3 A.M. – and just set at the table a-waitin', this terrible feelin' in the pit a my stomach.

Sure enough, not a quarter hour later, there come a knock at my door, and whenever I answered there stood a deputy. "You know a Cleophus Titsworth?" he asked.

"I surely do," I answered.

"Well, we're looking for him. We want to talk to him about a possible assault on his wife tonight."

I couldn't see no reason to lie. "He'uz here a while back, but he took off. He never said where he's goin'.'"

The cop was a nice young kid, and he believed me. He thanked me and advised me to tell Cleophus to get in touch with the sheriff if I seen him. He said there wasn't no charges, just a investigation. He said so long and I closed the door, but before I could decide whether to go to bed or not, I heard the door bein' knocked again.

I opened it and there stood that same cop. "I'm afraid I've got some bad news," he said real quiet. "I just heard over the radio that they found your friend's truck down at the bottom of China Grade. He didn't make the turn. He's dead."

All through the funeral and after, when folks was eatin' at the widder's house, I had this funny feelin' about what Cleophus'd told me that night. I mean, I never said nothin' to nobody, but I felt about like sockin' that widder woman, her makin' it clear to ever'one that she wasn't too sad about gettin' shed a Cle'. I knowed then what I had to do and I determined to do 'er. It'uz a gamble but I owed ol' Cle' that much.

First I killed me a bird and stuck Miz Titsworth's name in its beak, then I snuck it under her porch with the head pointin' north. That part'uz easy. Seven days later, it got tough. Like my ol' granny'd told me way back when, I boiled a cabbage in salt water, hopin' I remembered all the stuff I'uz supposed to do, then wrapped it in towels so it'd stay warm, and I drove fast over to Miz Titsworth's house.

It was after midnight, and Cle' had told me his wife slept real sound, but I's still worried whenever I jimmied the back door – a little trick I'd learned back in school. No problem, though. I sneaked into the room where she's snorin', her mouth wide open. I stood for a minute thinkin' of poor Cleophus married to that wolverine, then got on with it. I took this special vinegar I'd bought and real light made a teeny cross on each one of her shoulders, then on her forehead – her stirrin' just a little. I rubbed my hands in nutmeg powder before I finally unwrapped the cabbage and held it like a warm green crystal ball in front of me, the smell of it real strong.

Slowly, I lowered it toward her face and that gapin' mouth: slowly, slowly, not quite lettin' it touch her, liftin' it a little, then lowerin' it again, chantin' real quiet:

> Evil can't resist good,
> termite can't resist wood,
> night can't resist dawn,
> gone, devil, get gone!

I chanted that three times. Just when I was gonna start again, I heard this low moan, a choke, then Miz Titsworth commenced gaggin' to beat hell.

I was scared, but I stood my ground and for a minute I never seen nothing, just her buckin' there on the bed, mouth open, grabbin' at her throat, then I seen it, a long, yeller, puke-headed thing with big white eyes squirmin' outta her mouth, ugly as sin itself. The devil! I sprung back and dropped the cabbage. Shit! I never wanted no devil jumpin' into me.

After a minute, it dawned on me. That wasn't no devil. Couldn't be. It was a worm, I mean a giant worm. Lord, but it's a ugly booger. There I stood, not knowin' what to do. I's in too deep to get away.

That thing was half outta her mouth, squirmin' there like a sinner's soul, and Miz Titsworth seemed only semi-awake, gaggin' and scratchin' all the same. Much as I hated to, I grabbed that nasty thing – the worm, I mean – and give it a jerk. A bunch of it come out in my hands.

Miz Titsworth woke up then, seen me, then let out a war whoop. "You're the one!" she hollered. "You're the one that's been tryin' to kill me! Help! Po-lice!"

I never knew what else to do, so I held that half a worm out to her, it dangling with just the littlest jerks and jumps. Her hands rushed to her chest and she stared at it. After a minute, she gasped, "What *is* that thing?"

"It come outta you," I said. "It's what was chokin' ya." She stared at that worm and I stared at her. Wasn't nothin' else I *could* do, me expectin' the cops at any minute. After a minute, neither of us sayin' nothin', I just dropped that nasty thing right on the edge of her bed and walked out. To hell with it, let the cops come and get me. Anything'd be better'n her and her worm.

But to tell the truth, I never stopped worryin'. Even a week later, if I seen a police car, I ducked. Ever' time the phone rang, I flinched. I mean, the cops wouldn't have no reason *not* to think I's the guy they'd been lookin' for whenever Miz Titsworth had called before. But nothin' happened. No cops, no nothin'.

After a couple weeks, I relaxed some, still wary, still tryin' to figure out what I'd tell the sheriff whenever he come for me, but not duckin' no more ever' time a car passed my place. Course, I never seen Miz Titsworth either, not that I expected to, unless some deputy brung her. I mean, we never traveled in the same circles.

I's up at the Safeway on the top of China Grade doin' my grocery shoppin' that Saturday. I'd moved up there to a different apartment after Miz Titsworth caught me in her house. I just never felt real safe down below no more. Anyways, I's pushin' a grocery cart down one a them aisles, grabbin' this and that, not payin' too much mind to other folks – the store it was real full – when my cart run smack into another'n that was just bein' pushed around a corner. I looked up and there stood Miz Titsworth, us only separated by them two shoppin' carts.

I figured she'd start right in on me or commence whoopin' for a cop, one, so I hunkered down into my collar the way a guy does whenever he feels a punch whistlin' at him. Wasn't no place to hide. Our eyes they locked for a second and I seen – at least I thought I seen – somethin' flicker in hers. Not sayin' nothin', she pulled that cart back and skedaddled.

Me, I just stood there tremblin' like a mouse that had just escaped a gopher snake.

I never felt like shoppin' no more after that, so I hustled to the check-stand, paid my money, then hurried out onto the parkin' lot a-carryin' my bag a groceries. Just when I reached my car, I noticed this dark sedan settin' off by itself with these two eyes, scared-lookin' they was, just peerin' over the dashboard at me like some mad animal lurkin' in the dark: Miz Titsworth.

I'd had enough. I dropped my damn groceries right there in the parkin' lot and made for her. I don't know if I'd a socked her or told her off, but I never found out because that car it fired up so fast that all I could see was big white eyes as it blowed past me, them and a yeller, puke-headed blur. Jesus! I staggered back a step on the blacktop and stared after that thing in the dark car just fishtailin' away, off the bluffs down China Grade into the whistlin' white steam and boilin' black smoke.

THE KILLING PEN

Must of been late that summer when Sam Dawkins died, cause I still remember how brown the foothills and flats had become, and dull too, not like the gold of May or June. Even the warty old oaks on the knolls and in the arroyos and the clusters of willows around streams didn't add much color. The air was hot and heavy.

Grandaddy and me we'd found old Sam collapsed late that spring in the big stock barn, his eyes glazed, one of his legs jerking like a spine-shot buck's. Directly, Grandaddy and some hands put Sam in a wagon and carried him to town. It seemed like a long time before they came back without him. But he wasn't dead, Grandaddy told me, just real sick. They left him in the county hospital.

None of us knew exactly how old Sam was, but he was older than Grandaddy. He'd been a slave on my great-grandfather's spread back in East Texas before the war, and he was already a top hand back when

Grandaddy was just a boy. In the days right after the war, a lot of ex-slaves stayed on as hands, so Great-grandaddy had made Sam a foreman. "They don't make 'em no tougher," Grandaddy told me. "Ol' Sam could live on rawhide and sweat when he had to, by God. If you had some range cows lost out in the thicket, you'd just send ol' Sam and he'd drag 'em back."

Sam taught Grandaddy most of what he knew about horses and cows and men. He taught my daddy too, and he was teaching me and the other ranch kids. He was always telling stories and showing us kids how to do things.

One time Joaquin Dominguez he skipped school then faked a note so he fooled the schoolmistress. But he no sooner got away with it than he started bragging on himself. Then the teacher she got wind of it and whipped him good. Well, old Sam sniffed things out, so he herded a bunch of us kids out to the stock barn where it was cool and he told us a story his momma told him.

Back during the old days, he said, there was this here slave named John who got so he could sneak away from chores without getting caught. "One day John he hidin' out in the thicket, and he come across this ol' white skull a-layin' under a tree. Wellsir, that skull give ol' John a start, don't ya know." We all giggled. "Of a sudden, that skull speak right up to John and like to scare water out of him. 'Tongue brought me here,' it say. John he lit out fast." We all laughed and Sam he winked at us.

"John he tol' ol' Massa everything what happen, but Massa think John just tellin' a lie so's he won't get beat for runnin' off. John say he show Massa, and Massa he strap on his pistol and say 'Let's go.' By 'n by they come to the skull and John say, "Tell Massa what you tole me." Skull it don't say nothin'. Massa he gettin' hot." Us kids giggled, a little tense now since we all liked John better than ol' Massa whenever Sam told us stories about them.

"John beg that skull. He cuss it. He threaten. He do everything he can think of, but ol' skull just won't talk. Directly Massa pull out his gun and shoot John dead. Then he ride away."

We gasped, but before we could say anything Sam he went on. "No sooner'n ol' Massa gone, skull say to John: 'Tongue brought me here and now it's brought you.'"

All of us looked at one another, and Sam gave us the fish-eye. Then Joaquin he said, *"Yo entiendo."*

Sam waited for several moments, then he said: "Don' tell nobody nothin' you don' have to." He repeated it in Spanish just to make sure we all understood. We did.

As far back as I can remember Sam was always kind of bent and skinny with just a little gray fuzz on his head, not that we often saw it, for he wore his battered old hat nearly all the time. His hands were large and strong. He knew more knots than anyone I ever knew, and he could rope most anything. ("Sam can lasso horseflies," Grandaddy said once.) He didn't ride much anymore because of a stiff hip. Mostly he just took care of tack and helped Grandaddy break in new hands.

Afternoons you'd find Sam and Grandaddy playing checkers in the tack room, sometimes with Linc, the blacksmith, and a vaquero or two there just to give them unwelcome advice and listen to their stories. Often as possible us kids joined them. The stories were really something. "You call these things cows?" Sam demanded one time of a young cowpoke who'd broken his arm in a loading chute. "Back in the old days they was real cattle. Them devils stamp into a thicket and come out with a *tigre* hangin' off'n one horn and bear hangin' off'n t'other. I 'mind the first time ol' Jeff there" – he nodded at Grandaddy – "tried to tangle with one. You never seen such a bloody mess in your life." Grandaddy grinned under his curving mustache, but he said nothing.

The younger hands would brag about fights they'd had, but Sam he'd scoff. "Don't bother with no box-fightin'," he'd tell them. "If some ol' boy want a fight make him sorry. Find you a stick or a rock and bash 'im. Keep bashin' 'im 'til he ain't gon' bother you no mo'." The young guys looked like they wanted to laugh, but they could see Sam wasn't joking. And Sam could fight, or at least that's what Grandaddy told me. "He licked a hell of a lot of cowboys in his time. He was foreman and by God all the hands knew it." Grandaddy told me about a group of ex-Reb soldiers who "figgered they'd whup themselves a nigger and they picked Sam. Well they whupped 'im, but they picked the wrong nigger."

"They really whupped him?" I asked, not wanting to believe it.

"They whupped 'im bloody and near dead, but two of them *was* dead, and the other near it. Ol' Sam didn't play around none. He'd hit you with a horse, if that's all there was for him to use. And he could shoot a handgun mighty good."

Grandaddy turned real serious then: "You're a-gonna run this spread one day," he said, chilling my belly with the avoided realization that he too must eventually die, "and I'll tell you this: If you're a-gonna run a ranch you need the best vaqueros, not the whitest or the purtiest. The best. A lot of ranchers hereabouts wouldn't hire nothing but white cowpokes after the war. Fine with me. I hired the best and that's one reason we're still in business and most of them others're long gone."

Holidays, like Christmas or Juneteenth, Grandaddy threw a big dinner for hands and there was music and dancing and whiskey. Lots of things happened on those days, dancing and contests and no school, lots of things, but I remember most of all the stories Sam would tell when he was drinking liquor because they were so sad, and they were most always about slave days: those strange old days so long before I was born, those days that never seemed to die. He told different stories, but he always repeated one about the slave woman who kept having babies and the master just kept selling them away from her as soon as they were weaned. "Lawd," he'd say, "that po' woman just pine and pine." Sam's voice always turned to a mixture of pain and rage. "She have a new baby and she just determine ol' Massa ain't gonna take this lil chile from her." He kind of gulped and brushed at his eyes. "So she done the onliest thing she could figger: she give the baby pizen and took some her own self. Then she lay down and hol' her little baby to her breas' and they die."

That story haunted me. I dreamed of it, and worried over it. I couldn't imagine a woman who would *kill* her own baby. Not in my wildest thoughts did it seem possible. Whenever I asked Grandaddy about it, he answered only "Slavery," with a sort of faraway grunt. Then he added, "That's all past nowadays. Don't bother yourself none with them old days." But they did bother me.

A couple of weeks after Sam took sick, Grandaddy and Linc they brought him home from the county seat. One arm swung loose at his side, and he dragged one foot and leaned on a shiny new cane. Us kids rushed to greet him, but his face was a scary mask to us, with one eye and half his mouth drooping, so we pulled up short. Sam caught it. He saw the sudden fright in our eyes and it hurt him.

Grandaddy moved Sam into the main house with the rest of the family, into my daddy's old room. Sam took his meals with us, of course, but food dribbled out of his mouth and embarrassed him so bad, he found excuses to eat alone in the kitchen as often as he could. But gradually we all got use to each other again. Us kids we learned to understand Sam's newly slurred speech, and Grandaddy didn't let the old man just hide in his room. "You better get on out to that tack room before them young bucks wreck ever'thing. Half of 'em wake up in a new world ever' morning. Besides," he added, "there ain't nobody out there for me to whup at checkers." Sam fussed a little, but pretty soon he was back in the tack room.

My Uncle Jingles – Jacob, really, who was a doctor of veterinary medicine way up in Montana – was scheduled for his annual visit home. He was Grandaddy's only surviving son, so everyone was excited. Besides, he always brought presents. I had to clean my room specially good, and do my chores because Grandaddy was on the prod, checking everything. He had a prime bull calf moved into the killing pen next to the slaughter shed. It just happened that we had a lot of cows, some with suckling calves, on the large pasture bordering the killing pen, and that bull calf's momma stayed right next to the pen nuzzling her big old baby through the whitewashed fence.

We were walking out to the tack room after breakfast – Sam and Grandaddy and me – whenever Sam noticed the cow and calf close together, and he stopped. "Jeff," he called after us, for we'd kept on walking. We returned to where he stood. "It ain't right," he added thickly.

"What ain't?" Grandaddy asked.

"Looky there," Sam pointed his cane toward the cow and calf. "That's just what they done to my Momma and me. You know it ain't right." His face wore that expression of sad rage I'd seen before.

Grandaddy stopped dead. "Go on in the house, boy," he ordered me, and I snapped to it because his voice had turned low and ominous. I watched them out the window. They were talking, arguing almost, both men spitting violently on the ground.

I was baffled. Later, we ate a tense, silent lunch together, and after lunch old Sam he skipped his nap. Instead, he hobbled out to the killing pen and leaned on the rails. I followed him. "You musta seen a thousand calves in that pen before, Mr. Sam," I said. "Why does this one bother you?" His red-rimmed eyes turned toward me. "Some things don't strike a man till he ready to see 'em," he responded.

"Yeah . . ." I started to continue, but he cut me off.

"Ask yo' Granpappy," he ordered. He spent most of that long, hot afternoon, I guess, just leaning on the rails of the pen watching that cow and her bull calf.

Me, I wandered away, confused and a little sore, and found Joaquin. We mumbly-pegged and tried to make a straitjacket out of old harness straps and sacks. Finally we wandered over toward the tack room, stopping at the blacksmith's shed to talk to Linc, but he was quiet and tense. All the black vaqueros, in fact, seemed uneasy, like they felt involved in Sam's private anger. Eventually we reached the tack room and found it empty. I looked out back toward the killing pen and didn't see Sam there either, so Joaquin and me we started for the kitchen in hope of a snack when we saw what looked like a lone leg sticking out near the side of the barn.

It was Sam, crumpled and spraddle-legged: it looked like he'd tripped. His greasy old hat was off and I could see his fuzzy head bleeding bright where it'd struck the ground. He wasn't moving. "Go get Grandaddy," I told Joaquin. Something white-hot had commenced burning in the middle of my belly.

Grandaddy came right away and Linc followed him directly. They knelt next to Sam and Grandaddy felt for a pulse, then looked at Linc, Grandaddy's whole body, even his mustache, drooping; Linc nodded. "Dead," Grandaddy said finally, his pale eyes squinting hard, his voice sighing. Then he stood, looking very straight and tall, his tobacco-stained mustache twitching, and he walked, slowly at first, then fast, to the killing pen. He opened the gate and angrily shooed the bull calf with his hat until it returned to the pasture where the cow stood waiting. "Get in there, you little son of a bitch," Grandaddy said.

Grandaddy walked back to Sam, and knelt again next to the sprawled body. He took off his own hat and, real sudden it seemed, his head was resting in one hand and he was shaking right in front of all of us, a thin stream of tears streaming down one cheek. He reached for Sam and touched the chalky-dark face. "Damn it anyway," Grandaddy said. Linc was looking away. I stood next to Joaquin, too frightened to cry.

Grandaddy finally stood, holding Sam's battered hat in his hand. He cleared his throat, turned toward Joaquin and me, then handed me Sam's greasy old hat. "Grow into this, boy," he ordered.

ELEPHANT TIPS

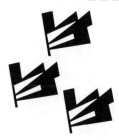

      I got me a job, man, a fuckin' gig. On my way to easy street – *E-Z Street* – because this dude I know, Tommy Giacomini, his uncle runs a classy restaurant out at the country club, and he's gonna make me a waiter. So I struts into Manuel's Chili Palace to tell my partners that will naturally be overjoyed, right?

"You what?" asks Big Cleve, who ain't worked since Nam, unless you consider breakin' and enterin' work.

"Got me a fuckin' gig, man."

"Sheee'."

Artie he just chuckles. He ticks me off sometimes, man. "Yeah," he finally says real loud, lookin' all around, "my man is moooving on up. He's going to circumcise elephants at the zoo. The pay isn't much, but he gets to keep the tips."

Everybody in Manuel's, even the ugly waitress, laughs to beat hell.

"You're a funny fucker, Artie," I tell him.

"What *is* your job, then?" He asks.

I tell him and he don't look so smart when he hears. He'd figured I'll be scrapin' up dog turds for the Parks Department or somethin', man, not a real gig, not a class one.

Cleve he says, "They need anybody else, bro'?" He's serious, man.

Before I can answer, Artie grins again and suggests, "Maybe Merlene here can give you some pointers." He winks at his honey, the waitress that has more tattoos than the three of us combined, and wrestles two weight classes above Big Cleve. She specializes in licking chili off her thumb after ploppin' a plate in front of a customer.

"Thanks," I say. "That'd be real nice." After she lurches away, I add, "Maybe she can teach me to walk like an orangutan too."

Cleve cracks up. "Chi-chi-chi!"

Even Artie smiles. "Hey, she keeps the kid in smokes," he says.

Just then T.J., lookin' like the ass end of bad luck, sways into the cafe. "What the fuck did we drink last night?" he asks as he climbs onto a stool. "I feel like shit."

His problem, man, ain't *what* he drank, it's how much. You drink that much *water* and you'll get sick. He was in the slammer for nine months, man, nine long months employed as a license-plate specialist, and he's been out for eight days tryin' to drink all the booze he missed while he was inside.

"You better slow down, my man," advises Artie. "You never see the kid putting away hooch like you. You never see *anybody* put away hooch like you. Your liver must look like a saddle."

"Fuck you, doctor," growls T.J. "Where's the fuckin' coffee? What's that fuckin' waitress doin'?"

"She's in back havin' her flea bath," I suggest.

"You guys are talking about the woman I love," grins Artie.

Big Cleve cracks up: "Chi-chi-chi! Man, the bitches you make it with."

Artie has an answer. "At least the kid makes it." We heard it a million times.

After T.J. puts the fire out with the brown water Manuel sells for coffee, we repair to the local Goodwill store so I can buy some waiter clothes, a couple used suits, a couple shirts, and these three ties. I let Cleve talk me into one tie with big Hawaiian flowers on it, and he promptly takes it out of my sack and puts it on when we hit the street. It looks great with his sleeveless blue workshirt, but his eighteen-inch biceps convince me not to say nothin'. "How's it look, bro'?" he asks.

"Fine as wine," I answer, havin' sampled his right cross on a couple occasions.

"Thunderbird wine," grunts T.J.

Cleve scowls, "Say, man . . ."

I'm not sure whether it's a comment on the tie or a request for a drink, but before things can get heavy, I say, "Look, once I make a little jingle, we can all buy some shit to wear."

"The kid needs some new threads," acknowledges Artie the great lady killer. Hell, he's the only one of us that's got any decent clothes, and that's because the badgers he loves up keep him clean. He's one slick chili choker, man.

T.J. and Cleve drop me off that afternoon – Artie havin' scheduled a rendezvous with the missing link – and we drive through these big gates and up a long, circular road with bushes that've been trimmed into shapes, like triangles and balls, alongside it. We can see golfers out on the hills all around, drivin' those funny little carts like they're all ice cream men, and wearin' fag clothes – bright little knee pants and pink sweaters and little caps, crazy shit, man; their old ladies must dress 'em. All the hogs in the parkin' lot are Cads and Jaguars and MB's, so T.J.'s Ford, which looks like Patton's command tank, it stands out.

I see these two security types eyein' the Ford when I get out, so I tell the guys to split and pick me up at seven because Mr. Giacomini is only usin' me for the early shift until I get broke in real good. I guess he don't want me spillin' gravy on somebody's pink sweater.

Inside, it's not like the mess hall in Nam, and it's damn sure not like Manuel's Chili Palace either. It looks like a fuckin' hospital, man. Tommy's there and he introduces me to his uncle that's wearin' a silk suit with a flower in his lapel, that introduces me to this guy named Earl, that reintroduces me to himself as "*Mr.* Romain" as soon as the other two are gone. He's gonna teach me how to wait tables. Earl turns out to be a snotty bastard, actin' like he can just barely tolerate me, and he damn sure doesn't wanna slip up and touch me or somethin', but I stay cool. I need the fuckin' gig, man. Besides, I think he's a fairy.

So after about an hour of instructions, ol' Earl he kinda sighs like he's done all he can, then sends me out to this table where three guys have just sat down. "They'll only want coffee or drinks," he adds, meanin' that I'm not up to carryin' a burger and fries. "Thanks, Earl," I say, thinkin' that the day will come when I'll serve him a fuckin' knuckle sandwich. He don't answer because he don't like me callin' him Earl.

I take three menus to the table and I say, "May I help you gentlemen?"

"A blonde for me and redheads for each of my friends," says this gray-haired dude in knee pants. Just my luck to get Bob Hope.

I smile, but don't say nothing.

One of the other guys says, "Coffee, please. What're you having, Ray?" Ray was having a draft beer.

"Do you have Pimm's Cup?" asks Bob Hope, his eyes all twinkly.

How the fuck do I know? Pimm's Cup? I don't know a Pimm's Cup from a jock cup. "I'll see, sir." I hoofs to the bar and asks. We do. So back I trot to the table. "Yes sir, we do," I say real polite.

"Well, that's a wonderful thing to carry. I'll have coffee." He grins like a shit-eatin' dog.

I try not to look at him while I jot the order down, then collect the three menus. I don't like people fuckin' with me, man. I don't fuck with other dudes and I don't want them fuckin' with me. But, I tells myself, he just saw I was new and wanted to have a little fun. Okay, I'll give him that one.

"What took so long?" Earl demands soon as I get back.

"That old dude sent me to look for Pimm's Cup."

"Dr. Gaspari is a card, but you've got to snap to it."

I'm about to snap him, put a fuckin' knot on his bald gourd, when he send me to another table, this one next to the big window where you can see most of the golf course plus the Sierra in the background. From inside this fancy place the mountains look real good. When you're out sleepin' under the fuckin' freeway like me and the guys've been, they look like freezin' to death.

This old dude is sittin' with a cherry chick, young with a body that won't stop. She's wearin' this low-cut dress and I'm standing over her, lookin' into her Pimm's Cups. The guy, that don't exactly act like her father, he orders cocktails while I eye his honey, thinkin', baby, I could make you forget that old fart so fast.

Back at the waiters' station, Earl is pissed: "You were *looking* at Mrs. Ruggles!"

"I sure as hell was. Is that his *wife?*"

"It most assuredly is! Don't you *ever* let me catch you looking at a woman like that again," he warns.

Now, I'd just about heard enough from ol' Earl. I can take some correctin', but this *warnin'* shit, well, it don't sit too good. "Lookin's not against the law," I point out, tryin' to stay cool. This gig ain't all I thought it'd be.

"It is definitely against the rules here for the help to *ogle* customers."

We're alone, so I ask real quiet, "What the fuck's the difference between a ogle and a look, *Earl?*" I spit his name so hard that he blinks like I lit a firecracker.

After a minute – it finally dawns on him that he's fuckin' with his pulse – he scurries away, sayin', "Mr. Giacomini will hear about this." Fuckin' fairy.

I deliver the cocktails and the guy nods. The chick, man, swear to God, she gives *me* the eye, that look that tells you if the time and place were right we'd be breathin' heavy. I get blue balls walkin' back to my station. And I also get blue, thinkin' about what money can buy. Well, fuck it.

Pretty soon, ol' Earl is back with this smirk on his face. "You are to obey me *or else*," he says. He looks like he expects me to faint.

"Look, asshole," I whisper, "I'll do what you say, but if you keep actin' like your shit don't stink, *somebody's* gonna knock a fuckin' hole in your lung and nobody, not even Mr. Giacomini, will be able to save your ass. Think about it, *Earl.*"

While he's blinking again, I head to another table where these four guys just sat down, and I'm wonderin' if I still got a job, but at least I'm happy that Earl finally understands what's goin' down. I can't figure people out, man. You try to do your work and they mess with you. The four guys all want draft beers, and one wants a club sandwich. When I get back to the station, I expect Earl will be gone, runnin' to report me to Mr. Giacomini, but he's not. "That was better," he says.

"Thanks," I say.

The way they do it, waiters don't go back to the tables to pick up tips – that's not classy, man; the busboys pick up what customers leave and put it in this box. That's why, when the next group comes in – two middle-aged guys in tennis clothes – I'm shocked when one of them says to me after I deliver their little bottles of water, "Would you like your tip now?"

"Well . . . sure," I stammer.

"Buy low and sell high," he says, and both of 'em crack up.

I just turn around and walk away, afraid I'll lose it, when I hear one of 'em say, "He doesn't seem amused." Then the other one says real loud, "He doesn't understand. They don't exactly hire geniuses here."

These are the jokers I fought to protect in Nam, that my buddies got killed to protect. I stalk back to their table. "You want that racquet stuffed up your ass, man?" I ask him, my eyes burnin' into his. I ain't kiddin' and he knows it.

He tries to grin his way out of it and, out the corner of my eye, I see his friend kinda scoot away from the table. "Now just a minute . . ."

"If you can't talk right, man, don't say shit to me."

He looks away, so I turn and walk back to my station. By the time I get there, those two guys're gone. Good fuckin' riddance. A couple minutes later, though, I'm on my way out, too.

This time it's Mr. Giacomini himself that comes stormin' up to me and calls me into his office.

"What did you say to Dr. Collier?"

"Who?" I know damn good and well who he's talkin' about.

"Dr. Collier, the gentleman in tennis togs."

"In what? *Togs?*"

Mr. Giacomini is this little short bastard with a big neck that smokes cigars; he looks like he's smolderin'. "Are you trying to provoke me?" he demands.

The truth is that I am. I mean, what the fuck, I can see that he's on their side, so why not? "Me? No," I says.

"You cursed at one of our best customers, and a close personal friend of mine. Don't you understand that these are people of the finest class: doctors, lawyers, businessmen? You can't come in here and act like a common hoodlum."

"Wait a minute, Mr. Giacomini," I tells him. "I was just doin' my job the best I could. If these people're so classy, why do they treat somebody workin' to make a livin' like he's a turd? If they're so classy, why don't they respect other people's feelin's? You got class mixed up with money, which they got. I know guys on the street that'll never do nothin' to fuck up another guy's gig, but these assholes . . ."

"That's the final straw," he says. "You can't even keep a civil tongue in your head. You're dismissed. I want you off these premises *immediately!*"

"Okay," I says, and I'm fingerin' the Goodwill trousers I just spent my last jingle on, and lookin' at this toad in front of me. "I'd rather not be a whore like you anyways, sellin' my respect so's I can get some doctors and lawyers to act like they like me."

His face turns purple and he jumps to his feet. "Nobody talks to Aldo Giacomini that way! You get your friggin' ass the frig outta here! I'm *connected* and I'll have you dumped in a friggin' lake."

The little wop has lost it. So I gives him one more shot: "Give me any more lip and you'll be *dis*connected, you sawed-off sack a shit." Then I glare at him a second and leave. After all I seen in Nam, guys gutted and kids burned and old people starved to death, this little fuckin' number in his silk suit isn't jack. I slam the door and walk away.

So ain't life grand. I start the day with my first job since Nam and I end it with the fuckin' Mafia on my ass. The more I think about it, I shoulda kicked Giacomini's butt, I mean if they're gonna put me in cement shoes anyway. But hell, he's Tommy's uncle and Tommy's a good dude. He lost his damn hand in Nam.

I get on the horn and call Manuel's Chili Palace and, sure enough, the guys're there. I tell 'em to come pick me up and to bring some fuckin' beer, since T.J. that I'm talkin' to, he sounds like he's already in the bag.

He is. I see his hog weavin' up the fuckin' road to the country club and this kid that parks cars, he says, "Jeez, it looks like that guy's shit-faced." So is Big Cleve that's sitting in the front seat with his eighteen-inch brown biceps hangin' out the window. He's laughin' at the fuckin' golfers in their turquoise pants and lavender sweaters. Soon as they pull up, I jumps in the back seat. "Gimme a fuckin' brew, man," I say.

Cleve passes one to me and says, "You see all these cats, dressed like a bunch a mo'fuckin' punks, man." Then he grins and asks, "Wha's happenin', baby?" Drunk outta his fuckin' gourd.

"The motherfuckers fired me."

"The mo'fuckahs do what?"

"Canned my ass."

"Why, man?"

"Because I told some snotty bastard I'd shove a tennis racquet up his ass."

Big Cleve grins. He likes that kinda action. "Where the mo'fuckah be? I kick his mo'fuckin' ass."

"Hold it," says Artie, who sits next to me in the back seat and who, as usual, is the great voice of reason. Also the great voice of chickenshit. Sometimes I'm glad I didn't serve in his outfit overseas, man. "Do not cause trouble here," he advises. "The kid does not need ninety days in orange coveralls at the county road camp. This is *the* club, where the D.A. and the Mayor and Police Chief, and all the money too, hang out. The kid says cool it."

"Fuck the kid," I say. "We gotta do *somethin'*. I ain't gonna back away from this place." I finish inhalin' beer number one and start on number two. "These assholes treated me like dirt, man."

"Why don't you guys moon the bastards on our way back to the fuckin' gate, man?" suggests T.J.

Cleve is one big grin. "Moon the mo'fuckahs. Right on!" He's already workin' on his belt. He digs it. His cinnamon rolls have been viewed by more people than any other buns in Sacramento, man. Fastest fuckin' moon in the West.

Sounds good to me, too, but Artie almost shouts: "Stop the car! Indecent exposure equals six months. The kid will walk back to town and be by the phone at Manuel's when you *locos* call for bail."

We're used to it, man. We don't even argue. He always pussys out. T.J. slows to about ten miles per hour, then says, "Hit the road."

"Hey, you're still movin'."

"It's a tough fuckin' life," grins T.J., real sympathetic.

"Hey, the kid could break his leg."

All of sudden Big Cleve speaks up. "Get the fuck out, mo'fuckah." Artie is interfering with the moonin', which Cleve is ready to launch.

Artie ain't too bad a fighter when you get him goin', but he don't want no parts of Cleve. He stumbles out and staggers, almost straightens to a jog, then jags until he tumbles on his face as we move away real slow. We all laugh to beat hell.

"Moon time!" calls T.J. as we approach this bunch a golfers right next to the road, and me and Cleve hang buns. They all look shocked. The next group does too, and we're havin' a ball, so T.J. hangs a left away from the gate. "Let's tour this fucker before we take off," he says. Me and Cleve open fresh beers, our asses nice and cool in the afternoon breeze. We're comin' up on this golf cart with these two dudes in it and for a minute I think one's that jerk doctor that got me fired, so I jam my butt so far out the window that I almost hit the driver with it. It's not him though.

Just then T.J. says, "The fuckin' pigs!"

Me and Cleve look around and, sure enough, a red light is flashin' behind us. "Let's get outta here," I says, trying to pull my ass in from the window, but I jammed it so far out that I'm stuck. Cleve is sittin' in the front seat drinkin' more beer, with his drawers down around his ankles. He wants to get as much brew into him as he can before the pigs nab us, man . . . if they do. Meanwhile, T.J. is makin' for the gate, not speedin', but gettin' there as quick as he can just the same.

Just when I'm about to get myself free from that damned window, I hear T.J. kinda sigh, "Ho-ly shit!"

I look up and see the whole fuckin' Sacramento police force waitin' for us at that gate. Red lights, blue lights, guys in bulletproof vests, shotguns, the whole fuckin' banana, man. I quit trying to wiggle my butt loose. Fuck it, man, there's no way to fight rich bastards. They always win. I shoulda just duked that faggot doctor when I had the chance.

"What'll I do?" asks T.J.

"Stop and show 'em you mo'fuckin' license," Big Cleve advises, gigglin'. He don't give a shit, man.

"I ain't got one," T.J. says, soundin' real tense.

"You in big trouble then, bro'," Cleve says, still gigglin'.

I can tell by the wind on my pearly white ass that we're slowin' down as we reach the road block, but I don't care either. "You'll probably get a fuckin' ticket," I add and Big Cleve spits a mouthful a beer laughin', man. He don't even bother to pull his fuckin' pants up.

"Let's all sing 'God Bless America,'" I suggest.

Cleve cracks up again: "Chi-chi-chi! Don' know the mo'fuckin' words, man."

Just as the car stops and the pigs come swarmin' up like they caught Public Enemy Number One, I sees Artie standin' by the gate, his clothes dirty from where he rolled, his hands stuck in his pockets, lookin' real sad. Fuck it, man.

GOOD-BYE, UNCLE SEAMUS

It's funny the things you remember about people. Sylvester Duggan was the first guy I ever saw sock a woman. We were at a dive on the east side celebrating a high school play-off victory, drinking beer and dancing with fancy women, a gang of us – Denny McCann, Sean Daly, Billy Dunn, Mike Shaw, Vester, and me.

Ves, an all-league tackle and huge by the standards of that time, was a gentle giant if ever there was one. Oh, he was a devastating boxer in P.E. classes – he'd battered tough-talking Denny, the only lad his size – but never had to fight otherwise, so never did.

Anyway, he was dancing with a cute little whore when a thick woman with tattooed arms and a face like putty swaggered onto the floor and punched the gal Ves was twirling. The aggressor screeched, "You slut! I'll teach you to steal tricks from me!" She grabbed the smaller girl's hair with one hand and began pummeling her with the other one.

For a second, big Ves just stood there looking like a confused angel, those red curls framing his freckled face. His erstwhile partner was crying, "Help me! Somebody please help me!" as the larger woman beat her. We all thought we were tough football players, but this scene was beyond us: the shrieks, the curses, the dark floor shattering with spears of light from the globe twirling on the ceiling. I, for one, was suddenly frightened, and I froze. But Vester moved.

He reached into the melee, grabbed the older woman's thick neck in one mitt, and popped her with the other, a short crisp left hand that anesthetized her mid-curse: "Son of a . . ." *thunk!* She fell without a quiver to the waxed floor, and nobody, not even the bouncer, laid hands on Sylvester.

Denny, known as "the flower" to his classmates in deference to a noxious habit of his, whispered to me, "It's a brute that'd hit a woman." He was still sore, I'm sure, because Sylvester had humiliated him in that P.E. bout.

"I think that woman's the brute."

He only snorted, "Hunh!" Then he loosed a fart.

That next year, over the protests of his family, Vester went away to college on a football scholarship instead of attending the seminary. You could hear the howls all over the neighborhood because his mother and aunts had assumed that he would become a priest. They never really forgave him. You see, when his father, Tommy Duggan, died – "It was the drink got him," my mother reported at the time – Ves was just a kid; his mother'd moved in with her two unmarried sisters, Rose and Mary Martha Wicklow, and the three of them conspired to raise the boy, to plan his life.

Sylvester was an exceptionally bright kid, it was agreed, and he was targeted for great things by everyone at St. Vincent de Paul School, but by the time he reached high school his brains had become a burden; he *had* to earn A's or he was considered a failure. And all those A's were pointed in one direction: I remember clearly his Aunt Mary Martha telling my mother, "It's a gift of God that will be given Holy Mother Church, isn't it?" I recall that especially, since it was said before noon mass the day after Vester had coldcocked the whore. "Our boy will be takin' the Holy Orders, won't he?" Mary Martha went on.

"A wonderful thing, isn't it?" my mother had replied, then she'd riveted me with her eyes. "There's some could learn from a fine lad like your Sylvester."

The irony, of course, is that now I *am* a priest – Viet Nam, what I saw there, sent me to the seminary – and Ves is a gynecologist out in sunny California. Even the black crows – that's what we called the nuns – would never have guessed that outcome, I'll bet.

For instance, I stood up with Ves when he married Maureen O'Connor. It was just before I went overseas and just after he finished his degree at Penn State and left for medical school at UCLA. In many ways, the ceremony seemed like a funeral. Although he was marrying a neighborhood girl, his mother and aunts were stone-faced because his marriage made it certain that he would not become a priest. They hinted darkly that Maureen had employed the darkest of passions, what they called "sec," to lure their boy.

"There's some don't need *that*, isn't there?" his mother said to mine the week before the wedding. I was driving the two ladies to an altar society meeting at the church, and before I could ask what "that" meant, Mrs. Duggan continued: "The flesh, it's the flesh and the divil that's taken our boy," she clucked and dabbed at her eyes. "It was them atheists at that college turned his head. Now, once he's lost his purity . . . like his father . . ." she muffled sobs with her handkerchief.

You have to understand that Vester's mother and aunts went to mass and received communion daily. They even dressed like nuns: dark clothing that covered their bodies, heads swathed in dark kerchiefs, worn rosaries in their hands, scapulars around their necks. They always planted themselves in the first row and were aggressively the first to stand, the first to kneel, the first to sit during services, their moves so certain that it was clear to all they were choreographed by some Higher Power. If an altar boy or – heaven forbid – a priest made a mistake the Wicklow women could be heard clucking. Until he went away to college, Ves had to go with them and if he didn't receive holy communion, they grilled him, so he always received.

In any case, I'll never forget Vester's bright-red face at his wedding as he knelt next to Maureen before the altar, listening to the soft, funereal sobs from his aunts and mother during the ceremony. His bride appeared stunned and Father Tim was angry. It was not an auspicious beginning, and the young couple made only a token appearance at their own reception in the Duggan flat, then quickly departed for faraway California.

During that period while Ves was in medical school on the West Coast, Maureen took a terrible working-over from her new in-laws: "She lured our boy with the flesh, didn't she." It was not a question. "*Sec.* No better'n a common whore. Not a bit. It was her fancy tastes took him out to *that* place, wasn't it?" Finally, old Father Tim spoke to them about the sin of scandal, and for a while they ceased attending St. Vincent, instead traveling across town to St. Mary Magdalene parish.

Sadly, Maureen was back three years later, with two babies and a broken heart. I don't know the particulars, but since her own parents were dead, she moved in with Vester's mother and aunts – they who had been vilifying her the whole time. After the divorce, they began referring to her as "his one true wife" instead of "that woman." Moreover, Mrs. Duggan and her sisters ceased speaking about their boy then and began to pray the death prayers for him. Because he and I corresponded, I knew Ves had eventually received an annulment – a tangle of church politics that I'd rather not get into – and remarried, that he was in fact living a remarkably conventional life out in exotic California: PTA, Sunday Mass, Little League, and a dog.

Just back from Nam myself, I spoke to Maureen immediately after she returned and she told me then only that she dreaded the winters here and the narrowness. When I asked why she hadn't remained on the coast, she looked away for a moment, then said only, "The children need family." Maureen had been taking classes at a junior college herself before the split, and she knew it would be tough to continue her education here, because there were far fewer such opportunities. I urged her to try night school, which was better than nothing.

When I returned to the parish a few years later as a priest, sad to report she had assimilated – dark clothes, dark demeanor – and her two children were being raised as Ves had been. She approached me shortly after I arrived, a pinched, smileless caricature of the Maureen I had known. She wanted me to intercede with the court that had granted Vester visiting privileges and that allowed him to take the children – a boy and a girl, named after their parents – during the summer. "He's no right to expose my children to *that* place." In fact, I told her, he had every right according to both church and civil law.

"He's fallen away and living in sin and I won't have my children exposed to him," she spat with the tone Catholics use when they're certain that clerics have gone soft. "I'll go to His Eminence," she warned. "It's that *California!*" She spun away and I've seen little of her since because, like her in-laws, she attends a Latin mass held weekly in the Knights of Columbus hall.

The parish itself changed dramatically during the years I was gone. It was now at least half black. When we were kids, it had been populated almost exclusively by shanty Irish, the second and third generation that had not managed to fully emerge from immigrant poverty, but by the time I returned, many of those families had moved to lace-curtain suburbs.

The parish was in disarray, and I found myself toiling in a different neighborhood, one that was haunted by racism both covert and overt, by a sense of hopelessness that led to drugs and casual sex, so I stressed revitalizing the schools to make them the focus of parish life. I wanted to thrust our youngsters, black and white, Catholic and non-Catholic, out of the terrible cycle of poverty that trapped them. Along with parents, I determined to make St. Vincent's elementary and secondary schools the finest in the city, and they're well on their way right now. We've won the Academic Olympics three of the last four years, and our basketball team is a thing to behold.

In any case, it's fortunate that the bishop backed my plan, because many older parishioners did not, deeply resenting my close ties with leaders in the black community, especially with clergy from other denominations. Many had also resented my even opening the school to non-Catholics, which is to say "them black Protestants," as Mrs. Duggan delicately put it. As a matter of fact, "Vinnie's," as we alums call it, had become underpopulated and was on the brink of closure when His Eminence approved my plan.

I'd hired a gifted Negro woman as principal after old Sister Mary Dominic retired, and the Irish really howled. Mrs. Duggan, her two sisters, and her daughter-in-law had written a joint letter to the bishop – he sent a copy to me – complaining that "Holy Mother Church" should concern herself with souls, not "race mixing." They predicted a spate of "mixed marriages," and they meant it both ways, I suppose.

Except to pick up and return his kids, Vester never visited the old neighborhood. In fact, he rarely came east at all; I knew from the occasional notes he sent me. Seamus Tynne's death finally brought him home for something like a real visit after all those years. Uncle Seamus, as we all called him, had been our high school football coach and P.E. teacher. He had been especially close to Vester, a second father to a boy dominated by women. After retiring, Seamus had remained in the parish, where he was a major figure in the Knights of Columbus and an invaluable aid to me. For a number of years after retiring, he had donated his time to organize and run a P.E. program at the grade school, helping those young black athletes as he had helped a couple generations of young white ones. I wrote to Ves, informing him of Uncle Seamus's death, and he called to say that he'd be flying in for the rosary, wake, and mass. Could I pick him up at the airport? I could and would.

Himself strode into the terminal, tan and bearded, leaner and more muscular than I'd expected, garbed in a stylish suit and tie. California seemed to agree with him. He looked, in fact, younger than he had ten years before. "Hey, Hollywood!" I called.

Vester stopped, grinned, then said, "Ah, the good father, you son of a gun!" and we shook hands, hugged, then shook hands again.

"How're my kids doing at Vinnie's?" he asked.

"They're fine as near as I can tell, top students and popular. Your aunts and mother don't trust them," I answered.

"That's a good sign. The kids sure seem great to me. I love to see them and they seem to have a good perspective. You know they've both decided to come out to California to college when they finish Vinnie's?"

"No," I replied. "How's that going over?"

"Like a turd in the punch bowl. But the law's on their side – our side – so they'll eventually join me, thank God."

"Poor Maureen," I said, and he understood.

"I'm sorry about Maureen. She's a fine woman, and now she's caught in everything I had to escape, and one day her own children will escape too." He shook his head. "I don't think she's ever understood how much it hurt when she left me without telling me why, but . . . I wish we could at least be friends."

I said nothing. That was private between them. If he wanted to discuss it, I would, but I wasn't going to push the issue. "It's not always fun being a grown-up," I said.

Driving back toward Uncle Seamus's wake, I told him that old Father Tim, now retired, was gravely ill.

"I'm sorry to hear that," he sighed. "Things change."

"Some things," I said.

"You still go down to the east side on weekends?" he asked innocently, his eyes creasing. "To minister to the whores" – he still pronounced it "hooers" in the old neighborhood fashion – "I mean. Like Pat when he sees a rabbi sneak into a whorehouse and says: 'Would you look at it, then, Mike. He ministers to his flock all week, then frolics with the fancy women.' A minute later they see a priest sneak in the same door and Pat says to Mike, 'Sure there must be sickness in the house.' "

"Oh, yeah," said I with equal innocence, "I spend a good deal of time on the east side. I've got to minister to *your* illegitimate children."

He smiled: "*My* illegitimate children!" Then he launched into another story: "Well, the priest says to the rabbi, 'Tell me, Goldstein, have you ever eaten pork?' Goldstein looks both ways, then nods: 'Yes, once, when I was young,' he says. 'And you, O'Reilly, tell me,' says the rabbi, 'have you ever made love to a woman?' The priest looks both ways, then whispers, 'Yes, once, when I was young.' The rabbi winks at him and says, 'A lot better than pork, isn't it?' "

I chuckled and shook my head, then dropped into the Mick dialect we neighborhood lads had always employed when together: "Arghh, boyo, sure and it's a *praist* yer talkin' to. And it's a mind like a racehorse ya have: It runs best on a dirt track."

"And do ya remember who told me that very tale these fifteen years past, then? A certain feller that's wearin' the collar now," he countered, "and foine broth of a lad wi' the lasses in his day."

"Sure 'tis the divil himself talkin'."

"That's what me mither says."

"Your mither," I replied, "says I'm the divil because I don't speak the Latin and I do speak to them *Knee-grows*."

"Are they black Protestants, then?"

"The blackest," I grinned.

"Arghh. At least they ain't orange." We both laughed at that one. He changed the subject: "Is this to be a drinkin' wake, then?"

"'Tis that, knowin' Seamus Tynne. He'd spin in his grave if forced to depart dry."

"Indaid he would. A foine man. One of the foinest," Ves nodded, and I heard sadness in his voice from years of exile when he had not visited the old man who had been his real father, that man now dead. "I'll have no trouble prayin' for him, will I?" he added. We said no more for a while.

"You going to visit the kids while you're home?"

He nodded. "I'll call tomorrow after the burial. No need alerting the enemy that I'm here."

The rosary was uneventful. As was customary, the body was laid out in an open coffin in the parlor of the deceased's house, which was crowded to bursting with faces black and white. Vester's various womenfolk wouldn't be attending services for the man who had coached their boy to the football scholarship that had "stole him from Holy Mother Church," although Denny McCann, alias "the Flower," who had been trying to keep company with an indifferent Maureen, would likely show up.

Even without the Wicklow women, the soul of Uncle Seamus was given a solid boost toward the heavenly reward we all expected it would receive. After praying the rosary, folks had dutifully filed through the kitchen to collect food and drink. It was a while before the affair thinned, but when it did, I was left with most of the Knights of Columbus – in their formal regalia, complete with brass buttons, plumed hats, and swords – old teammates, plus a few neighborhood layabouts eager for free drink. It seemed a propitious time to begin the toasts, so I ushered most of them into the parlor where Uncle Seamus lay with an angelic look on his tough old mug.

"Boyos," I said, raising a glass of Bushnell's finest, "here's to the coach who made us champions. May his flowers always bloom; may his feet never stink; may his eyes never cross; may he always have drink." Laughter and applause, plus a loud, collective slurp, followed my toast.

Vester was next: "Here's to a lad who was foine wi' the ladies, the Mollies, the Sallies, the Maggies, the Sadies. Here's to a lad wi' a brogue and a wink, who taught us to win and taught us to drink. Here's to a lad who never gave up, I honor him now wi' the tilt o' me cup." More laughter, more applause, and many cups tilted.

By then tongues were loose indeed, and one toast followed another, some smooth, others crude, but all at least mildly funny and all sincere in their appreciation of Uncle Seamus. The several new black members of the Knights seemed to especially enjoy the toasts, and Robert Reed, whose two boys had been coached by Uncle Seamus, offered one of his own: "Here's to a man that had him some soul, who called all the plays and paid all the toll. When he meet his Maker, may his Maker say, come on in and join us, champ, time for to play." I waited until all the oral poets seemed to have exhausted their creativity before making the announcement I'd been saving for just the right moment.

Standing over the coffin, I raised my hands: "Boyos!" I called, "I've something special to tell you." They quieted and gathered around. "It was Uncle Seamus's last request that I present his sword" – I picked up the ceremonial weapon in its sheath from atop the closed half of the casket and held it in both hands – "to the lad he believed was the finest he ever coached." I paused for effect, and names were whispered all around me. Finally, I announced: "Sylvester Duggan!"

Applause and shouts of congratulations mingled with friendly barbs – Billy Dunn: "He couldn't carry my jock!" Sean Daly: "He *needs* a damn sword! Mike Shaw: "That bench warmer?" – as Vester, grinning from ear to ear, but with glistening eyes, accepted the ornate instrument.

Then a boozy growl cut through the others: "He don't deserve it! He's fallen away!" It was Denny McCann, drunk and sounding angry. His presence, save for an occasional noxious aroma that filled the room, had been happily ignored. Now he bulled his way through the crowd, his plumed hat askew, his face like a tight red balloon. He was a big man,

Denny, a big man gone to fat, and he wedged a large space in front of the coffin, across it from Ves and me, then growled, "You're not in the Knights, ya bastard. You're livin' in sin out in that damn California! Look at ya, wearin' them fairy clothes. Gimme that!" He reached across the coffin and tried to grab Seamus's sabre, but I quickly moved in front of him.

"Cool off, Denny," I advised.

"And you, a man of the cloth, defendin' that bastard that's no better'n a Protestant." Denny pushed me aside and drew his sword, it dull as his wits, but a dangerous bludgeon.

"Put that down," warned Vester, shrugging those muscular shoulders. He did not back up.

"I'll settle your hash, ya queer, ya!" cried the Flower, and he waved his weapon while everyone on his side of the coffin scrambled to avoid the wild swings.

"Damn!" I heard Robert Reed grunt when he dodged.

Vester ducked and blocked a blow with his own sheathed weapon and I hit the floor. I heard two more sharp *clanks!* while Denny huffed and swung his blade, then a loud *smack!* followed by a dead *plop!* when the Flower hit the floor across from me, his plumed hat landing three feet away.

I climbed to my feet, and Vester was shaking his head, puffing more from excitement than effort, a look of disgust on that freckled face framed with fading red curls, and I heard Sean Daly from the back of the room whistle between his teeth and call, "Did ya see that left, then? It sure wilted the Flower. Uncle Seamus would've loved it." He was correct, of course, and laughter sprinkled the room, then grew to a roar. "And the good father, scramblin' for his ecclesiastical life!" added Sean. More laughter.

I grinned. "I was just down there givin' the last rites to poor Denny." Another roar. When it subsided, I continued: "Wee Sean, on the other hand, instead of defendin' his fellow Knight, Denny, was on his way to Atlantic City as fast as his size sixes would carry him when the good doctor here applied his anesthesia." More laughter.

"Was the good doctor just drummin' up business, then?" called Billy Dunn, as Vester examined the prostrate Flower.

"He's okay," called the medic. "Just resting."

"And does Dr. Duggan specialize in kayoin' his patients, then?" asked Billy, a copper who's seen a few scraps in his day.

Mike Shaw almost sang an answer: "Oh no! I believe the lad's got another professional interest." Giggles and guffaws from the crowd.

"And what *is* the good doctor's specialty, then?" winked Billy.

"The same thing it always was," wee Sean replied. "He's a lad whose dreams've come true." Another roar.

Standing beside me, Vester smiled and raised his hands over his head like the champ. At the same time he whispered out the corner of his mouth to me, "I *wish*," and his eyes rested momentarily on Uncle Seamus lying placidly amidst the clamor.

MADSTONE

Well, hell, I never believe them vaqueros. I mean they're good workers and all, but *superstitious*. Me, I don't never fall for none of that stuff. Like the night we're workin' on coffee and swappin' stories round the fire back when old Eight Ball Kelley was bear sign artist. Now Eight Ball he's a broke-down cowpoke from East Texas, ghost country, so you know he ain't no great shakes with haints and such. No man on earth can scare him, no critter either, but a haint turns him pale blond. He's plum levelheaded next to them vaqueros, though.

So this night me and Eight Ball and about four vaqueros is all squatted, chawin' tobacco, and damn near havin' to chaw the coffee too, it bein' the bottom of the pot, when these here big white owls kinda fluff over us quiet as beer farts, more like reverse shadows than birds, if you get my meanin'. Just as old Eight Ball is about to finish the story he's been draggin' out, I noticed them Mex'cans has quit breathin', then so does Eight

Ball, cause them vaqueros they of a sudden show more eyes than face.

"Los Chisos!" barks Jesse Avilos, then every one of them boys taken off like wolf-spooked jackrabbits.

There we sets, me and Eight Ball. "Mex'cans," he chuckles, then he hauls for his bedroll, so there sets me all alone. Just when I'm fixin' to turn in, here comes Ramon Dominguez, the foreman.

"Where's all the boys?" asks he.

"They got spooked by some birds," says I.

"Birds?" He pours hisself some coffee.

"Yeah," I tells him. "Big white owls they looked like."

He squats there next to the fire for a spell, rollin' that coffee around in his cup, his eyes narrowin', his head tiltin' just a little. "Los Chisos?" he asks me.

"That's what old Jesse said."

He groans, "Madre de Dios." Then off he runs, not even botherin' to eat his coffee first. Well, hell. I turns in. I have to ride drag next day, so to hell with it.

Mornin', old Eight Ball can't raise them four vaqueros nowheres. Pretty soon, up rides Ramon with the night guards. Eight Ball tells him about the missin' men, but Ramon says he already knows. He says they're sick, took with *la luna*.

Eight Ball he's kind of the crew doctor too, so him and me we rides over to the gully where Ramon tells us them vaqueros has hid their bed-rolls, and sure enough they're all cooned up with chills and fever. "This don't look like no moon sickness to me," declares Eight Ball. "Naw, looks like grippe. Nothin' I can do. Let 'em rest some. Leave somebody back to watch 'em. They can catch up."

Just when we're fixing to haul, up canters Ramon with this here stray man that's been ridin' the grub line of late. He's a Mex'can too, named Cruz. They dismounts, so old Eight Ball and me we dismounts too. Ramon leads this stray man over to the boys and they talks some, Ramon askin' Cruz if it was too late (Eight Ball he winks at me), and this Cruz an-swerin' real solemn that no, he figures *maybe* he might pull 'em through. He never says *what* he's pullin' 'em through, but I sees Eight Ball roll his eyes, and I figures maybe we oughta stick around.

Well, hell, while old Ramon tethers their horses, and I sees to ours, this stray man he fishes in the roll he takes off his mount (it, the mount I mean, lookin' more wild than tame, and him, Cruz I mean, lookin' to me like he belongs in a gun outfit). Eight Ball keeps a close eye on that stray man, and he tells me that all this Cruz takes from his roll is a rosary that he kisses and puts around his neck, and a white silk kerchief.

Directly, old Cruz drops to his knees and starts prayin' next to them four sick vaqueros, and fiddlin' with that silk kerchief. I can't rightly savvy him, then I catches on that he's sayin' his prayers backwards. Ramon, by then, is on his knees too. My knees is a little weak because everything of a sudden feels funny, though I figures it's just the sight of two growed men actin' so silly.

Eight Ball catches on to that funny feelin' too, and he jabs me and says, "Looky there." The stray man he's tyin' little knots in his kerchief while he chants them prayers. Every time he finishes one of them knots, Cruz lets out a war whoop that likes to scare water out of me. "That's another'n," Eight Ball he says, and I can tell it's gettin' to him cause his lower lip looks bigger and bigger.

When Cruz finishes the thirteenth knot, he howls even louder, then collapses limp as a old man's pecker. Me and Eight Ball runs to help Ramon tote him, then I notices that more than three of us is workin' on Cruz: It's them four vaqueros, all fit and ready to cut a rusty caper.

Eight Ball he takes off. I mean he's *gone*. I stands there a minute real casual, then tells Ramon I have to get gone too, not that he pays any mind to me, he's too busy slappin' them four boys on the back and proppin' up that stray man. I catches up to Eight Ball about a mile from where we'd been, and that old mossy mare he rides is puffin' to beat hell. "Slow up!" I calls to him, but he keeps his head down and his butt up. "Whoa, dammit!" I hollers, and he finally seems to notice me, then he looks back over his shoulder, his eyes all over his face. Finally, he slows down some. But just some.

"What the hell's wrong?" I asks him.

"What's wrong?" He looks at me like he figures me for crazy. "Them boys took with grippe, and that witch change 'em, that's what's wrong. I don't study no devil!"

I can't help but laugh. Well, hell, I'd just saw what Eight Ball'd saw, and I admit it's a mite weird, but it's just a damn Mex'can trick and I told him so. Hell, he'd rode with Mex'cans as long as me, but he won't hear nothin' I say. "Them boys have grippe," he keeps repeatin', "and now they cured." I can't reason with him, so I gives up.

Three days later I'm ridin' point through scrubby brush when I hears a big commotion in a thicket up ahead. I rides up to it real quiet, then dismounts and creeps through brush until I sees a prairie wolf kinda staggering against a piñon tree, its head lollin' funny, a greenish-white froth on its mouth. I ain't but ten foot from that wolf, but it never even notices me, it worryin' that tree right smart. It's took with hydrophobia I sees right off, madder'n a gut-shot grizzly. Well, hell, I ain't no great pal to prairie wolves, but I don't like to see no critter suffer like that, so I steps out from the brush and levels my pistol at that poor devil, me fixin' to put him out of his misery.

But my handgun misfires and that wolf he sees me. I cocks my pistol again – the wolf staggerin' in my direction – and my damn gun misfires again. I cocks it once more and it fires this time, killin' the poor critter just after it bites my left leg.

I sets down then, knowin' that goddamned wolf has killed me just when I'm fixin' to help him, knowin' I'm gonna go crazy in a couple weeks and chaw dirt and bite folks then die in the awfulest way, and knowin' there ain't nothin' can be done. I looks at that bite on my leg and at that wolf's carcass and at my damned handgun that's let me down. Well, hell, I figures, might as well make it clean. I puts the muzzle against my head and squeezes the trigger. The sonofabitch misfires.

I puts it against my head once more, then bang! I'm on my butt. Miguel Ybañez, that's been ridin' swing behind me, has kicked the pistol out of my hand and caught my head too. "Qué pasó?" he asks. I nods at that wolf, then points at my leg. "Aye, Madre!" he says. Then we hauls toward Ramon and Eight Ball and the chuck wagon.

It's funny, really, that even when you know good and well that somethin' won't kill you for a spell, you still get all faintified. By the time we gets back to camp, I can't even stand up. I just slumps against one of the chuck wagon's wheels. Eight Ball makes a poultice as quick as he can, but he never looks too happy. Ramon takes off in a hurry.

I'm still there propped against that wheel with Eight Ball's poultice on the wound, him trying to get me to drink some coffee, when up rides

Ramon with Cruz, that he's hired on by then. They come right over to where I'm sprawled and that stray man takes the poultice off my leg. (Eight Ball disappears when he sees Cruz.) Well, hell, that stray man he looks into my eyes, then back at that bite, then jumps up and trots to his saddle roll.

He comes back with a funny lookin' rock or some such. Ramon says it's a madstone, took from the belly of a deer and that it can suck the poison out of a wound. What the hell do I have to lose? Cruz kneels next to me and commences jabberin' some kind of prayer, swirlin' that madstone round and round his head with both hands while he carries on, then he puts it right smack where that wolf bit me.

The stone sticks like a leech, hanging there by itself, and I feels this powerful pull. I kinda jumps, but that stray man tells me to set. All the time that stone is suckin' and pullin', I can feel it. It even looks a little like it's gettin' bigger, like dry bread soppin' in soup. But I never says nothin' cause I'm flat scared by then.

I don't know how long that stone is on my leg, but directly it falls off onto the white silk kerchief that Cruz has put under it. "Leche!" He hollers, and here comes Miguel Ybañez with a pail of hot milk he's just took from the fire. The stray man drops his madstone into the pail, careful not to touch it, and the milk directly turns green. "Veneño," says the stray man, grinnin' for the first time. Ramon and Miguel they both laugh.

"You feel better?" asks Ramon and, you know, I do. "Finish your coffee, wrap that wound up, and get back to work," he orders. "We got cattle to drive to Bakersfield." Then them three Mex'cans rides off, the pail of green milk going with 'em.

Soon as they're gone, here comes ol' Eight Ball. "Now what you think?" he asks.

Well, hell, I know he's fixin' to give me a bad time, so I just shrugs and says real casual, "You know how them Mex'cans is."

He pours me a fresh cup of coffee, lookin' at me all the time. "I knows how *you* is," he grunts. Then he fills his own cup, shakes his head, and says, "Loco."

RETURN, PRODIGAL

They'd all but given up on him, the critics had I mean; they'd written him off. After all, when a potentially outstanding artist is roasted by reviewers, then takes a job at a hick college, well you naturally figure he's thrown in the towel.

But Gio Leoni was no ordinary artist. Those of us who knew him weren't surprised when his name appeared in the *Times* a couple of years after he'd quit San Francisco. It was a small story written by Ron Kinney, the art editor, saying that Gio claimed to have developed a new genre, something he called "holoform." Kinney referred to Gio as an "erstwhile boy wonder who claims to have developed an ultimate form of organic art." The story featured a small photo of Gio wearing a cowboy hat.

The new art form would be first presented at a show here in the city, at Beddecker's, the very gallery where Gio's last exhibit had been held, the one so badly slammed by Ron Kinney and company.

Well, great, I figured. Anything that brings Gio back to town is okay with me. You've got to understand that Gio and I became close friends as undergrads at State College. Both of us had been married – both since divorced – and both took advantage of the GI Bill. We swilled gallons of wine together, and wenched together, and solved the world's problems several times over. And we've picked one another's livers more than once too. We had one running argument that lasted about three years. He could never understand how I survived a chemistry major. "Too stifling," he'd say. "It would kill my creativity."

"Oh, balls!" I would delicately answer. "What you need is some scientific discipline to free your cluttered mind."

"Free!" he'd shout. "Free! You don't know the meaning of the word!" And then we'd be into it till the wine ran out or dawn forced us to call it a draw.

I remember one evening when I argued for science as a creative endeavor, telling Gio that Art (with a capital A) had vitiated due to its own incest. Did he ever blow up over that. "Artist die for art," he shouted. "Art lovers die for it. But people only die *because* of science, not for it." That got to me, so we again debated all night, but the point is we never really got angry.

Another thing we disagreed on was his second show. He had received favorable reviews with his first set of displayed paintings, but scheduling his next showing so soon after the first, and at a big gallery like Beddecker's – well, I sensed disaster. And I was right. Gio was experimenting with a fly-sprayer for all his paintings at that time, spreading an incredibly fine filigree of feeling on massive canvases. The trouble was that critics seemed unable to see merit in anything but little, gutsy pseudo–Van Goghs and something they called "organic art," what the hell ever that was. Gio's work was doomed, but he said no, they'll recognize originality when they see it.

Well, the critics didn't recognize any originality in Gio's second showing – they characterized his work as "contrived and weak" – so he and I had to go into hock to pay his outstanding debts and let him get away for a while. He took an artist-in-residence position at Desert State College over near Bishop and, save for an occasional note, disappeared. One letter, I remember, tersely stated: "I'm into something good now, an original synthesis," but he never explained the synthesis and I knew better than to push him.

Came the *Times* article, though, and I knew I'd see him soon – probably a phone call in the middle of the night would rouse me and I'd hear his Groucho Marx voice: "Hello, you fat kike," he'd say with great reverence. "If you can stop playing with yourself long enough, come get me. I'm at the airport." I would reply with an accurate description of his mother's vocation (and avocation) and would then drive out to South City and pick him up. We'd probably be debating before my car had traveled a block.

Sure enough, one night just as I crawled in bed to enjoy an Agatha Christie, the phone rang. "Hello, you Zionist bastard," Groucho's voice said. I cut him short: "You have the wrong number," I replied in a thick pasta accent, "this is the Italian-American Civil Rights League. Who you want us to kill?" Gio broke up. "Aw," he chanted, "your momma's a tool grinder. I'm at the airport. Come get me." I fetched him home.

Gio was pooped, but we stayed up and drank rot-gut wine and talked. I finally found out what his latest creation was and, I have to tell you, I was astounded. He claimed he got the idea from me, with a little help from Bernard Berensen's writings and Kenneth Clark's. He said that the last two had shown him that new insights in one art form are quickly adapted to other forms. "You know," he said, "you develop something like baroque or rococo in one genre, and pretty soon you've got correlates popping up all over, right?" I nodded. "Well, you add a little McLuhan to the other two, and your own brilliant insights, of course" – I blushed appropriately – "and it just seemed to me that the world was waiting for someone to put it all together at once.

"Well, we've got the technology now to do just that, so I have. Remember all that crap you used to throw my way about the creative potential of the sciences. Okay, I've taken you up." He suddenly metamorphosed into Bela Lugosi: "Meester RRRenfield, I haf created a moonstair," he leered, rubbing his green hands all the while. Then he flew into the kitchen and poured himself another glass of Red Mountain blood. "How the hell can bats drink wine hanging upside down?" he asked.

"They have hollow legs," I responded with scientific gravity.

"Oh," he said, climbing down from my chandelier.

I kept pushing Gio to tell me more about this thing he called "holo-form." He said it would replace Lydia Pinkhams in the hearts of the people. "It's better than hash, grass, and lucky number score cards," he claimed, rolling Jerry Colonna eyes.

"I believe, Great Mufti," I salaamed, "but what the hell *is* it?"

Finally he said that he had created a total artistic experience. "Holo-form is a piece of living sculpture. I mean you can see it and touch it, right? But you can enter it too. And once you get inside," W. C. Fields said, "you will experience thrills and delights, de-lights." He placed his top hat on the end of his cane and staggered through the room juggling two small boys and a dog. "And as for you, my little Jewish poltroon," he said, "I hope a sexually crazed Arab voodoo queen sticks pins in the crotch of your likeness." W.C. teetered into the kitchen, goosing himself with the doorknob, then returned holding a full glass. "Ahhh," said he, "spiritus fermenti."

"But what the hell's inside?" I asked.

"Nuns!" Gio answered surreptitiously. "Wildly passionate nuns driven into a sensual frenzy by a nude photo of the Marquis de Sade!" He sobbed, his face in his hands. "Oh, my secret is out. Pray, kind sir, I was not always as you see me now." He wiped his hands on a cat.

"Peter Sellers," I said.

"You saw that one too. Good. One of the all-time greats. Well, anyway, about holoform, you get caressed by warm, slick membranes when you're inside." Within, he told me, holoform was precisely the temperature the computer at his college had advised. Moreover, a gentle electronic music played just what the computer ordered. And there was more: The dark-ness within holoform was livened by a light diffuser prepared by a physics prof at Desert State that shattered and blended colors. And a couple of organic chemists at the school had developed a pleasant musk aroma that was, as Groucho put it, "verrry stimulating" (he raised and lowered his eyebrows several times). "To women, it smells like primed man; to men, it smells like primed woman."

His last revelation was that a mild hallucinogen was sprayed into the air within holoform. "But cool it," he requested, "it's slightly illegal." In fact, before the night was over, he made me promise not to tell anyone anything about holoform. Both Peter Lorre and Sydney Greenstreet aided him in convincing me I'd best not squeal.

While he brought several of his other things – some conventional sculpture and chronology of his paintings – along to help fill the gallery, there was no question that holoform was the whole show. I asked him if he wasn't counting too much on one piece, and for a moment he flared at me: "Haven't you understood anything I've been telling you? There has never been anything like this. *Never.*" He quickly cooled off and said no, he'd thought about it a long while before making a public announcement, but it was also a question of time, for he knew of several other artists working on similar projects and he keenly understood the value of being first.

Gio spent most of the next couple of days at Beddecker's preparing holoform and the other pieces for the show. Evenings we partied with old pals, including some women I'd somehow foolishly forgotten. Every morning, my mouth tasting as though a marmot drive had passed through it during the night, I'd creak out of bed and find Gio brewing coffee with chocolate in it. He showed no signs of wear. "Work! Work!" he'd say, stalking the kitchen, raising his eyebrows and puffing an imaginary cigar.

On the evening before the show was to open to the general public, there was the usual reception for the select few, mainly critics, plus a sprinkling of fellow artists and, of course, a gang of edible models. Liquor flowed freely, and funny little cigarettes were puffed openly, while the crowd milled around the massive holoform, which stood draped in the middle of Beddecker's main gallery room. You could tell everyone wanted to get started, but Gio guarded his creation like a new father. About the time various critics began glancing at their watches, Herman Beddecker and Gio called everyone to the sculpture and without fanfare, Gio pulled the cord and holoform was exposed.

Wow! The entire audience gasped. It was an earth brown monolith, shaped with the muscular smoothness of an animal form, yet unlike any animal I'd ever seen. I found myself immediately attracted to it. I was standing right next to the holoform and to me it seemed to be pulsing, so lifelike was its exterior, and I thought I heard a vague purring sound, probably feedback from the microphone Gio had used in assembling everyone.

"Well," announced Gio in his usual off-the-wall manner, "let's allow the gentlemen of the press to explore the de-lights within holoform first. Mr. Kinney?"

Dapper Ron Kinney separated his plump form from a tall black girl and, with bemused grin, gave us a thumbs-up and slipped into holoform's glistening crease; I caught a flash of pink as he entered; the purring and pulsing increased slightly. Gio let Kinney have holoform to himself for several minutes, then let other critics enter. I could see Gio's satisfaction as the gentlemen of the press disappeared.

"Give them time to really dig," Gio ordered. "The rest of you can join them in a few minutes. More drinks?" So we all drank until Gio finally gave us the go sign.

I entered first, sliding tentatively into the dark crease, blinded until my whole being suddenly lifted: tingling, tasting, smelling, existing pleasure. Soft, warm sides pressed gently on me as an odor awakened my body. Passionate breath engulfed me; my being orgasmed.

Outside again, I needed a nap. Everyone glowed. "That thing's gotta be illegal," whispered a blonde model I'd been trying to score with all evening. "It's too *good.*" And I knew what *good* meant. Did I ever.

One artist friend of Gio's and mine kind of leaned on me and said, "My God, he's actually done it. It *is* a total experience. It's like your first hit of smack, only better. A total experience. A new space. I can't get over it." In fact, everyone who was willing, or able, to talk praised Gio and his holoform. Herman Beddecker looked like one big grinning dollar sign. What a night for Gio! What a comeback!

When we finally returned home, Gio and I enjoyed a nightcap – morning-cap, really – and gabbed for a few more minutes. We rehashed the whole show, step by step, word for word. "You really showed those smug bastards," I told him. "You made them back off."

"One of 'em, anyway," he answered.

"One! All of them. Every damned one! Man oh man, were their mouths open," I told him. "What ever happened to Ron Kinney? Did he rush out to retract a postdated review? He's famous for writing reviews before he even attends shows, you know."

"I know. But that dude has filed his last public crucifixion." Gio looked drunkenly conspiratorial. "Arrrrrgh," breathed Long John Silver, "can ye keep a secret?"

"What do you mean? Do you think you can get his job?"

"Arrrrrgh, who needs his job? I've got the lubber a'ready. Er at least me holoform has. Arrrrrgh."

"Got him?"

"It ate him."

"Ate him?" He was putting me on, per usual.

"Aye, boots, buckles, and all. Arrrrrgh. The boots be tastin' better than his wormy carcass did."

He sounded too serious beneath Long John's speech, and I felt a bubble of doubt growing in my throat. "What do you really mean, ate him?"

Gio poured himself another stiff brandy. "Man," he said, "you are one dense dude. Ate him. Devoured him. Gobbled him all gone. Dig?" He shook his head at my imperception.

"But . . ."

"Look," he said with painful patience, "holoform is alive. How else do you think it can do all those things at once? The critics wanted organic art, didn't they? Well now they've got it. Let's see what the sons of bitches do with it."

I could see he was serious. "What the hell are you saying? You mean you killed Kinney?"

"I didn't lay a glove on him."

"But you say he's dead."

"Maaan," answered Step'nfetchit, "he ain' jus' daid, he *et!*"

"Then how did the rest of us get out?"

He poured more brandy. "You really don't know much about nature for a guy with a Ph.D. It's like a big snake, it only eats about once a week, usually a dog I get at the pound. Old chubby Kinney will last two weeks, I bet." He chuckled. "It's no sweat. I just let it get good and hungry and I can feed it anything I want."

I stood and stalked the room, growing more aghast as the impact of what he revealed struck me. I turned to face him several times but could say nothing. "The police are sure to find out," I finally sputtered.

"Why?"

"Why? Because they'll find the remains, that's why."

Again he laughed at me. "There aren't any," he said, "at least not any that the police will recognize; just a fine gray powder that looks like ashes."

I stood again and walked to the window, then returned to my chair. "But you can't just let it devour critics. It . . . well . . . it just isn't *right*."

Gio looked at me rather sadly, shaking his head a bit, then he finished his brandy and stood. "Why not?" he finally said. "Critics have been devouring artists since day one."

THE LAST ROUNDUP

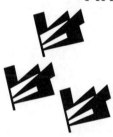

"Come on, all you cowboys and cowgirls," urged that announcer's voice from the radio, "join us at the Last Roundup Saloon in Modesto for the wet T-shirt contest next Saturday night. You cowgirls can win a hundred dollars cash if the judges select you, and all entries will receive free Last Roundup T-shirts."

Some real fast country music without no sangin' come on, then that announcer's voice it talked again: "Don't forget, the wet T-shirt contest at the Last Roundup Saloon in Modesto next Saturday, cowboys and cowgirls, with live music for your dancing pleasure."

"That there's where I wanta go," I said to Uncle Fud Murray that was sippin' coffee at the counter. He's a ol' fart, Uncle Fud, a ex–ranch hand with nothin' to do in Oakdale but drink coffee at the Big Or'nge where I work and bullshit. Usual, he tells some purty good stories too, but sometimes he acts downright devilish.

"You ain't no cowboy, Delbert," he snorted, "and Judas Priest you don't look worth a shit in no T-shirt anyways." Before I could answer him back, ol' Fud went and switched to what he'd been a-talkin' about: "Yessir, just like I's sayin', it's kids nowadays look too damn much alike. A bunch of damn Barbie dolls. Hell, whenever I's a boy back in Bowlegs, folks had character. Like my Aunt Mabel Proudy that had a goiter on her neck the size of a mushmelon. Wadn't nobody else in Bowlegs like her. Anybody seen that goiter, even if they never met 'er before, they knowed it was Aunt Mabel.

"And Dad Murphy that had buck teeth he could play a pianer with, and him a pinhead to boot, but that never slowed the ol' boy down. Run him a good feed bidnis and had fourteen younguns. Went around in the tiniest Stetson you ever seen, like a doll's."

"I look a hell of a lot better'n you do in a T-shirt," I finally got a chance to say. I wasn't lettin' any Fud Murray get the better of me. "Besides, that man he was talkin' about gals in wet T-shirts."

"Ya don't say?" Fud grinned, winkin' at Jake Garcia, this cattle rancher that was settin' next to 'im, and I think he was a-kiddin' me. Just when I's fixin' to answer him real snappy, he started again.

"There was Mutt Powers that had a face like a Mexican Hairless and could yodel better'n any white man in Oklahoma, and Wilma Watson with a harelip that could dance real good, and Tody Parker that had pockmarks on his face so it looked like somebody'd shotgunned him. He owned about half the county. Them folks looked like folks, not plastic dolls." He paused and slurped some coffee and nodded at Jake like he just proved somethin' real important.

"Nowadays," Fud went on, "all these damn kids got braces and that plastic surgery stuff and all. Judas Priest, it seems like there's a doctor behind ever' bush, and the kids they come out lookin' like Dee-troit cars, all the damn same, a-thankin' they're purty, but how can they be purty if they're all the damn same is what I wanta know?"

"That man said they got a band and all them cowboys and cowgirls are a-gonna be there," I said.

Uncle Fud grinned again at Jake.

"Besides," I added, "they even got a mechanical bull at the Last Roundup."

"Bet them cows truly 'preciate that," Fud said real smart-alecky. "Is it like one of them vibrators or what?"

"Huh?" I said. Jake was laughin'.

"Besides," added Uncle Fud, "there's a whiteface bull down the road worth ten thousand dollars. Out to stud."

"That's where I'm a-goin', anyways," I told him, not givin' in.

"Out to stud?"

"Huh?" I said.

Jake was laughin' louder: "Hah! He-he-he!"

"Yessir, out to stud, this boy, and hung like a boar mouse," added Uncle Fud.

"I never said that!" I snapped quick as I could.

"Hah!" Jake busted out even louder. "He-he-he!"

Uncle Fud wouldn't let go, talkin' faster 'n faster. "Gonna service all them little heifers at the wet T-shirt contest."

"I never even said that!"

"Hah! He-he-he!"

"Gonna make that mechanical bull look like a hobby horse!"

"Hah! He-he-he!"

"I never said that!" It's hard keepin' up with him oncet he gets goin'. Just when I's about to sock Fud, in walked that family, and him and Jake clammed right up, but they kept lookin' at me through their eyebrows and I seen their eyes a-laughin'.

Anyways, a man and a woman – they both ordered big or'nges – plus two little knob-knockered girls and even littler boy that looked like he set fire to haystacks for fun – them three had Cokes – set in a booth by the front door. Bigger'n hell, them kids had more chrome in their mouths than a Cadillac does on its grill, and you shoulda seen the I-told-you-so look ol' Fud give me.

By the time them folks left, I wasn't so sore at Uncle Fud no more, and him and Jake was carryin' on about them kids and their braces. "Like a bunch a damn robots," Fud concluded, "all of 'em look exactly alike."

For a minute or two nobody said nothin', me happy for the silence, then Jake said, "Wet T-shirt contest, huh? I've never seen one a those." He sounded interested.

"They got a live band and ever'thang," I added.

"Didn't thank they'd have a dead one, did ya?" Fud asked.

"Huh?"

"Ladies in wet T-shirts, eh?" Jake kinda sighed, tappin' his cup for a refill. While I scrambled over to the pot, then filled his cup, he kept talkin' real quiet: "Wet T-shirts. Uh-huh. Well, boys, let's go take a look at those women in wet T-shirts. Uncle Fud, can your old heart take it?"

"You bet!"

"How 'bout you, Delbert?" he asked me.

"You mean it, Jake? You really gonna take us to the Last Roundup clean over at Modesto?"

"Yeah, I am. I'll have my stock moved by then. Why not?"

"Oh, boy!" I felt about like sangin'. "Boy, oh boy!" I really wanted to see one a them real cowboy places and this was my chance.

I never thought Saturday'd ever come. That ol' week it just dragged and dragged, with me ever bit as excited as the time I went to Disneyland. After work I'd go to my trailer and try on that dandy straw hat with big feathers in front that I'd bought last winter in Fresno. I'd look in the mirror and see that I looked just like the guys in the movie had, like one a them guys that drives a four-wheel-drive pickup, the kind that sets so high off the ground you need a stepladder to climb into it, the kind with white writin' on the tars and all. I'm a-gonna get me one a them someday, too.

Anyways, come the big night – it still light, of course, 'cause it was summer – up drove Jake from his ranch in his pickup, in two-wheel drive with mud and cowshit on the tars, and so low I could step right into the cab. Well, he'd probably have to park down the road from the Last Roundup, so none a them cowboys or cowgirls would see what we was drivin'.

Soon as I popped into the cab, I noticed what Jake was wearin': a suit and tie topped by a green baseball cap with "Skoal" wrote on the front of it. Oh, hell. "Jake," I told him, "you gotta go home and change clothes. You gotta dress like a cowboy to go to the Last Roundup."

"I got my good boots on, Delbert," he answered, sounding a tad pissed. "Besides, if I turn this truck around, it ain't goin' nowhere but home."

I felt about like spittin'. "Couldn't you at least go home and get your hat?"

"I ain't got but two hats. My good one's out being blocked and my work one looks like, well, a work one. I'm driving to Modesto. You can stay or go. Make up your mind."

Hell, he was ruinin' ever'thang. Here we was going to a high-class cowboy and cowgirl joint, and he was dressed like a damn clodhopper. Just when I's about to really tell him off, Jake said, "Where in God's name did you get that war bonnet, anyway?"

That done it. "I . . . I . . ." I couldn't thank a nothin' to say right then, so I made my mind up to travel with him, but not to talk. I'd show Jake Garcia, by God. "This here's a real cowboy hat," I finally told him. Then I give him the silent treatment.

It never lasted too long, though, because that damn ol' Fud came out from his trailer dressed more like a rodeo clown than a cowboy. He had on these baggy slacks, a white Western shirt with red and green cactuses on it that musta been all the rage back about 1940 whenever ol' Gene Artury wore the same thang, yellow shoes like nobody else ever wore, and one a them Smokey-the-Bear hats rangers wear, the kind with dents on the side. "He ain't goin!" I told Jake, and I meant it too.

"Hell, he's all dressed up," Jake answered, never crackin' a smile.

Fud swang into the cab, smelling like a barbershop. "All right, boys," he announced, "let's have at them wet T-shirts."

"You ain't going!" I told him plain and simple.

"Somebody ain't going if you don't shut your face," Jake growled at me. "I'm getting tired of your bellyaching."

"What's a matter with Delbert?" Fud asked, grinnin'.

Well, I wasn't settin' with them two at no Last Roundup. I just made my mind up I'd travel with 'em, but that was all. I was through with 'em. Then I noticed ol' Fud eye'n my clothes real close. "Judas Priest!" he spouted. "Where'd you rustle that getup, Delbert?"

My getup! I's fixin' to tell him off. Before I could, though, he got that motor mouth of his to workin'.

"Hell's bells, you're just a-provin' what I said the other day about young folks all lookin' alike cause if they cain't change their faces, then they try to dress alike: flashy pearl-button shirt, big ol' belt buckle, hat that dips down in front and back and – boy howdy! – how many chickens had to die so's you could wear them feathers? You look like you's stamped outta the same machine as all them citified peckerheads.

The Last Roundup 105

"Why, ol' Tody Parker that owned half a Bowlegs, he's a real cowboy from the git go, and he wore a derby hat from England. Nobody else had one. Whenever they seen a derby hat around Bowlegs, wadn't but one guy they knew could be a-wearin' it: Tody Parker."

Even Jake got into it, adding: "Look at ol' Fud's hat. I'll bet you don't see another one like it in Modesto."

I's just fixin' to say somethin' real clever to shut 'em up when Jake he changed the subject and commenced talkin' about how he's gonna buy a Brangus bull to toughen his herd and that led Fud back to Bowlegs and a guy that used a Brahma to service his whitefaces and stuff like that. I let 'em go on, but I never forgot. I's fixin' to tell 'em off but I's afraid I'd lose my ride. They was damn lucky, I'll tell you that much.

The band it was real loud in the Last Roundup, and the joint was real crowded, and I was right about how cowboys dressed, by God, I seen that directly. Jake he fetched us three beers from the bar and found us a table next to the dance floor. He's a big ol' boy, Jake, neck like a bullfrog and arms bigger'n most guys' legs, so he's good to follow in a crowd. To my surprise, nobody give him and Fud the horse laugh for bein' dressed so funny, at least not that I noticed anyways, and one little ol' cowgirl winked at Fud and said sweet as can be, "Love your hat. It's outrageous." She never said nothin' about my sombrero.

We set there for a while, music loud enough to knock the fillin's outta your teeth boomin' from these great big speakers on the sides of the band-stands. All the musicians was hippies with long hair and beards. But cowboy hippies, by God, with feathers on their hats and ever'thang. Jake he tore off pieces of a napkin and stuffed 'em in his ears. "Where the hell's the women?" he asked me. "I don't see anything but a bunch of pencil-necks in cowboy costumes."

For a fact there wasn't a lot a cowgirls showin', and the few I did see had droves of cowboys around 'em, but at least they knew how to dress, not like some folks I could mention.

We's on our second beers whenever they started that mechanical bull-ridin' contest, and had just ordered our thirds whenever the damned thang went and broke down, spittin' sparks and smokin' so bad this one cowboy got his butt burned, fancy chaps or not. Fud went crazy, cacklin' like a damn hen. "Ya reckon it's got the bloat?" he asked Jake, who laughed too. "It sure blowed a parful fart!" said Fud. Then he turned to me: "Where's all them gals at, Delbert?"

"They're a-comin'," I snapped, but to tell the truth I's a little worried myself. Thangs they wasn't exactly like I'd thought they'd be and I's afraid of the raggin' them two would give me whenever we got back home.

Just then the announcer, this fat guy in a sequined suit, he called for the wet T-shirt contestants to report to the bandstand, and everbody give a big war whoop. I could tell it's mainly what they'd been a-waitin' on. Like a mir'cle, a line of gals appeared up there, signed on, and he give each one a T-shirt, then they disappeared into the john to change while the band commenced playin' softer than before and even Jake took out his earplugs. Meanwhile that announcer he said funny thangs like "These ladies wanta get something off their chests" and "Hope you boys don't miss any points of interest," real clever stuff like that. I's laughin' to beat hell whenever the gals come out from the can in their T-shirts, but Fud looked half-solemn and Jake just looked.

The announcer and a helper had spread big ol' mats on the dance floor and they had these pitchers a water on a foldin' table they'd set up. "All got the same T-shirts on," said Fud, soundin' kinda breathless, "just like I said, all trying to look alike," but it never sounded like he meant it, his eyes massagin' them gals.

The man commenced pourin' water over the front of the first little ol' gal, a real cute redhead, and her cupcakes they stood straight out under that clingin' shirt. I heard Uncle Fud gasp, "Judas Priest!" whenever she danced a few steps to the music.

The next cowgirl's bigger'n the first, with black hair and real crisp eyes like flint. Once they got her good and damp, her cantaloupes just glistenin', she danced a bit and I heard ol' Fud gasp, "Jud-das Priest!" Jake hissed, "Now that's my kinda woman," his own eyes locked on her.

Number three was another blackheaded gal, the kind with banana boobs that pointed left and right once her shirt was wet, and bounced in opposite directions whenever she danced. I liked to slipped off the table where I'd climbed to see better, and ol' Fud did fall, moanin' "Juuu-das Priest" just before he landed with a thud! It never killed him though, and he bounced back onto that table like a tennis ball. He sure as hell wasn't fixin' to miss nothin'.

The only blonde in the contest was number four, and her little lemons pointed damn near straight up at the ceilin' fan when her shirt was wet. Once she was dancin', them little boogers jumped like ground squirrels in a bag, and old Fud timbered again, calling "Juuu-dass Priest!" as he fell.

That's when this cowboy standin' next to me, he turned and growled, "Get that old fart outta here before somebody kicks his ass."

Jake, who'd been too busy devourin' them gals with his eyes to pay much mind to Fud, heard that guy, and said, "What?"

"You heard what I said, man, get the old fart outta here right now or I will." That young buck he had a lotta beer talkin' for him. "He's buggin' the hell outta me!"

Well, Jake's blood was already warmed a bit anyways, so he just looked that cowboy in the eye and said, "Mind your own business." From the way he said it I knew he wasn't gonna say no more, so I slipped off my good cowboy hat and surveyed the crowd: Young buck had four pardners all ballin' their fists, all of 'em beered up and brave.

Directly there was only three total because Jake he blasted young buck to the floor so quick I never seen the punch, then he put a choke hold on another'n and crumpled him too. Two others they jumped on his back, and I peeled one off with my beer bottle, and damned if ol' Uncle Fud didn't kick the other'n in the nuts and fold him up. There wasn't but one left and when he seen Jake comin' for him he took off like a spooked quail right through the wet T-shirt contest, knockin' the announcer and his helper ass over teakettle in the process.

Even the bouncer, whenever he come for us, he give Jake a wide berth. "Sorry, boys," he said, a real big guy that looked like a horse trailer, "house rules. All fightin' and fighters outside."

"You kickin' out those punks that started it?" Jake demanded.

"They're gone," answered horse trailer.

"Then we'll just join 'em in the parking lot."

Horse trailer nodded. "Good. We don't want any trouble with you boys."

Before I realized what happened, we's out in the parkin' lot, but them other guys was nowheres to be seen, though two of them big four-wheel-drive pickups with fog lights on top and chrome exhausts they roared out just as we hit the pavement. "I reckon them tough cowboys swallowed the olive," Uncle Fud observed.

"Let's go back inside and see who wins the wet tit . . . I mean T-shirt . . . contest," I suggested.

"They won't be letting us back in there tonight, Delbert," Jake told me. "We're kicked out."

"Kicked out! I left my hat in there."

"Judas Priest," spit Fud, "just when it's a-gettin' good."

We climbed into the cab of Jake's pickup, me feelin' so bad about my lost hat I couldn't even talk. Finally, I asked, "Are you sure they won't let me go back in for my hat?"

Fud shook his head. "Not after the way you operated on that one feller's carbunkle. Sweet as a surgeon and with a beer bottle too."

"That great big bouncer'd put a dent in your head if he saw you," added Jake. "You're better off with a head than a hat, feathers or not. Besides, they'll probably save it and we can pick it up next week."

"Next week?" I asked.

"Next week!" gasped Fud.

"Hell, yeah," Jake chuckled. "I wouldn't want to miss out on all those cowboys and cowgirls. Speaking of that, Fud, I've got one question for you."

"What's that?"

"Do you still think all young folks look alike?"

Fud broke out laughin'. "Judas Priest, I's talkin' 'bout faces, not knockers. I bet if there's a way to put braces on 'em they'd do 'er, but for now there's still somethin' to be said for the way they are. There's still a little variety left, by damn."

"Yeah," I stuck in real quick.

"You got me there, Delbert," he admitted. "You sure as hell got me there," pattin' me on the back.

I felt better all the way home.

STOLEN GLANCES

"Hey, you!" He heard the voice and turned. Across the street he saw the blue blur of a man, who began striding toward him, so he stopped and lowered his plastic bag of aluminum cans to the sidewalk and waited, his eyes lowered.

"Let's see your ID," the policeman demanded.

Up close, Winfield could see well enough to tell this man was young, despite his rough voice. "I got this," he said, and he handed the policeman his discharge paper.

"*You*, a veteran," sniffed the cop, his tone saying it all. Then he handed the frayed paper back. "Where're you livin' at?"

"I'm on the road right now," said Winfield.

"You got a job?"

"I collect these cans."

"Yeah, and steal anything that ain't nailed down. You just keep movin' on, buster, if you don't want hard time. We don't tolerate vagrants around here."

"Yessir." This kid was young enough to be his son. He surely hadn't even been born when Winfield was dodging bullets across France and Germany.

"Now move it."

"Yessir." He hefted the plastic sack and shuffled toward the bridge under which he'd stashed his pack and bedroll, mumbling to himself: "Before you was even born. . . . You need to treat me like a man, not a damn bum," he demanded, one arm flailing, his voice rising as he continued walking. All around him, colored blurs moved to sound, but he concentrated only on each step. His belly boiled, though, for he resented the implication that because he was on the street he was automatically a thief. If he was, he wouldn't be scrounging for these damned aluminum cans. He was a working man out of work.

"Buster!" he spat. "I'm not no buster. I got a name."

What really burned him was the kernel of truth in what that cop had said: he had, just lately, twice stolen pairs of glasses, so guilt compounded his outrage. He knew a real thief wouldn't feel guilt, but that was no solace. "Damn son of a bitch!" he heard, then realized it was his own voice. He was shouting as he walked, and other pedestrians were swerving far around him. Well, to hell with 'em. "Christ on a crutch!" What did they know, anyways?

He wasn't any damn thief, but his eyes were going and he had to see. He had first realized something was wrong when, watching television at the farm near Red Bluff where he'd picked two summers before, the screen had never seemed to be properly focused. At a flophouse in San Francisco he'd had a fistfight with a wino who insisted the TV was okay. After that, when all the other stiffs had agreed with the wino, he realized something wasn't right with his eyes.

Only when everything lost focus did he lift that first pair of glasses from the assistant preacher at the Fresno Rescue Mission. They'd made things look different, longer mostly, and they'd swerved his brain like cheap wine. He returned to the softened edges and blended colors that had gradually become his world, though he kept those glasses just in case.

He stole a second set from a flophouse manager near the railroad yard in Dunsmuir. He liked them better because they flattened and curved what he saw like a funhouse mirror. He often wore them when he walked through city crowds, laughing at the bulging clowns all around him.

Glancing up before crossing the main street, he noted patches of color, thousands of patches, seeming to glow in the afternoon sun. For a moment he smiled. Then one suddenly flashed green and he crossed the street, looking at his own shoes – he could still see them, even the laces – and he pulled at his beard. "He he he!" he chuckled as other walkers delicately skirted him.

Under the bridge, he fumbled a can of chili from his pack and opened it with his pocketknife. Then he carefully scooped the cold beans into his mouth with the blade – they would be his only meal that day and he didn't want to drop even one. From the shade in which he sat, he could see an orange tone settle over the late-afternoon landscape on both sides of him. He liked it, a cantaloupe color that livened the gentle tans and browns of the vacant lots, the vague outlines of buildings beyond. Even in the bridge's shade, the growing glow warmed him.

How many bridges? How many years? There had been jobs after the war, some good ones, but always someone seemed to invent a machine to do what he did, and Winfield had to move to something else, to start again, until one summer he'd found himself, a veteran of W. W. II, picking grapes next to guys who couldn't even speak English. And he had been married for a while, until the day his stepdaughter'd told her mother and him about her dream, and Winfield had reflexively interrupted the girl: "I never touched her!" They both – the daughter, the mother – had gazed at him with surprise, then sorrow, knowing immediately that he had. He'd departed that night and never seen either again. Departed for bridges. Departed for years.

"Son of a bitch!" he shouted. "Bastard!" and his voice echoed from the bridge's cement piers across the lapping water. Then he noted what could have been a large shadow slinking across the far lot toward this very bridge. It was the movement that first alerted Winfield. He could not clearly discern a shape, but the way the thing was approaching – like a damn coyote – warned him. Keeping his eyes on the approaching dark form, he placed his knife on the earth next to him, bolted the rest of his chili, running one finger carefully around the inside of the can, then licking it so that no morsel would be lost. All the while he followed the prowling motion, the blemish moving over the golden lot, until it paused in the sunlight just outside the bridge's shadow and assumed the large, loose figure of a man.

Entering the shade, the coyote was again difficult to see, although he was close enough for his breath to burst white-port sweet on Winfield. "Hey, brother," the bearded and bespectacled face called, and the older man felt the coyote's eyes scanning him, searching his kit. "What you got in that plastic bag, brother?"

"Just got me some cans," Winfield grunted.

"Hey, brother, you're gonna share 'em, aren't ya?" The false friendliness of the coyote's voice hung more ominously than a threat. He was big and assured, this coyote, and Winfield felt peril as tangible as the heavy odor of the man's body, but he also felt something else, and he welcomed it: a scavenger's scorn for carrion.

Winfield had not survived on the streets for all these years without learning how to deal with danger, so he immediately rattled the bag of cans with his right hand to distract the younger man while slowly moving his left down his side where his knife lay shielded from view.

"What else you got, brother? What's in that pack? That's a good bed-roll," crooned the cocky voice.

While the coyote jostled Winfield's sleeping bag, the older man carefully lifted the knife.

The coyote's wide face was much closer now, and Winfield felt his pack being tugged. "What's this here?" The younger man was in no hurry. He was confident that he could do anything he wanted. "Hey, brother, you got some beans it looks like." He had pulled open the pack's top and was rummaging through it.

Silently, Winfield opened the blade.

"How 'bout money, brother? You been workin'?" It was a demand, not a question.

The knife was poised.

"No talk, huh? You one of those crazy bastards? Only talk to yourself? Well," the coyote's voice deepened to a growl, "just gimme that bedroll and pack before I fuck you up, brother. And gimme your fuckin' money too."

"I ain't your brother," Winfield hissed. "I'm a veteran. I got a name."

The coyote chuckled as he leaned forward and grabbed Winfield's sleeping bag; his pale face was inches from the old man's but he did not seem to know the knife was coming until he lurched back and screamed as his face peeled open. "You fucker! You cut me, you fucker!"

"I got a name," the older man repeated in a tight whisper as though talking to himself, his blade balanced at his side.

Half the pale face poured crimson as the coyote – still backing away – touched it, looked at his stained hand, and screamed once more as though he couldn't believe it – "You cut me, you fucker!" Then he scrambled from the bridge into the fading orange light of the lot, seeming to dodge aimlessly in the decaying light like a gut-shot dog.

"Son of a bitch!" Winfield shouted. "Bastard!"

After a second – still twisted by tension – he hurriedly secured his pack, tightened his sleeping bag, then hoisted them. He needed to travel before the cops got curious about that yelping coyote. He had just moved when he felt something under his right knee and reached down: Glasses, the ones the coyote had worn, and they weren't broken.

Hesitating a moment, he held the spectacles in one hand, then he put them on and stared out into the light, but immediately covered his eyes with his hands – the images were like razors. He blinked and thrust his fingers under the lenses to rub his eyes. Once more – slowly, gradually – he opened them and gazed tentatively toward the light, his eyes little more than slits.

Through lashes, images again sliced at him as though someone had etched each shape, sharpened every edge. They hurt. Far across the lot loomed the distinct edges of distant buildings, and in the nearby lot were the filthy clumps of gutted cars, clumps of garbage – here an old mattress, there a deteriorating shopping cart – and the crazed figure of a large man, his face masked with blood, running and screaming.

Averting his eyes, he noted that the nearby walls of the bridge's cement abutment were covered with imprecise drawings of women's bodies and of vast, erupting male sex organs, with boasting messages and telephone numbers. Feces had been smeared on the cement surface to shape a swastika. In front of him the river water was gray with what appeared to be turds floating in it, along with a dead fish.

"This world is ugly. Ugly!" he declared.

Winfield removed the glasses and flung them into the water, rubbing his eyes again, then he turned toward the soft, the comforting blur of the lot and began walking toward that great orange glow beyond, hefting his plastic bag of cans and treading across the bare lot toward the vague distance.

"I'm not no Buster. I'm a veteran!" he proclaimed, one arm punching the sky.

THE SOUVENIR

"Do you think I could talk Myrtle into flyin'?" the white-haired man chuckled, and his wife – her own hair a shade of blue invented in a laboratory – smiled primly, still not confident of her new teeth. "That's a fact," she lisped, adding, "Baldwin ain't gettin' me to climb into nothin' I cain't climb out of." She smiled once more, her dentures even and white.

They sat in a clattering railroad lounge car, sipping coffee and talking to another couple – the man bald, the woman also sporting blue hair – while the train swept them up the heart of California's San Joaquin Valley, acres after endless acres of reclaimed desert now green as a tropical rain forest on both sides of them, the engine's silver snout plunging everyone north toward San Francisco.

"So you folks're from Bakersfield," observed the bald-headed man.

"Oildale," Baldwin corrected.

"It's the same as bein' from Bakersfield," recorrected his wife, shooting him an annoyed glance. "He always says Oildale, but it's just part of Bakersfield. Anyways, we're not original from there. We come out from Checotah in '37, me and Baldwin, just married and too young to have good sense."

"We're natives," interjected the other woman.

"Ain't that nice," observed Myrtle tonelessly. "Anyways, Baldwin found work in the oil fields and he's been at it ever since, forty-two years up till he retired last March, workin' for Shell Oil. Not like some of these youngsters jumpin' from job to job. *If they work a-tall.*"

"Isn't it the truth," agreed the native woman, whose teeth seemed to fit securely. "Dan just retired too. He was a salesman for Ward's."

"Uhm. I bet that's inter'stin' work," lisped the new teeth.

The bald man nodded, his eyes twinkling.

"The stories he could tell!" remarked his wife.

While the women continued talking, their conversation drifting toward grandchildren, then recipes, finally to the fact that ladies in San Francisco always wore hats and gloves. The two men sparred for topics, touching on the general rudeness of the younger generation, the fact that *some people* should be forced to speak English if they want to collect welfare or vote, and the assurance that Muhammad Ali couldn't lace up Jack Dempsey's gloves. There was a pause, then the bald-headed man asked, "You folks get up to Frisco often?"

"Naw, not for years," Baldwin replied. "Me and Myrtle just thought, why not? It's time to travel some." He smiled and his own large yellow teeth gave him the appearance of a happy mule. He shifted his heavy shoulders. "Yessir, why not? But do you think I could talk her into flyin'?"

The salesman's smile faded into a knowing scowl. "Well," he intoned, "you won't know Frisco. It's been taken over by beatniks and hippies. Our daughter lives up in El Cerrito and she took us over there last summer. You'll really be surprised at what's on the street."

Again the yellow teeth grinned. "Well, I don't mind if I do see me a hippie. Like I told Myrtle, I'm gonna get my pitcher took with one a them boogers for a souvenir."

His wife, although in the midst of a list of grandchildren's accomplishments, remarked, "You *are* not." She smiled at the other woman, raised her eyebrows, and sighed, *"That* man." The lady with the fitted teeth chuckled knowingly.

Baldwin ignored them. "Yessir," he continued, "seen some a them suckers on TV, but I never seen a real one. I'll find me one, though, and get my pitcher took."

His wife paused, glancing first at him then back toward the native woman. "I *swear,*" she said. Once more the other lady nodded and chuckled.

They detrained at Oakland, bidding good-bye to their new friends, whose daughter met them with a car. Then they walked to a waiting bus that would take them to the terminal in San Francisco, Myrtle scurrying ahead, pillbox hat firmly planted atop her blue hair, white gloves covering her hands. Once Baldwin had plopped into the seat beside her, he asked, "What 'uz the big rush? You damn near run to the bus."

"*You* may not mind bein' stared at by coloreds," she responded tartly, "but *I* do."

"Oh, hell, them boys wasn't starin' at you."

"Hah!" she snorted, and he patted her hand. A few moments later, as the bus wound its way toward a freeway, she observed, "You'd think we was in *Aferca* is where. The co-*loreds!* I never seen so many. Just look at 'em." Baldwin also stared out the window at the dark faces and strange costumes, examining houses and stores and cars, all of it as alien as another nation. "Ain't this somethin'," he said to himself. "Would you look at that!"

Soon the bus swerved up onto the freeway, then across the Bay Bridge, muddy water swirling far below them, and Baldwin felt his stomach lighten. His wife stared stonily ahead. "Looky at that water," he remarked, but she ignored him. He knew she hated bridges.

At the terminal in San Francisco, they gathered their suitcases – him commenting again that she'd brought enough clothes for a month – and asked the Amtrak man how to get to the Busby Hotel, where they had reservations. He instructed them to walk to the front of the building and hail a cab. "How much'll that run us?" asked Myrtle, but before the man could answer, Baldwin had departed for the front of the building; abandoned, she rushed after him, holding her hat on with one gloved hand while she caught up. "Would *you* wait!" she demanded.

They had only walked a short distance in the large building when they saw the first one, a young man dressed in Army fatigues, a pirate's red bandana around his head, and no shoes. "L-O-V-E" was printed neatly just above his eyebrows in green. "Looky there, Myrtle," Baldwin said, his yellow teeth exposed in a great grin, "a hippie. I believe I'll go get my pitcher took with that sucker."

His wife, who cringed from the oblivious young man, hissed, "You *will* not," and increased her pace slightly, but Baldwin stopped and followed the buccaneer with his eyes. *"Baldwin!"* Myrtle cried, torn between the desire to escape this building and the need not to be alone.

While the older man eyed him, the pirate twice accosted people, demanded money, and received it, the donors scurrying away as though embarrassed while the young man with L-O-V-E on his forehead counted the bounty in his hand before thrusting it into a pocket, then scouted for other potential patrons. "Would you *look* at that," observed Baldwin. "Them folks're givin' him money," he grinned to Myrtle, who tugged desperately at his arm. "Come *on*," she urged.

Baldwin had to hurry to keep up with her, his eyes nonetheless scanning everything, everyone. He nearly ran into a post when a long-haired colored girl in a 1940s dress passed them. "Would you *look* at that," he remarked, but Myrtle didn't answer. Just before they reached the heavy glass doors at the front of the building, Myrtle swerved to avoid another barefooted youngster, a girl dressed in jeans and an old blue work shirt. The youngster wore flowers in her hair and no gloves. "Peace," she murmured as Baldwin passed, and he showed her his yellow teeth.

Just as Myrtle and Baldwin emerged from the building, the lone taxi they had sighted through the large glass doors, and toward which they had been hastening, pulled away. "Now what?" asked Myrtle, sounding heartbroken.

Her tone caused Baldwin to wink at her. "Oh," he observed, "I reckon there's more'n one taxi in Frisco. Another'n'll be along d'rectly." He put down the two suitcases and opened the smaller one.

"Now what're you doin'?" asked his wife, her voice still ragged.

"I'm gettin' out the Brownie so's you can take a pitcher of me with a hippie."

"You *are* not."

"I sure as hell am. I never come clean up here not to get my pitcher took with no hippie." His tone was firm.

"*Baldwin,*" her voice raised an octave, "you *are* not."

He had just removed the camera and rezipped the bag when he felt his wife's gloved hand grip his arm. "What?" he asked, not looking up. When Myrtle didn't reply, but only squeezed his arm tighter, he glanced up, annoyed. She nodded to their left, where a pale girl stood with one bare hand extended. Someone had drawn a red-and-blue star on one of her cheeks. "Got any spare change?" she asked dreamily.

Baldwin felt his wife shudder. He examined the girl, young and thin with dark eyes and hair, no makeup except that star. She wore a kind of smock over faded jeans that had brightly colored patches on both knees. Around her neck hung a string of eucalyptus buds. "Want your pitcher took, little lady?" he asked.

For a moment the girl didn't reply, then she asked, her voice slightly less dreamy, "Do you got a quarter?"

Myrtle's grip tightened and the lines at the corners of her mouth slashed downward as though extending beyond her chin into the pavement itself. "*Baldwin,*" she begged.

"Right over there by the flower stand'd be good," Baldwin told the girl. "My wife here can take the pitcher."

The girl blinked. "What's wrong with you, man? Don't you even got a dime?" Her voice had hardened considerably, and she edged a step away from the muleface.

"Come right on over here, little lady," Baldwin insisted, grabbing the girl's thin arm and leading her to the flower stand, dragging along his wife, whose glove seemed welded to him. "You get right there, and Myrtle here'll snap our pitcher."

"I *will* not."

"Hey, man!" the girl protested, her dark eyes wide, her voice grown rough.

He thrust the camera toward his wife, who suddenly dropped his arm and hurried back to their suitcases. "Myrtle!" he called, but she refused to even turn around and acknowledge him, standing like a gloved, hatted statue facing the street. "Damn it, anyways," he said.

"Tommy! Tommy!" he heard the girl call, and he followed the line of her vision until he saw slouching toward them the same red-bandanaed pirate in Army fatigues he'd noticed earlier. The buccaneer seemed in no hurry, but when he arrived, he extended his hand. "Got any spare change, man?" he asked in a tone that sounded more like "Stick 'em up."

Baldwin handed him the camera. "Back up there by the curb so's you can get them flowers in," he said.

"Huh?" responded the pirate.

"Hey, man!" the girl seemed to moan.

"And make sure you get us in that little square," Baldwin ordered. The buccaneer blinked his eyes, then backed up to the curb.

Baldwin turned to the girl. "Smile, little lady," he directed. She smiled the way a fighter does when he's caught a good right hand.

"It won't work," the pirate said.

"You never wound it," explained Baldwin patiently. "Wind that little doodad on top. Yeah, that's it."

Again the two smiled, and this time there was a soft snap. Over the photographer's shoulder, Baldwin could see his wife's blue hair and white hat like a blossom decorating the background. He retrieved his camera, still grinning, and said, "Much obliged." He returned to his wife.

The pirate followed him, but the girl kept her distance. "How 'bout that spare change?"

"What spare change? I ain't got no spare change. I worked for what little I got and I need it."

The buccaneer stared at the large, white-haired man in front of him. "Okay," he said, "then how 'bout our modeling fee?"

"Your what?" Baldwin stared at the L-O-V-E on the younger man's forehead.

"Modeling fee." The pirate's eyes narrowed; his jaw thrust forward.

For a moment, the old man seemed stumped. His wife hissed out of the corner of her mouth, "Bald-win, give 'em somethin'."

"Modelin' fee, eh?" Baldwin chewed on it like a fresh tobacco plug, and the pirate boldly stepped closer until his hand almost touched the older man. Then the mischievous mule grin reappeared: "Well, since you took the pitcher and I's in it, you owe *me* a modelin' fee."

"Bald-*win!*" insisted his wife.

"Hey, man! I want my money!"

"Your money! You got some money?" grinned the hulking old man.

"Tom-*my!*" the pale girl called to the pirate, keeping her distance.

"Yessir," said Baldwin, "I never knew they paid no modelin' fees in Frisco or I'd a come up sooner."

The buccaneer's mouth hardened to a gash. "Okay, man, I'm calling a cop."

Still smiling, the old man pointed across the street. "Want a cop? There's one right over there. Hey, officer!" he shouted.

The pirate and his lady immediately fled into the terminal, eyes wide as they glanced back over their shoulders, even though the policeman didn't acknowledge Baldwin's call. "Would you *look* at that," the old man observed. "I guess they never wanted no cop after all."

For a long moment his wife did not speak, then she said slowly, "I just *hate* it whenever you act like that."

"Like what? We come up here to have fun, didn't we?"

She clattered her new teeth at him, too exasperated to speak. It seemed that a cab would never arrive. Baldwin was unconcerned. Grinning, he scanned the area, the assorted cars and people, then his eyes locked onto a bewhiskered specimen wending his way toward them from the far corner. The man wore an ankle-length overcoat that sagged like an elephant's skin, and he sipped furtively from a brown paper bag. He appeared to be carrying on an active conversation with himself, complete with shouts and angry gestures. "Would you *look* at that," Baldwin said, then he handed the camera to his wife, who absently accepted it, her eyes straining for a glimpse of a taxi. She no longer cared how much it might cost. When she finally darted a glance toward him, her husband was moving toward the man in the overcoat.

"Baldwin?" she called.

"I'm just gonna go have me a word with that booger," he explained over his shoulder.

"Bald-*win!*"

SOJOURNER

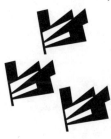

We are only sojourners on this Earth,
waiting to be called Home.
    Rev. Gary Chu, Pastor, Stockton,
    California, 1981

Afternoons he liked to face the gradually lowering sun, to feel it smooth his ridged and canyoned face, soothe his sightless eyes. Lulled by its warmth, he registered shrill voices of children from the playground and allowed them to evoke the one shrill voice he'd not heard for more than half a century, that he could never again hear but would never cease listening for. Beyond, just over the levee, sucked the great river, the Sacramento. During such somnolent moments he imagined it was the mighty Shuang sweeping past.

So, so far away, all of it: his land, his life, his people. Yet never deserted. He carried all within, where he could often return, especially on long, warm afternoons.

He had traveled to this heathen land originally in search of the golden dream. Since his older brother had occupied their ancestral home when their parents died, Wing Nu set out in search of his own best opportunities, first as a laboring peasant in the fields of others until great floods destroyed crops and forced him to eke out a subsistence cutting wood in Fukien's nearly denuded hills.

Tied to no man, he was young, sinewy, and clever, clever enough to realize that his abilities would be wasted in Fukien unless nature itself changed dramatically, something he neither expected nor bothered to hope for. He could do any job and do it well, and he could both read and write a bit, but what was the point if work promised no improvement in his conditions?

He had heard, of course, of the mountains of gold across the sea. Rumors of great fortunes spread where poor men gathered, gossip of kinsmen who had migrated and, within a week, gathered enough gold to return home rich beyond the dreams of the emperor. For a woodcutter, however, the very trip to the mountains of gold was hopelessly expensive.

Gnawing himself within, he stalked the lanes of his village seeking a loan, but could arrange none. Then he saw the posted sign:

Laborers wanted for California in the United States of America. There is much work. Food and housing supplied. Wages are generous. There is no slavery. You will be treated considerately. All is nice.

The ship is going soon and will take all who can pay for their passage. Persons having property can have it sold for them by my agents or borrow money for passage against it from me. I cannot take security on your wife or children but if you are a good worker, I will loan you passage money which you repay from your wages in California.

The ship is substantial and convenient.

The poster was signed "Ah Chang," and an address in Fuchou was listed below the name. Wing Nu read the poster to himself, then read it aloud to other men gathered around. He reread the part that began, "I will loan you passage money," and the men gathered round him chattered excitedly. He had no money, but he was a good worker and an educated man. He would climb those mountains of gold.

Voices, voices, voices:

"What else could I do? Crops had failed and floods had ruined our field. There was no wood left to cut in the hills. What else could I do?"
Lu Ng, laborer, Sacramento, California, 1854

"I remember the mornings on the river at home, the sounds of women calling to one another, the laughter of children. I miss them most."
Ying Nu, laborer, Auburn, California, 1856

"My father sold me when I was nine. He had no choice."
Jade Ping, prostitute, San Francisco, California, 1858

From downstream the old man heard the hoarse hoot of a steamer's whistle, and he strained his ears for the slap-slap of its wheel churning through the water. Before his eyes had dimmed he had much enjoyed pausing in his work to watch the large white ships that plied the Sacramento, and had been amused at the sometimes rude gestures and shouts that passengers made at the lone man waving to them from a field. These Americans, he had thought, so immature, so uncertain, so frightened.

Like the red-faced man who had confronted him at Silva's Bar on the Consumnes River. "I don't give a good goddamn what the law says," the Yankee had growled to the constable, "I say when American miners quit, these goddamn chinks gotta quit too. They got no goddamn business workin' longer'n white men. It ain't natural!"

"Well," chuckled the constable, whose main occupation appeared to be avoiding mayhem to himself while breaking up fights, "seems like to me, Jake, it was you told me a Chinaman couldn't work as long or as hard as an American whenever these boys come to the diggin's. Said they was too little and weak and dumb. I recollect you sayin' how these little fellers'd burn out in no time."

Wing Nu stood impassively before the two men, lightly holding a spade. He understood enough of their difficult tongue to know he was in danger, and he was prepared to defend himself.

"I don't know why a bunch of goddamn Chinee pirates can come from nowheres and dig American gold and take it back to their king or who-the-hell-ever."

"These here little fellers all pay the foreign miners' tax, Jake. And look what they're scrubbin' dust from. Why, you boys finished with this bar months ago, claimed it was played out." The constable's arm gestured at the pile of tailings on which the Chinese worked. "Hell, they're workin' second-hand gold."

"First-hand or second, the boys deputized me to come stop these damn chinks from workin' overtime and to make 'em observe the Sabbath like Christians. Hell's fire, ain't no human bein' can work like these heathens. There's somethin' wrong with 'em. They don't have feelin's like normal folks. They ain't human, and we can't have 'em workin' when we ain't."

The constable rocked on his heels. "Wellsir, I disremember you boys holdin' any church service on the Sabbath."

The big man's neck swelled like a horned toad. "This ain't no damned joke! The new miners' law at Silva's Bar is that no goddamn chink works longer'n us Americans work or they'll all lose a hell of a lot more than their pigtails."

Still grinning, the constable had turned toward Wing Nu, who acted as captain of the Fukinese miners. "You heard 'im, Chinaman. No more work until I say so." Wing had merely nodded, his gaze straight and un-blinking. He had to acquiesce, but he did not want these Americans to think they intimidated him. In fact, they reminded him of a Northern Chinese he had met on the boat to California. That man, expensively dressed and traveling on the upper deck, had spat that Wing and the other Fukinese were barbarians and had laughed at their plight. When the Northerner's remark was translated for him, Wing had struck the man. These Yankees, however, were too numerous and too well armed, so Wing Nu kept his counsel.

Three weeks later, carrying only what they could secrete on their per-sons, all seventy-one Fukinese miners were driven from Silva's Bar by a mob of drunken heathens. The volunteer fire department marching band and drum corps had accompanied the grim procession, and their presence probably saved many Chinese lives, for the music lightened the mood of the drunken Yankees, who contented themselves with cutting queues and a few slaps and punches to keep Wing Nu and his friends moving.

Voices, voices, voices:

"We had saved enough so that all four of us could return to Canton rich men, but a Yankee bandit stole it from us in broad daylight. When we complained to the sheriff, he laughed."

Yu Wang, laborer, Reno, Nevada, 1866

"They are in many respects a disgusting element of the population but not wholly unprofitable."

Editorial, *Record-Avalanche*, Silver City, Idaho, June 23, 1867

"No one bothered me, except when they were drunk. Most people left me alone, and I avoided them. I became a Christian."

Au Li, herbalist, Mariposa, California, 1871

From the labor contractor's office across the street, the old man heard voices of laborers returning from the fields, piling out of wagons in mid-afternoon, then drifting in small groups toward saloons or camps or the park where Wing Nu rested. Many of them spoke tongues he did not understand – Spanish, Portuguese, Italian – and they smelled unlike the people he knew well. But he did understand their toil and their fatigued relief at the workday's end.

Despite the congratulations and cries of envy from other Fukinese laborers, there had been little triumph in Wing Nu's step that first morning following his return to Mr. Schmidt's farm outside Stockton. True, he had visited his small village in Fukien, a rare enough occurrence in itself. Moreover, he had married and sired a son there, the cause of great celebration among his fellows.

But a more harsh and immediate reality made it impossible for him to rejoice: He was back in California while his wife and son remained in China. One part of him acknowledged his good fortune, while another ached for his wife and the little brown bundle he feared he would never again see.

At least he knew they would be well cared for. Each month he turned most of his wages over to the *hui kuan*, his clan, which in turn forwarded it to his village. The question of whether he would ever see his family again was entirely up to him. He would work. He would save. Someday he would return to his village a wealthy and respected man.

It would take a great fortune, though, to accomplish that, as he had learned on his first visit home. With nearly 1,500 American dollars he had saved or won gambling, Wing Nu had assumed he could return and remain. But his money had disappeared more quickly than he had imagined possible.

Conditions had changed, and the entire country seemed to be run by soldiers and petty officials. He had been forced to pay off a minor magistrate and the man's lackeys in order to leave the port. Then his aging uncle had to be rescued from bankruptcy. He loaned his older brother a substantial sum. When all was done, he had barely enough money left to marry, buy a small house, and provide for his family when he finally returned, far too soon, to the gambling halls and whorehouses and opium dens of America.

Back in California, he knew his next fortune would come more slowly than his first. There was no more gold to be dug. He would now dig another man's vegetables or irrigate another man's fields. On the boat taking him away from those he loved, he had fantasized that one day his son would join him and help accumulate wealth for the family.

That had only been a dream and, standing in the searing sunlight of a San Joaquin Valley morning, his comrades still teasing and praising him, everything and everywhere else seemed unreal. The ache in his loins was real, the ache in his heart was too. In front of him, heat waves shimmered from Mr. Schmidt's fields, and Wing Nu strode forward, certain in his secret self that he would never see his wife and son again, not in this world anyway. That realization was his first death.

Voices, voices, voices:

"I liked working on the farm. It was good work, outdoors, with animals. If only my family could have been with me, then I could have been truly happy."
Lin Ho, laborer, Fresno City, California, 1879

"We cut through mountains for the railroad, chipping stone, blasting it, hauling it away. We spanned rivers. It was hard, but I was young and strong. Afterwards I was able to return home."
Pyau Ng, merchant, Kwantung, China, 1881

"They killed my brother and they tried to kill me. I was beaten. My queue was cut. I was stripped and my clothes were thrown into the stream. They left me to die, but I did not die."

Woo Soo, laborer, Rock Springs, Wyoming, 1885

Caught in a dragon's bowels, Wing struggled with the bulky sacks of laundry, sweating, almost unable to breathe. No longer young, he was wearied by the tough toil. His eyes had so dimmed that he could not do the farm work he preferred and, forced into this humid basement to earn a living, he could no longer hear birds sing or feel breeze on his skin. Another part of him died then.

Nonetheless, he toiled, struggling through hissing, grinding mechanical monsters. Through the bragging of fellow workers, through the steam that seemed to enter and sap him, he labored. He was trapped in these bowels, but it had been the only job the *hui kuan* could arrange for him, and he had to work. That much was certain.

Each evening he bumped through crowded streets to the small alleyway cafe where Fukinese workers gathered to eat and talk about home, then he would slump on to his tiny room, too exhausted to even try to read the newspaper the restaurateur saved for him each week. Less frequently, he would visit a fantan parlor, more for companionship than gambling. For the same reason he would occasionally patronize one of the bordellos so available in Chinatown. Somehow, even they brought little joy.

Although he had plenty of people to talk to in the city, plenty of people who could understand his feelings and hopes, he felt trapped here. All his life he had loved the outdoors. Now only once a week or so could he wander to the new park being built near the levee on the town's west edge and gaze across the river at the open land beyond. Those were the best times of all.

Voices, voices, voices:

"It is quite simple. We provide entertainment for lonely men. In exchange, we earn a profit. Occasionally we must protect our interests, but we are not violent men."

Lin Jay, Tong leader, San Francisco, California, 1893

"Cities are filthy, but what choice have I? I cannot operate my business without customers. Besides, I can speak a civilized tongue again here, and perhaps begin a family."

Yang Lee, laundryman, Los Angeles, California, 1899

"I am strongly of the opinion that, but for the presence of the Chinese, California would not now have more than one-half or two-thirds of her present population; Chinese labor has opened up many avenues and new industries for white labor, made many kinds of business possible."

Alva Griffin, State Senator, Sacramento, California, 1903

Meeting Mr. Reilly had been one joy of his late years. Retired like himself, Reilly also had no family and few friends, and he was also blind. Every sunny day, the old Irishman's servant deposited him on a bench in the town's square – it was there the old men met – and he would sun, chatting with Wing Nu as the outer heat fought their dimming inner fires, two travelers near journey's end.

Each had trouble understanding the other at first, although both spoke English, "or so we t'ought," chuckled Mr. Reilly. Both were immigrants – each regaling the other with tales of his youth, of strange green lands and long-dead friends – but Reilly's fortune had been considerably better than Wing's: He owned a restaurant and a home and several rentals. Still, aging and alone save for his servant, ignored if not disdained except by those coveting his property, his emptiness was no less. For him, too, the golden dream had come to dust.

While Wing yearned for the wife and child he'd not touched for over fifty years, Reilly – who'd never married – pined for a girl he'd left in Ireland half a century before, "gone dead in the convent these twenty-seven years," and for the children they'd never had. Rich or poor, loneliness was the same.

But the two men did not mire themselves in maudlin memories. Having acknowledged the pain of estrangement, they found many lively topics to discuss, conversing through most afternoons, laughing frequently about episodes from their lives or those of others, debating points of religion or philosophy or politics, resolving nothing. It was the fray they enjoyed, the respect each paid the other's ideas. Those conversations were the liveliest moments either man experienced anymore.

Passersby often noted with amusement the two old men who had never seen one another animatedly debating in near-incomprehensible accents the doctrine of Original Sin or farm labor practices. From a distance, in fact, it was difficult to notice their physical differences, and their tones revealed little.

Voices, voices, voices:

"No greater scourge in the history of mankind has been recorded. The heathen mongol must be stopped. He breeds like an animal and soon Christianity and Democracy will be dead. If the Chinaman is allowed to resume his invasion, the White Race faces mongrelization."
Benjamin Franklin Burns, Congressman, Washington, D.C.
October 9, 1906

"All we do is sit. No family here. Just us old men. Just us. I only hope to return home someday."
Ko Yip, retired, Seattle, Washington, 1914

"Edward, my son, returned home from school crying yesterday. He said a gang of bullies had chased him and called him 'Ching-chong Chinaman.' We must move to a better neighborhood."
Mrs. Lin Chen, housewife, San Francisco, California, 1918

The aging man trudged the stairs to his room, resting every few steps, his breath seeming to grow shorter each day. Fumbling his key into the lock, Wing Nu snapped the door open, entered, then closed it. Evening had come. He felt the slight chill and heard the sounds of night begin to replace those of day, traps and carriages rattling by on the street below, and even a few automobiles.

He slumped to his bed and sat for several moments before stretching out. It had been a full day for an old man far away from home. Yet – and only fatigue prompted such a question – where was home? He had lived three-quarters of his life in California. He knew its rivers and fields better than he had ever known Fukien's. With his wife dead and his son disappeared, his only true friend remained here in Sacramento.

It was no question, really. America had tolerated and used Wing Nu; it had never accepted him. Only dreams of Fukien motivated him. He was Fukien: It dwelled within him, as tangible as the bed on which he rested, and soon his third death would free him from this tiny room, this alien town. Then the *hui kuan* would transport his body back home, to the soil that had given him life. Then, at last, he could rest.

Still, lying in darkness, nearly asleep, hearing familiar sounds from the street, smelling familiar odors, feeling a familiar breeze, it was difficult to separate places, as though there were only one place with many names, one life with many journeys, and he – this weary sojourner – was about to begin another.

WIDDER MAKER

Things they's a-jumpin back in them days. Ever'one fig-
gered there was oil under their land, and wildcatters was a-raisin' rigs so
fast the whole of Kern County looked about like a forest. Me, it was just
my luck I hired on to a dirt-poor wildcatter out of McKittrick who run
this here old cable tool rig, and I mean old. He couldn't pay nothin',
but he kept us in grub, and us roughnecks was a-gonna get 5 percent of
whatever we struck. It beat sittin' on our butts.

Brownie, the wildcatter, he had this arrangement with a farmer whose
place was right next to where the Shell done real good, so we commenced
putting up that big damn rig, workin' our tails off while that farmer he just
stood around spittin' tobacco juice on the ground and figgerin' how to
spend the oil money he'd make. He never offered us no water or nothin'.

Whenever we was hoistin' the walkin' beam into place, Brownie's
A-frame just a huffin' and puffin', damned if the cable didn't bust and

bite ol' Clarence, this colored boy from Langston that was on our crew. Well, the farmer's wife she carried ol' Clarence in the car to the county hospital. That left us one man short just whenever we needed everyone most, so Brownie he asked that farmer to come give us a hand, but not him. Naw, he just sucked on his tobacco quid for a spell, then turned and grinned. "Well?" ol' Brownie'd asked. That farmer he kindly puffed up at Brownie and barked: "I'm payin' you boys to do the oil work. If you can't handle her, I believe I can find me another outfit to drill here."

Well, he was right about findin' another outfit. It was a good spot and we all knowed it. So Brownie he just turned around and stuffed a little more snuff under his lip and we all went back to work. And I seen that farmer just a-grinnin' while we liked to killed ourselves getting that damn rig together.

If Brownie hadn't been down on his luck, that farmer'd of been one big bruise, but when you're eating the labels off last week's bean cans, well, you just take them thangs, but you don't forget 'em. Ain't none of us forgot 'em. We was sure as hell happy that next week whenever ol' Clarence got back.

Before long we was makin' hole, that big ol' mother hubbard just a bitin' through clay formation. Brownie he spent about his last buck to have a mud smeller come check what we was a-bringin' up. Well, that geologist he said it looked good, real good. He figgered we was only a few hundred foot from makin' a strike. But it was a long ways when we was out of casin', then we lost our damn bit in the hole and had to fish for it. I commenced wonderin' if maybe we wasn't lookin' for farmer's sand.

All the time we was workin', that farmer he's a-hangin' around, like a fly on a manure pile, buzzin' and settin', then buzzin' some more, givin' all the advice he could think of. Lefty, this other ol' boy on the crew, he said there wasn't nothin' worse than a sorry farmer that figgers he's about to get rich. But that farmer's wife she was nice. Ever' once and awhile she'd bring us out a pot of coffee. She knowed we wasn't eatin' too good, so she'd carry sandwiches or pieces of pie to us. Her and Brownie used to talk a little each time. She was real nice.

One mornin', just about the time we'd of been switchin' towers if we'd had any relief, that lady brought us out some coffee. Us guys had been fishin' out our bit again, and we was wore to a nub. We seen her comin' and ol' Lefty he said, "Damn, but I might could drank me a little coffee. Don't reckon she's poured any whiskey in it do ya?" We all laughed, but Brownie he said we'd earned us a little drank, and that he had some whiskey in his locker, then he walked over to this old trailer we used for a doghouse. Just about the time Brownie disappeared in the trailer, here come that farmer snortin' across the field from his barn. He hollered to his wife to stop. She was close to us, but she stopped, and her old man run up to her and commenced chewin' on her about how we was lazy and hadn't got him no oil and how he was fixin' to run us off and hire on this here rotary outfit he'd heard tell of. Well, she said she'd fixed the coffee for us because we'd worked all night. He slapped that coffeepot out of her hand and it spilled, then he socked her on one eye.

"Hold on!" I heard this voice holler. It was Clarence. Well, let me tell you, you don't wanta tangle with ol' Clarence. He's the stoutest ol' boy I ever seen in a oil patch. He never fought much, but when he did, boys, he's like a badger on a dog. Clarence stood right there on the edge of the floor with his big brown finger a-pointin' at that farmer, and he said: "Pick up that pot."

The farmer he glared at old Clarence. "Mind your own business, boy," he spit.

Oh, Lord! There goes our job, I figgered, so I just sort of leaned on the headache post to watch Clarence swarm the booger, but before ol' Clarence ever got to the farmer, here come Brownie from out of nowhere, a-snortin' like a gut-shot bear and wham! one-punch coldcocked the farmer, that bastard fallin' plop like a road apple.

All that time that farmer's wife hadn't moved. She just stood there holdin' her eye where he'd smacked her. Brownie turned to her, and Clarence he handed her the coffeepot. I could tell just lookin' at 'em that all three of 'em knowed we was through, and that Brownie'd probably lose his rig too. It was sad, but I felt kinda easy for some reason, like what the hell. Lefty he poked my ribs and hissed: "Ya know, I believe it's worth it." Then he sent a brown stream of tobacco juice into the big hole in the middle of the floor.

Whenever that farmer he come to, he commenced screamin' for us to take our rig and get our tails off his place or he'd have the sheriff after us. But he never got too close to Brownie, or Clarence either. And he never pushed his wife again. He just give her the evil eye, then stomped off.

Well, after Brownie'd made sure that farmer wasn't fixin' to beat his wife up, he come back to the rig, draggin' some from the night's work and from what he was a-thinkin'. He called us all together and he said, "Boys, I surely hate to tell you this, but there was show in the mud on that bit we just brought up. We're sittin' on a pool right now. What I figger is that it'll take that numb-nutted farmer an hour, or maybe two to fetch the sheriff. If we're lucky, we can have a strike by the time the sheriff gets here, which means we get our money no matter what. But we've gotta bust our butts if we're gonna finish before he gets back. Are you with me?"

"Let's make hole!" ol' Clarence he sang out, so we got hot after it.

About an hour later – us not more than inches from pay – here come that farmer with this here big old hayseed deputy trailin' along behind him. Lefty he stalked out to meet 'em because Brownie was a workin' on the long tail. They climbed up onto the floor, that farmer nosin' around while the sheriff he asked who was in charge. "I am," Brownie called, shuttin' the engine down and turnin' to the farmer. "I wouldn't get too close to that hole if I was you," he advised real quiet. "That's slicker'n snot, a real widder maker."

The farmer, feelin' real smart alecky with that deputy backin' him, just sneered: "I'll do what I damn well please." He stepped to the edge of the hole, turned around and kindly nodded his nose at Brownie, then he slipped.

Now the hole you dig with a cable tool rig is one hell of a lot bigger than what you dig with a rotary, but it ain't all that big either. A guy has to be pretty lame or unlucky to fall into one. That farmer he hit the rim of the casin', hung there a second, then slid into the hole. I seen his fingers grab at the edge, then just slide loose. We could hear some funny thunks and whacks while the booger fell, then nothin'.

Everbody, even the deputy, they run to the hole, but not too close; we all knew there wasn't no hope for the farmer. "Damn!" the deputy he said from where he stood just a little further back than the rest of us. "That's awful."

"Hardheaded," Brownie told him, shakin' his head. "He never would listen to nobody."

"What do we do now?" asked the deputy.

"You're the sheriff," Brownie told him. So the deputy he told us to stop diggin', and he hurried back to town.

The next day a man from the county attorney's office come out and talked to all of us, and had us sign these papers about how the farmer got killed. Then he talked to the widder woman. Brownie he went over too and explained how we was just ready to strike pay. It turned out that the farmer he was as broke as we was, and about to lose his place to boot. His widder never even had money to buy him a funeral. So Brownie he made her a proposition. A couple days later she got the go-ahead from the county attorney.

"We're cementin' it," Brownie told us.

"Hell," I said, "we don't need to stabilize it. We're right over the damned oil."

"That's part of the deal," he explained. "And that's gotta be done by noon."

"Why?" I asked.

"We're havin' a funeral."

Just after we pumped the cement down, me addin' some panther piss to make it set quicker, up drives this here fat preacher in a big black A model with three more cars a-followin'. Out of them cars pops a bunch of stringy ladies, and fellers with tan faces and white foreheads. Most of 'em was carryin' flowers. Directly, here come ol' Brownie out of the doghouse, all dolled up, with even a necktie, and joined them mourners up on the floor next to the hole right where we'd sprinkled sawdust, a real solemn look on his face like he was going to Sunday meetin'. Us boys we was standin' in our work clothes a little behind them church folks, fig-gerin' we'd watch the show, but ol' Brownie he turned around and hissed at us: "Get outa here."

At first we just stood there, confused, but ol' Brownie he glared at us, so we slipped on back of the long tail and watched the best we could. Well that tubby preacher he commenced jabberin' and I swear I figgered he'd never quit. He told how Brother what's-his-name was strong in the church and a good provider and kind to his wife (that widder kindly daubed her eyes whenever he said that; she had pancake makeup on the one her late lamented had blacked) and how he tithed whenever he could. Ol' Tubby he preached about the Kingdom of Heaven and Original Sin and how Jesus died for all Mankind, then he got going on Jews and how they not only crucified Our Lord, but how they kept decent folks poor with their banks and how Roosevelt was a Jew, and he was just getting started on the Pope of Rome whenever ol' Clarence he started the engine, and the rig took to shakin'.

Well that near scared the water out of them folks, so the preacher cut hisself off, and the funeral it ended with folks droppin' flowers down the hole. Just as they was leavin', I seen Brownie squeeze the widder woman's hand.

We never made but about a foot of hole through that farmer's carcass before we hit crude, a nice pool opener. And I knowed of a sudden that ol' Brownie'd found hisself a rich widder. The other boys knowed it too. Ol' Lefty he sang out, while we was finishin' Brownie's bottle after we'd capped the hole, "You know, Push, while I was a-pilin' sawdust on the floor for that funeral I noticed how it looked slicker'n usual, like some-body's poured top oil on it, and casin' looked like maybe some petroleum jelly might've been rubbed on it."

Brownie just looked at Lefty, the teensiest grin on his face, then he said, "Well, I hope you cleaned it up. I wouldn't want nobody to slip and fall."

ROAD KILL

. . . This is what I told her:

When I was a small child, my mother read to me from a book called Animals on Parade. *It was my favorite, with bears and elephants two by two, with leopards and camels, mice and ducks. For years thereafter, I would dream of animals parading, great highways of them. And I dreamed of marching along, one hand gripping the small fingers of a raccoon, the other clasping the ebony claws of a crow.*

As I grew older and studied biology, zoology, and evolutionary theory in college, my animal dream deepened. Soon great legions of rats, of bats, of gnats extended beyond vision or memory, toward prehistory; rows of buzzards and lizards and wizards, animals all, extending back to the dawn of time, to a primordial puddle where a mutual and schizophrenic ancestor somehow divided, actualizing its illusion of separate species. And in

*my dream, that same single-celled maniac dwelled still within each of us,
constituted our shared biology.*

I tried to explain it all to my wife that morning . . .

It's strange. You whiz along at fifteen, maybe twenty miles
an hour, eyes squinting ahead, legs pumping, and you don't realize how
much you're seeing until after you've seen it. That cat was no more than
a sliver of vision, since I was really pumping – head down, butt up – at
that point, just over the Copeland Creek bridge on a slight downhill. It
might not have registered at all except that it had been knocked completely off the road and lay on the shoulder with its head protruding onto
the blacktop bicycle lane, as though it was resting.

A couple of hundred meters down the road I knew it had been a tabby
wearing a collar, and still intact. That last may sound like a cruel thing
to say, I guess, but when you bicycle everywhere as I do, you get used
to seeing road kills, sometimes dismembered by impact or repeated im-
pacts, or flattened like furry Frisbees. When I began commuting on my
bike, the sight of dead animals on the road initially shocked me. It was the
only place I'd ever see the corpses of animals wild or domestic, and the
whole deadly process seemed a terrible invasion of the animals' privacy,
and of mine.

At the least, our own separate deaths – that final moment when our
shared heritage is least deniable – should somehow remain private, even
sacred. But people get used to things, or at least I did, and soon I would
slip past the gray ruins of an opossum or the fragrant carcass of a skunk
with only the slightest acknowledgment. Only unusual cadavers grasped
my attention then: the slim form of a ferret, the askew feathers of a
pheasant, the small smear of a skink – those I'd notice.

Aside from the oddly consistent remains of birds looking like feathered
teardrops, opossums dominate road kills around here, grinning at eternity
like they've played a joke on it. Skunks are second – you smell them a
furlong away. Domestic cats are a close third. Gopher snakes, especially
in spring, are common. There are a few deer dead on the road each year,
and even a few dogs. Once I saw the small, dead, unmarred form of a
rubber boa, and it caused me to stop my bike and gaze with unaccounted

sorrow at an animal so rare that had lost the long gamble of existence, not to a predator who would use its flesh but to a car driven by a person who probably didn't know boas occurred. During certain times of the year, smashed salamanders and toads can turn bicycle lanes hereabouts into slalom courses.

And, driving to the store a couple of years ago with my little girl in the car, I hit a cat. It leaped from between two parked cars and the wet smack of the impact told me it was dead. In the rearview mirror I saw it thrash for several seconds, then lie still. I didn't want Denise to know what had happened, so I didn't stop – the cat was dead, believe me, I could tell. But I told myself that if it ever happened again, I'd stop.

So after passing that other tabby's body that Monday, I had thought of it for several seconds, registering clearly its unmarred face, its open eyes, and the repose of its body. There had been no dark halo of dried blood; no creamy intestines had lain exposed to the air. Then I returned to the personal problems I had been chewing on that morning and continued my ride to work. It was brisk and I remember thinking how good a cup of tea would feel when I reached the office.

I ride that route to work three times a week: Mondays, Wednesdays, and Fridays. On Tuesdays and Thursdays I travel an alternate course just to break the monotony, and I can't remember even thinking about that dead cat the next day, although I may have passed an opossum or two, their button eyes dull, on my alternate route. I don't give much attention to road kills. My life is so busy that I use the rides as a kind of meditation, almost consciously emptying my mind. Many days I've arrived at my office with no memory of having traveled there.

Wednesday I was pumping hard as usual, trying to cleanse myself of thought or worry as I sped north and zinged over the Copeland Creek bridge. That tabby had been completely out of my mind, and I was wheeling so close to the bike lane's margin that I had to swerve to avoid hitting its head and spilling. For a flash my attention captured that furry face as I maneuvered around it and its eyes stared back at me, or seemed to. I eased my tempo. The body had not moved, of that I was certain, but the cat's eyes in that instant had seemed not dull with death but sharp with the familiarity of one creature recognizing another. No, that was nonsense. It was just the way the head was positioned, as though resting, I told myself, but I nevertheless imagined I had even seen an appeal in those eyes. Still, the possibility . . .

A quarter mile down the road I stopped and looked back. There was the small, dark lump on dirt next to the bike lane just this side of the bridge. It was impossible, and I was late for work. The crazy things you think about. But what if it *was* alive, maybe paralyzed, what could I do? I asked myself as I continued toward my office.

Well, I could do nothing but kill it, put it out of its misery, and in so doing discomfort the hell out of myself. I could just picture myself kicking its head as cars whizzed by and drivers gawked. No, thank you. Nonetheless, the remote possibility that the cat might be alive ate at me all the way to work, but was quickly and mercifully forgotten once the day's business began.

You'd think that I would have at some point returned in memory to an event that had troubled me enough to stop my bicycle, but I didn't. In fact, I forgot entirely until Friday as I sped to work and once more was startled by the bright eyes of the motionless tabby. Immediately something lurched in me and I eased the rhythm of my legs. But, of course, if the cat had been dead on Wednesday – or even if it hadn't – it would certainly be dead today, so I squinted and pumped even harder than usual, seeking to submerge my doubt in the effort, but a question blossomed as I drove myself harder and harder, trying to concentrate only on my burning thighs: Why were there no flies?

After a pained instant, the answer comforted me. It was the morning chill. Flies don't appear that early in the morning during the fall – too cold. I accepted that notion, and whatever comfort it contained, until I arrived at work and was swept into my business world.

Each weekend, I take one long bicycle ride – something over fifty miles. My wife laughs and calls it my "postman's holiday," since I ride the bike to work all week, but I really enjoy the workout as well as the scenery of those journeys, which I vary considerably, often driving the car great distances so I can pedal through unfamiliar terrain. Sunday I did something unusual; I decided to pump out past the research institution where I work, then over the mountains east to the next canyon and loop home.

That afternoon, I swung onto the familiar course, riding easily to save my strength for the tough hills ahead. Again, my mind pleasantly empty, I crossed Copeland Creek bridge at a relaxed pace. Then I was alongside the cat, a little startled to see the animal still lying as it had been, and startled too that I had managed to forget it, for this time it was swollen and covered with flies. I stopped my bicycle, returned to the carcass and saw with piercing clarity that the head had moved or been moved slightly, as though something had released and allowed it to roll a degree or two to the side. Its eyes were closed.

For a moment I could only stand there, filling with a grief inchoate yet certain. Ahead the horizon seemed to spread and narrow like a squinting eye, into a final twilight, and my breath began to catch and surge. As I stood over the animal's body, a car slowed and a teenage driver called, "Gee, mister, did your cat get killed?"

"No," I choked, and he gazed at me a moment longer, then pulled away. I walked to the soft soil a few steps from the road and gouged a shallow hole with the heel of my shoe, then pulled the cat's body by its tail to the small grave. I covered it as best I could, then placed rocks over the mound. I did not add flowers, although some yellowish blossoms grew in a ditch nearby.

Instead I climbed back onto my bicycle and turned toward home, pumping harder and harder, trying to deflect questions that rumbled through me. Twice I veered in front of cars, nearly causing accidents, but even the squeal of their brakes didn't touch me. When I walked into the kitchen, my wife smiled over her shoulder and observed, "You're home early. Have trouble?"

I didn't reply.

After a second, she turned to examine me, then asked, "What's wrong?"

I tried to answer but could produce only raw sounds, like an animal drowning in its own blood. "The parade," I finally choked, then I told her . . .

ROMAIN PETTIBONE'S REVENGE

My older sister, Marie, always wanted to play doctor. She was the neighborhood's physician in back rooms and garages and lofts, behind pied bushes and fences and drawn curtains. As her little brother, I was often the patient, and her girlfriends were often attendants, as they poked and probed and squeezed my meager equipment.

Marie, the doctor, took great pleasure in making pronouncements like, "That's where Momma had the doctor cut his nozzle off. That's why it's so little. He can't even have babies when he grows up!"

"Oh, yes, I could!" I insisted.

"Cannot! Boys can't."

"Could too."

The other girls joined in: "Nuh uh! No you can't either."

"See, Romain," grinned Marie.

"I'm telling Mom . . ."

"You gotta be kidding!" interrupted the large lady named Flame. "You've *gotta* be kidding!"

Oh, man! I would get *her* mad at me.

Flame's thick arms, scrolled with tattoos, hung from a sleeveless leather jacket. She wore five rings in each ear, and another glimmered from a pierced nostril. "This is sexist shit!" she thundered. "Are you gonna let him *read* this sexist shit here?"

Having been so rudely halted while presenting my childhood memoir to the creative-writing class, I was stunned and waited for the professor to rescue me. That tweed man suddenly looked like a disoriented duck, so I sank into my seat.

"Well . . ." mumbled the gray-haired professor. He blinked several times and seemed to search the room for help.

The woman was so much bigger than me and so much angrier. "I won't have this *boy* definin' me. I won't be *aborted* by this *boy*." Even her fists were large.

I slunk lower.

No one responded for several moments while the tall, decorated woman glared at me, then a guy named Chad leaned forward and seemed to smile like a serpent as the gold ring he wore in his right ear glinted. He intoned: "Pettibone is like giving offense. He's like reflecting the *patriarchy*, offending Flame. He's like offending *me* too. He's like offending all *progressive* people. What're you going to do about it, Professor Litwack?" Chad tugged his sparse beard as he spoke.

"Ah . . . what exactly do you find offensive?" asked the teacher. He looked like he craved a drink.

"His sister examining him, hah! Who'd examine *him?*" demanded Flame.

Chuckling rippled through the class, but Flame halted it. "What's so funny? Inappropriate laughter gives offense too. What if he was insultin' an African American?"

"Yeah," added Chad. "What if the patriarchy like attacked our righteous black brothers and sisters!"

"Stay out of this," Flame snapped at him.

Zondra, the only black woman in class, agreed. "Flame's right. This is clearly a women's issue, Chad."

"Excuse me," ventured the professor, "but did you say 'Afro' American or 'African' American?" Was he trying to change the subject?

Flame did not laugh. "'Afro' is old," she said patiently. "Just like 'black' is." She glanced briefly at Chad.

"I was afraid of that," admitted the faculty member.

By then I was nearly out of my seat, not up but down, slumped to a mere puddle.

"What're you gonna *do*, Dr. Litwack?" demanded the tattooed woman, and by now Mary Alice, Fay, and Betty had joined Zondra and her. "Yeah, what? Who empowered this little patriarchal, gynophobic, phallocentric *boy* to write about women? Do you endorse this oppression?"

"I like don't," ventured Chad. "I *really* don't."

"Well," hesitated the professor, "I'm certain that Mr. Pettibone didn't mean . . ."

"I'm certain the dean'll be delighted to deal with this *boy!*" asserted Flame. "We've got a code here at San Francisco State to protect women and other ethnic groups from oppression."

Other *ethnic* groups? How did women get to be an ethnic group?

"What about the writing itself?" the professor tried to direct discussion back to the course's ostensible subject.

"Where'd you get that word 'pied,' Romain?" demanded Fay, the self-appointed expert on all technical matters.

"*Webster's Third International Dictionary,*" I snapped. She wasn't much bigger than me.

"Well, it's a dumb word and your writing sucks."

"Thank you for sharing," I replied.

"And you'll notice that this *boy* endorses the patriarchal notion of family that imposes the false notion of heterosexuality on the younger generation. What about that, Dr. Litwack?" demanded Flame.

There were only four men in the class: Chad, me, and two jocks – one black, the other white – who slouched at the back of the room wearing baseball caps backward and, as usual, saying nothing. Chad, the resident Sensitive Male, physically moved his desk away from mine. "Yeah, that stuff's like *real* hurtful, Romain," he said. "It sounds like the *patriarchy!*"

Finally I sat up and said, "Look, I just wrote the paper I was assigned.

All that stuff really happened. It's *you* women who're sexist. Reverse sexism is still sexism. You can write anything you like, but because I'm a guy, I can't!"

At first Flame's biceps bulged and I thought she'd punch me out for sure, but she turned to Zondra and sneered, "Sexist! Us! Hah! There isn't any such thing as 'reverse sexism,' *boy*, because sexism and racism were invented by white males, so *reverse* sexism and *reverse* racism can't exist. They're myths."

"Right on!" agreed Zondra.

Chad was rapidly nodding his scraggly beard. "Like straight shit, sisters," he cooed, "straight shit," and I at least had the pleasure of seeing Flame shoot him a dirty look. Chad blinked, then quickly added, "Especially colored women!"

Now Zondra's eyes snapped at him.

"I mean colored women of color! Women of color!" he quickly recovered. "That's what I *really* meant."

"Ah, perhaps, Pettibone . . ." the professor was saying, but I cut him off.

"This is bullshit! All I did was write what you assigned, an honest memoir. What about the First Amendment in this class?"

"The First Amendment only applies to *proper* perspectives, *boy!*" Flame explained. "We have a code to protect us from harassment and oppression now."

"Protect *you?*" I said.

As I left the Humanities Building that night, the black jock stopped me. "Hey, Pettiboner," he said, "how many feminists does it take to screw in a light bulb?"

I shrugged.

"The answer is 'That's not funny.'"

The two jocks laughed, but I didn't.

My interview with the dean was brief and to the point. "I've read the offending material, Mr. Pettibone," she said. "It doesn't appear to me that you necessarily intended to harass or give offense, but you have to learn to be more sensitive to the feelings of others. Understand that no matter what newspapers say, females and other Third World people still grow up in profoundly oppressive circumstances, so they naturally are sensitive when they feel themselves attacked."

I was genuinely grateful for her moderate tone. "I appreciate that, Dr. Hoover, but all I'm trying to say is that generalizations may or may not be true in individual cases. My sister's a lawyer. She can buy or sell me . . . as she reminds me regularly," I smiled. "She was student body president in high school . . ."

"That section of your essay . . . the part about your sister . . . was particularly disturbing, Mr. Pettibone."

I nodded. "It was troubling to me too, Dr. Hoover. That's why I wrote about it."

The dean stood, walked around her large desk, then leaned on it as she addressed me. "You're an intelligent young man, Mr. Pettibone, and you've got to understand that anecdotes like yours distort the weight of evidence and dilute the devastation that sexual harassment has caused and is causing women and other ethnic groups. It can lead to false consciousness."

False consciousness? I missed the point, I guess, so I said, "I'm not sure I understand why I shouldn't write what really happened."

Dr. Hoover sighed, then an edge entered her voice. "What I'm saying, Mr. Pettibone, is that your truth may not be true. It may be the product of false consciousness because it obscures the larger issue."

"Oh," I nodded. I was finally getting the message – nothing I said in my defense would be significant. Still, I tried one more time. "I'm really not trying to cause problems, Dr. Hoover, and I'm grateful for your patience, but it just seems to me that we're trampling on individual liberty for everyone when one group can create guilt just by claiming to be offended – the accusation becomes the guilty verdict – but members of another group can never be offended no matter what's said or done to them. I mean, it seems to me that the notion of individual liberty is sweeping the whole world right now – all over Eastern Europe, in China . . ."

"What's your point, Mr. Pettibone?" The edge in her voice grew sharper.

"How can anybody be free if others are oppressed – men or women, nonwhite or white?"

Once more, Dr. Hoover sighed. "Don't you recognize that the term 'individual' is racist and sexist? Who's *really* in charge under the guise of 'individual liberty'? White males. We're working toward a more humane, more compassionate collective consciousness here at the university." She walked back around her desk and scrawled something on a large yellow legal pad. "I was going to simply forget this incident, but it seems clear that you'll need to spend a little time in one of the sensitivity sessions mounted by the Women's Studies and Ethnic Studies departments."

Wow, I was thinking, I already feel like I've been mounted. All those 1960s radicals like my mom and her boyfriend couldn't win with Marxism in the streets or at the ballot box, but it sure seemed like they'd worked their way in here. I was lucky I wasn't paraded around campus in a dunce cap with slogans from Chairman Mao tied around my neck.

Well, I laid low for the next couple of weeks, but I did read some stuff in the library that I'd heard Flame and Zondra and the rest refer to in class. Was *that* ever an eye-opener. I really *was* lucky not to have been pilloried and paraded. Fortunately, Flame and Zondra lightened up on me almost right away. One of the jocks made the mistake of opening his mouth, and he said something about "disabled," so he became their focus: "differently abled" and "ableism" were tossed around, and "lookism" was added for good measure. Chad was smart enough not to join in this time because, I suspect, he knew the hulking jock would make *him* "differently abled" if he shot his mouth off.

But I didn't forget the Hitler Youth attack by Flame, Zondra, and the rest of the bigots. I had a plan.

My nemesis was due to present her childhood memories, I knew, and I'd overheard her talking to classmates. Flame was in the class primarily to make everyone else watch what they said . . . or wrote, not to do any writing herself, so she seemed to be trying to finagle a way out of doing the personal memoir assignment. I would help her. First I obtained Flame's telephone number from the student resource center, then I called.

As I had hoped, an answering machine replied: "Hello. Myra, Jane, Ashley, and Flame aren't in. After the long beep, leave your message and we'll get back to you." Beeeeeep!

Disguising my voice, I announced: "This is the English Department.

Professor Litwack's creative-writing class has been canceled this week. It will meet next week at the usual time. Thank you."

Stage two was to type up a brief memoir and put Flame's name on it.

My mother was short. My father was tall. He took advantage of her height to embarrass her. One day when I was little we were driving along Highway 99 and a song called 'As Time Goes By' came on the radio. He said it was his favorite one, and he pulled the car over to the side of the road, got out, and then opened Momma's door. He took her hands and pulled her out of the car and began dancing with her there on the side of the road while the radio played. Momma laughed and laughed, but I felt so sorry for her.

Drivers of cars passing by honked and waved, and Momma was laughing, but I could tell she was so humiliated. My sisters and me hid ourselves in the backseat until the song finally ended and they at last stopped dancing. We looked up and he was kissing her right there in front of everyone – imposed himself on her in a kind of public rape, and she was so intimidated that she smiled and kissed him back.

He was crazy. And mean too.

He could be real mean. If my sisters and me asked him to stop at one of the Big Oranges along the road, he'd say no, that he was going to make us each a pine float when we got home. Then, when we got there, he'd float a toothpick in a glass of water. That was the famous pine float.

One Easter he gave us pet bunnies. They were so cute. He barbecued them that Labor Day. That's how mean he was. Poor Momma. Poor us.

I attached a note, ostensibly from Flame, explaining that she was ill but would still like her paper critiqued by the class, then I put it in Professor Litwack's mailbox.

The following Tuesday, after we had read "Flame's" essay, no one seemed willing to speak up, so the professor finally observed, "That scene of the mother and father dancing alongside the road was delightful and original, don't you think? A little gem."

"I suppose the public humiliation of a woman might appeal to some men," said Zondra, and I thought I heard Dr. Litwack groan.

"What do you think, Mr. Torrelli?" asked the professor, clearly trying to avoid Zondra's path.

Chad looked around. He was a counterpuncher, not a leader, so this role was threatening to him. "Well . . . ah . . . I . . . ah . . . appreciate that she like reveals the . . . the *heightism* her family like suffered. I mean . . . ah . . . like her mother was real short."

Ah! My opening. As the shortest person in the class, I was ready. "Short!" I shouted. "Short! Don't you mean *vertically challenged*, Chad?"

"Yes," added Fay, none too lofty herself, "vertically challenged, Chad."

I heard the two jocks chuckle, and I added, "That's a *very* oppressive thing for you to say, Chad. And a hurtful thing for Flame to have written. Maybe the dean should be alerted to this."

Zondra, saying nothing, stared at me.

"Oppressive . . . ," stammered Chad. "Oppressive! I can't be oppressive. The patriarchy *is* oppression!" he declared and glanced around for support from the women.

"Wait a minute!" I demanded. "What's this patriarchy you're always talking about? Isn't it white males? You're a white guy, Chad, or had you forgotten?"

"Yeah . . . yeah . . . but I'm not the patriarchy because I'm . . . I'm in touch with the woman within!"

"I think you're in touch with the nitwit within," I snapped, and the whole class broke up, even nervous Professor Litwack.

"Nitwit!" Chad protested. "Nitwit!"

Everyone ignored him.

"Well, Mr. Pettibone . . ." said the prof, still chuckling.

"Flame can certainly say 'short,'" Betty interjected. "She's not trying to preserve the supremacy of tall white heterosexual males. They're the only ones who misuse language, who *can* misuse it."

Chad said nothing.

"As an ethnic group," I asserted, "we vertically challenged people are often ignored. It's a very hurtful form of harassment."

No one commented, but I thought Zondra's eyes were twinkling.

"She did say 'pet,' though, instead of 'animal companion,'" pointed out Mary Alice.

"Speciesism," I snapped.

Zondra was still staring at me. She knew. Oh, well, too late now.

"Flame *can't* be guilty of speciesism. She was just showing herself using the words back when they were imposed on her when she was little," suggested Betty. "She'd *never* say 'pet' today."

"Well . . . maybe so," agreed Mary Alice.

"What's a white male like you think, Chad?" I asked.

He squirmed, then sat straight. "Hey, I'm like an ethnic minority too. I'm like bisexual."

"Say, Romain," I heard Zondra's husky voice call. "What about the writing? Do you like the writing?"

"It's very effective." What else could I say without getting into trouble?

Fay had no reservations. "I think it's *real* good. Real revealing. It just shows that you have to suffer to write truth, that's why guys can't write good – the male power structure."

"I'm like bisexual," interjected Chad, his confidence rebuilding.

"She does use accusative pronouns in nominative positions," pointed out Professor Litwack.

"Perhaps from a white male perspective," snapped Fay. "Women're breaking that oppression, creating a new syntax of honesty."

"It still sounds like poor grammar to me," said the professor. "Not *gravely* poor, of course," he quickly added.

"Yes, it *would*, wouldn't it?" Fay responded.

Zondra still gazed at me. "What do you think, Romain?"

"I think Flame's in a whole 'nother space."

"For sure," agreed Zondra, grinning at last.

Then I added for the class to hear, "She sure devastates the patriarchal notion of family, doesn't she?"

"Oh, she *does*," agreed Mary Alice, "and that's the biggest rip-off of the whole male-imposed heterosexual conspiracy."

"I'm like bisexual," Chad said.

"We *heard* that before, chump," growled Zondra.

"Yeah, chump," I added.

Then the classroom door burst open, and Flame stood there for a moment, hands on her hips, decorated arms flexing. All eyes snapped toward her as she said, "Well."

My heart sank.

"We've just been discussing your essay, Ms. Leibowitz," explained Professor Litwack.

"You have?"

"Yes, and the consensus has been quite positive."

"It has?"

"I didn't know you were such a good writer," said Zondra.

"It's quite promising," Dr. Litwack smiled. He seemed relieved to have so positive a greeting for her.

"What exactly did I have to say?" Flame asked, her tone surprisingly moderate.

"I like the part about your father the best," Chad offered.

"My *father?*"

"What he did to your mother," Mary Alice added.

"What'd he do?"

Zondra began chuckling. "He was bad," she said, "a *bad* dude."

"Yeah, he was," agreed Flame. "He was pathetic, in fact."

Ah, the old Flame was back. For a moment, I thought she'd slipped into humanity. But I said nothing. This wasn't going the way I'd planned.

"His like heightism," offered Chad.

"He was a sawed-off little dude," said Flame.

"Vertically challenged?" asked Chad.

"Short as a toadstool, *boy.*"

"Oh . . ." choked Chad, "like short."

Professor Litwack glanced at his watch, then announced, "It's time for our break. May I see you for a moment, Ms. Leibowitz?"

The rest of us repaired to the hallway or rest rooms, the smokers wandering outside. Zondra called me as soon as I left the room. "Say, Romain!"

"What?"

"She's gonna find out."

I shrugged. "Find out what?"

"She's gonna find out and when she does, you're meat."

"Hey, Zondra, I don't know what you're talking about."

The black woman only smiled. "Okay," she said. "But she's still gonna find out."

I turned and slowly walked toward the men's room, hoping to reach it before Flame left the classroom. Just as I pushed the door open, I heard that voice: "Where's Romain?"

I didn't even pause to wash my hands but pushed open the far window and eased out. I walked rapidly across the large quad toward the parking lot on the west side of campus, glancing over my shoulder frequently. Just as I reached the student union I saw them, a mob of females pouring from the humanities building with a tall, sleeveless figure in the lead.

Oh, damn! I began to lope, passing the gym, the R.O.T.C. building, the crumbling education hall. But when I looked back, the mob was closer and there were more of them, enraged women seeming to emerge from each structure to join Flame's pursuit: fat and thin, tall and short, young and old, black and white, brown and yellow, red and . . . was that *the dean* I saw dashing from the administration building to join the vigilantes? Was that *the dean* who was carrying a rope?

I sprinted then – knees up, arms pumping – right past my car because I had no time to get in, start it, and drive away. Pulling hard, I circled back toward the football stadium, where I might be able to escape among the trees, but the feminists were closing on me as my legs thickened. I hit my afterburners and managed to accelerate once more, but I could sense Flame, huge as an eagle, swooping toward me.

I could feel . . . or almost feel . . . her breath, all their breaths, and I was getting in *real* close touch with the chicken within.

Hellllllllllllllllllllllllllllllllllllllllllllllllllllllllllllllp!

SCUFFLIN'

for Bob Young

'Mind me of a story: This Eye-talian, this Jew, and this colored boy, they killed in a wreck, you know, so they go up to Heaven and St. Pete he say, "You better *have* you some money to get in here. You better have you ten thousand dollars." Now them three they just scuffle to stay alive, you know, and they ain' got no bread. That Eye-talian he start cryin' and carryin' on, so St. Pete he let him in. Then the Jew he start barginin' – "Will you take seventy-five hundred?" – till he wear ol' St. Pete out, you know, and Pete he let him in, too. Finally, St. Pete he look around for the brothah but he can't see him nowheres, so he ax this angel, "Where that black boy go? Might as well let him in too." Angel he say, "You gon' have to find him you'self. He out lookin' fo' a co-signer."

Get it?

'Mind me of the time that little white hooker come in my liquor sto'. She park a bad Continental out front, you know, and she ax can she use my telephone. I know she gon' make a contact, that's why she ain' usin' no phone on the street, so I say, "Sho, baby, but I be a bu'iness man, you know, just scufflin' to get along. It gon' cost you." Now she a sweet-lookin' little thing, Jim. *Sweet.* When she say to me, "I'm a woman," and wiggle that tight little ass, I damn near gives in. But I say, "I *got* me a woman at home, and this be bu'iness, baby. We talkin' money."

Little who' she smile and say, "Doc, you the smartest man I met down here." She use my phone and, you know, after a while a cab come by and pick her up and she leave her bad hog at my place. When she come back, she give me fifty dollars cash money. And she keep comin' in, usin' my phone and pretty soon we gets tight and she give me the money *and* the booty. Get it? You take care of bu'iness, bu'iness take care of you.

Some dudes on the street, you know, they come in and borrow a little gamblin' money from me. I don' make no big loans – too easy to get caught doin' that – but I lets a cat have a dollar for a dollar-and-a-half, and they always pays me back. Folks know they got me if they needs some bread, no references. So they pay me soon as they can, you know. Not many problems when you take care of bu'iness. 'Mind me of the time this boy come in and say he need two hundred dollars. I say, "Man, you don' need no two hundred. That cost you too much: hundred skins a month. I don' hold no long paper."

He say, "Got to have it, Doc. Jew Baby gon' sell me a bad Bonneville for two hundred down and twenty a month."

"Twenty a month fo' *how* long?"

"Five years."

"*Five years!*" I say. "Man, that's a rip-off. Don' let no Jew Baby talk you into that."

"Hey, man," he say, "you *got* you a car. You got you a Caddy. I got to have me some wheels too, man. *Got to.* Jew Baby put me in some wheels for two hundred."

I say, "Looky here, Richard" – his name Richard – "looky here, when the dude give you one of those dollar-down-dollar-till-you-die deals, you got to *die*, man, to end it. Get it?"

"I needs my wheels, man," all the boy say. "I got me a family, man. Got to have my wheels."

Well, the boy never leave me sho't befo', and he be workin' steady, you know, so I goes against my judgment, but I tells him make sure the car cold – get it? – then see will Jew Baby take three bills cash. He come back and say Jew Baby take fo' hundred. I say, "The mothahfuckah take three-twenty or he better not show his white ass in this neighborhood no mo'." Richard laugh, then he go see will Jew Baby take three-twenty. Jew Baby, he ain' no fool. He take the three-twenty and Richard get a hog.

The mothahfuckah turn out to be hot. Jew Baby just change plates, he don' even file the serial number, so my man, Richard, you know, he drivin hot. Then I knows why Jew Baby give in so easy. "Richard," I say, "I tol' you the hog no good if it ain' cold."

"Jew Baby say it cold."

"The mothahfuckah *say* it cold?"

"That's what he say." Richard low, man, low as a snake's balls. He can't drive his hog, you know, and he in debt up to his ass.

I thinks for a minute, then I figure, what the fuck, man. Got to teach Jew Baby to treat people right, you know, if he want to work the 'hood. Hate to get into it, but I got to. "Where the mothahfuckah stay, man, that shootin' gallery on Fifth?"

"Yeah."

"And he still keep those two gray punks to guard him?"

"Yeah."

"All right, brothah," I say, "go home and get clean, clean like a mothah-fuckah, then come back here with yo' Bonneville. We gon' visit Mr. Jew Baby." I don' tell Richard, but he got to be clean, you know, so nobody get killed. You start some shit dressed all funky, dude kill you in a minute. You come on clean, dude got to think. Anytime I raise sand, I get clean. My five-hundred-dollar suit say you ain' dealin' with some street bloods, Jim, you dealin' with trouble. Get it? When you scuffle to live, you learns the edges.

I tells my clerk to watch the sto', then I calls in some tabs – these three big brothahs name Harold and Skeets and Tyrone, you know, they join me. They happy to pay off, so when Richard get back, I tell him to follow my Cadillac to the shootin' gallery. Now when you sees four black dudes in three-piece suits drivin' through this part of town in the middle of the day, man, ain' but two things they can be: cops or trouble. Lots of eyes follow us, you know, and they all happy when we slide on past 'em.

Like I figure, Jew Baby's punks don' give us no shit when we gets there. They back off and look at my mens and don' say shit. Good thing, too, cause I knows Tyrone carryin' – Tyrone *always* carryin' – and I believe Harold and Skeets carryin' too. I walks right up to Jew Baby and gets in his face. "Why you sell my man a hot car?" I ax.

J.B. he look, you know, real sleepy like always. "Nobody made the nigger buy it. He got what he wanted." I start to answer, but Jew Baby he cut me off: "You don' wanna mess in this, Doc. It ain't your business. People get hurt when they mess in other people's business."

"Looky here, Jew Baby," I say, "don' threaten me. Don' say shit to me. I *cut* yo' mothahfuckin' ass, mothahfuckah. And if you don' want yo' mothahfuckin' tongue on the flo', don' never call nobody nigger. Bloods decide who be a nigger. Don' need no offay punk to say shit." The cat, you know, he make me hot and I be fingerin' my steel. I keeps a .357 in my sto', but I carries a blade and I be cuttin' dudes before any Jew Baby born. He damn near in the 'mergency room, man, whether he know it or not. "Don' say 'nigger' to me never no mo'," I warns the mothahfuckah.

"I got friends downtown," Jew Baby say.

"Dead mens don' got no friends, mothahfuckah, 'cept the mothah-fuckin' undertaker," I tells him.

He stand there, not movin'. I know he carry a piece, but he know I can cut him and I got four dudes with me. He also know he fuck up when he call Richard nigger. From outside on the street I hear two mens holler at each other. Winos. "Well?" I say.

Jew Baby, he reach into his pocket and peel bills off his roll. He hand me three-twenty. "I want a receipt," he say.

"Give the mothahfuckah his keys," I tells Richard. He toss 'em to the white dude. "That yo' receipt," I say. "Now I gives you some advice. Number one, do not never make me come down here no mo'. Number two, do not never threaten me or my mens again. Number three, if you wants to work down here, you got to give somethin' back. You got to give people some respec', man, don' be callin' nobody no nigger and takin' they money. You can make you a buck-and-a-half on a buck if you gives somethin' back. Most these folks just scufflin', man. You still make money and you make friends. But if you sell hogs hot, you know, and tells lies and rips peoples off, you dead. I don' have to kill you, mothahfuckah, 'cause the street kill you. Get it?"

When we leave I takes the boys to Smokey's Bar-B-Que and buy some good hot links, and I tells Richard if he learn his lesson, he don' owe me no interest. Richard he say, "Doc, you the man. Next time I listen." Well, I likes that, you know. I likes a young man can learn. But this the last time. He got to pull himself out the shit if he get in it again. We feelin' loose so we get to jivin' and Skeets he say he hear Jew Baby a punk. "Don't surprise me none," I tell him. "He don' straighten his act out, he be a *dead* punk." And he were, just a year or so later, pigs find his body in the alley behind the shootin' gallery. Some dudes, you know, never learn.

'Minds me of ol' Happy. He a white cat stay down here in the lot next to my sto'. Dudes got some ol' couches, you know, and chairs there and they play a little whis', some coon can, some bones. Drink a little pluck. Hap the onliest gray dude stay there all these years. At first some young bloods, you know, rough him up, but Hap he fight back good for a dude without no legs. And when these kids steal his wheelchair, you know, I go gets it for him. I tell 'em, "Boys, the man got guts. Give him a chance. Don' make me come back no mo'." They young, but they smart. They leave Hap alone after that.

Well, Hap he ain' like no Jew Baby. He live on that lot, you know, and he sleep on cardboard boxes with the colored winos and he share his little short dogs and his big long dogs with 'em, drink from the same bottle. He scuffle down to the Union Mission every day for his vittles, then back he come to the lot. He never play no games – all the bread he snag go to wine – but he hang around, you know, and joke and give other dudes a taste. He never come in here axin' for nothin' free, but I slips him a taste from time to time, and I ain' lettin' him go a day without eatin'. If he broke and in bad shape, you know, I hires him to keep an eye on things a while. Last winter I give him a poncho that fit over his chair for when it rain so bad.

And Hap a heavy cat, too. He say some deep shit, man. He not like all those fools hang around talkin' to theyselves, lookin' through they eyebrows waitin' to kill somebody – mumblin', mumblin'. All them dudes they let outta nuthouses, you know, they too crazy to be afraid. When they jumps you, you got to kill 'em. Anyway, Hap he a stone wino, but heavy.

One day I tells him I don' drink and I don' force nobody to buy, but liquor, you know, my bu'iness. I been feelin' a little low that day, man, 'cause some cat call me a booze pusher and I don' dig no kind of pushers. Hap smile and he say, "You a friend to me, Doc. I know it's hard being friendly to drunks. We don't think sensible. I could be in a veterans' hospital right now, but they won't let me drink. I'm a alcoholic, out and out. I'd rather be on the street drunk than in the hospital dry. I want my freedom, and that means my freedom to drink. You never forced nothing on me."

"I never know you a vet, Hap. You lose you legs in the war?" I ax.

"No, I come home whole. But I got in this car crash right afterwards – I was drunk – and ended up like this. My own fault."

"How come you to stay here?"

"Don't take offense, Doc, but when you're crippled and an alcoholic, you feel comfortable with niggers. You know a little bit about all they been through."

I think about it a minute, you know, and decide he one white dude can say 'nigger' to me. I say, "I 'preciate that, Hap, but don' it get lonely, man?"

He look away and say, "Yeah, sometimes. Sometimes. But I ain't complaining. Life's *supposed* to be tough. Jesus could only redeem us *after* his suffering, right?"

"You right," I answer, marvelin' at what Hap just say. He heavy. "You sho' right. It's got to be sufferin' in this worl'," I say.

Life get tougher for ol' Hap d'rectly because two of those mumblin' mothahfuckahs kill him and steal his wheelchair. They take his coat, too, and his poncho, and they leave him behind one of the couches. I find him next mornin', you know, all cold, all alone, and he look real small, almost like a little baby child there without no legs. Pigs catch them two mumblers right away, and they put 'em back in the nuthouse where they belongs, but the mothahfuckahs out again now. They stays away from here, though, because somebody cut 'em if they come back. They crazy, not stupid. A good ol' dude, Hap, and heavy. Best white cat I ever know. Onliest one, you know, that understand what it all about.

'Mind me of a story ol' Moms Mabley tell. Moms say this white dude and this brothah arrested for killin' and sentenced to get hung. Well, come close to hangin' time and the white boy, you know, he cryin' and beggin' and carryin' on. Finally, the brothah he say, "Act like a man and stop all that bawlin'. Why don' you straighten up, man?" White dude he wipe his tears and answer real hot: "Easy for you to say. You *used* to it."

Get it?

HIS WAYS ARE MYSTER'OUS

Glendon was gazing toward the Tehachapi Mountains after having begun irrigating that morning when, with a sudden grip of recognition, he realized that it wasn't a sunrise he was watching at all, it was God Hisself revealed in His Golden Splendor just to him. "Thou art my Prophet," he heard a voice boom. "Preach my gospel. Convert sinners. Take wives unto thyself. I wilt send thou Signs." The young man's thin knees buckled, and he collapsed like a drunkard's dreams.

When he came to, he found himself sprawled on a dirt bank next to the irrigation ditch, his shovel beside him, his billed cap knocked askew. The sun was over the mountains, and an unfamiliar lightness buoyed his body. "I cain't believe it," he whistled through his teeth as he straightened his cap. He had never been an especially religious person, although he had been marched to Sunday School throughout his childhood, so he could not understand why he had been Chose. His Ways Are Myster'ous, Glendon had often heard the preacher at the Free Will Gospel Church of God in Christ say, and it was true. It was surely true. Rising, he bathed his face in the clear water gurgling through the ditch, then turned toward the house. "I just cain't hardly believe it," he repeated.

In the bunkhouse kitchen that morning, he poured himself a cup of coffee and sat at the table, still trying to understand the Miracle that had occurred. The radio was blaring country music, but it now sounded profane, not entertaining, just as everything around him looked dull after the Grandeur he had witnessed. He said nothing, and finally Mrs. Watson, who was cooking, commented, "You're mighty quiet this mornin', Glendon."

How could he tell her? He sighed then announced, "I seen God a while ago."

"Sure you did, honey," replied the older woman without turning. "Want some grits with them eggs?"

"I really seen Him. I had me one a them revelation deals."

"Sure you did," agreed Mrs. Watson, plopping two fried eggs like the greasy eyes of a hanged man onto his plate.

Glendon stared at the eggs – were they a Sign? – then at the woman's broad back. "I'll take some a them grits, please," he said, having decided to disclose no more about his Mission, not right now at least. He had not been told to announce his prophecy yet, so he decided to wait for another Sign.

A moment later the other two irrigators, Manuel and J.R., strode into the room, poured themselves coffee, then scooted up to the table. "How they hangin', Glendon?" grinned J.R. The Prophet winced at the implied profanity, and J.R. seemed to interpret his expression as a greeting.

"Ola, Flaco," grinned Manuel.

"Say, Miz Watson, you sweet thang," called J.R., "when you gonna break down and step out with me?" He winked at Glendon and Manuel. He was a rough cob, J.R., and a womanizer, who seemed to take pleasure in pushing others. Glendon was always uncomfortable around him and his aggressive, mocking ways.

"When I get that desperate," the elderly woman parried without turning, "it'll be time to put me in one a them old folks' homes."

The irrigators laughed, but Glendon remained silent. What would be the next Sign, when would it come?

"Que paso, Flaco?" asked Manuel.

"Oh, nothin', but I'm gonna take some wives unto myself."

J.R.'s brows raised. "Say what? *Unto* yourself."

"Some *wives?*" asked Manuel, smiling.

Glendon nodded. Maybe he shouldn't have told them.

"Well, I hope they're better'n that warthog you took unto the dance last Saturday," grinned J.R., who always seemed to accompany the prettiest ladies.

No, he shouldn't have told them. They weren't ready. He'd wait for a Sign. Just as he finished eating, Mrs. Watson said, "When you're done, honey, I got a grocery list for you. Take the pickup into Arvin."

Becoming a Prophet had not lessened Glendon's appetite. He engulfed a second serving of biscuits laden with bacon gravy. "I swan," clucked Mrs. Watson, "if you don't eat for two, and slim as you are! If I's to eat like you, I'd weigh a ton."

"Instead of half a ton," whispered J.R., and Manuel nearly fell off his chair.

Not dignifying the remark with so much as a smile, Glendon stood. "Well, I gotta go get them groceries so's I can be back in time to change my water," he announced, letting J.R. know that he would have nothing to do with such comments. Taking the pickup's key from its hook, Glendon moved with detached dignity, his eyes scanning for a Sign.

"What's wrong with him?" he heard J.R. whisper to Manuel.

After a pause, Manuel replied, "Loco in the cabeza," and they both laughed.

"Leave the boy be!" hissed Mrs. Watson, and the two men quieted, still grinning at one another, while Glendon climbed – slowly and gracefully as a Prophet should – into the battered truck and clattered away toward town.

His market cart was loaded with supplies when he approached the checkstand and, as usual, picked up a copy of the *Enquirer* to scan while he waited for the clerk to check his groceries. The headline immediately leaped at him and he all but staggered; he didn't know what it meant, but it was clearly a Sign: "SIAMESE TWINS FACE FIRING SQUAD. One

Brother Guilty of Murder." It was like they were the only words on the page; all the other print could have been gibberish. His chest tightened and he gasped.

"You buyin' that paper or rentin' it?" asked the clerk.

"I'll take it," the Prophet replied huskily. Even his voice was changing, he sensed, deepening in response to his new role. "Did you read that deal about them two brothers that're stuck together and one's gonna get shot?"

"Huh?" the lady replied, not looking up.

"Well, they're just like me and you, stuck unto sin." The words came out of him without thought, as though some Greater Voice spoke through him.

"Thirty-seven eighty-eight," she said with a tired smile.

"Verily I say unto you . . ." the Voice spoke through him.

"There's other people waitin'." The woman's eyes narrowed and so did her tone.

"Oh," Glendon said. He paid quickly and carried the groceries out to the pickup, then hurried back to the ranch. He would teach them, all of them. He would spread the Word.

As soon as he had arrived and unloaded the groceries, Glendon hurried to his cabin, where he read and reread the mystical article, the Sign. Finally, remembering that he had to change the water on the sugar beets, he stood and headed for the door. On his way out, he spied something moving on the brass doorknob that the boss had installed when he had lived in this very cabin years before, and that Glendon kept polished. Squatting and squinting, he realized that it wasn't a bug as he suspected, but a curved reflection of his own angular form, yet there was more: next to him, attached like a swerved shadow, was a dim being, ominous and vaporous. He recoiled and swatted at it, but hit nothing; it was incorporeal and could not even be seen except in the polished brass.

Staring at the image once more, he noted that a tiny wizened face stared back at him, and that the thing itself was small, just the vestige of an evil twin – and that, Glendon realized, was why he had been Chose; he had his own evil twin under control, squeezed down to a nub. The evil face in the doorknob was surely the next Sign: folks're all stuck unto sin just like the mystical voice at the grocery store had said, and they gotta get shed of it to enter the Kingdom. He, Glendon Leroy Stone, had been Chose to spread the Message because His Ways Are Myster'ous, His Wonders to Behold. Glendon beheld himself and his pitifully shrunken evil twin once more in the knob, then hurried to the sugar beet field.

At lunch the Prophet kept his Message to himself because J.R. would make a joke out of anything. He realized that he should start converting the people nearest him before Spreading the Word, but couldn't figure how to avoid J.R.'s sharp and taunting tongue, so he sat tensely at the table, barely able to finish his second helping of chicken and dumplings, when J.R. suddenly jumped up and exclaimed: "Hell's bells! I forgot the water on the milo!" then sprinted out the door, leaving Glendon and Manuel alone at the table. His Ways Are Myster'ous.

The Prophet immediately faced the remaining irrigator and asked: "Do you believe on the Lord Jesus Christ?"

Manuel, whose mouth was full, mushed, "Humph?"

"Have you been washed in the Blood of the Sheep?"

"You mean the Lamb?" Manuel asked.

"The Lamb?"

"Hey," Manuel said, "I been baptized. I been confirmed. I go to Mass every Sunday. How 'bout you, ese, I never see you goin' to church."

Glendon did not dignify Manuel's smirk with a reply: He had been Chose and that was that. Then the Voice spoke through him: "Verily I say unto you, we are all born as twins, Good and Evil, stuck unto one another, and to enter unto the Kingdom, we gotta get rid of the Evil half."

"What?"

"The only guy born without this evil twin deal was Jesus Hisself!"

Manuel's brows knitted and he put his fork down. After a long pause, he asked, "What about the Blessed Virgin Mary?"

For a moment the table was silent, then Glendon responded: "She wasn't a guy."

Something in Manuel's eyes changed as he agreed, "That's right, she wasn't."

Glendon felt Manuel's gaze, felt it as he never had before. There was something new in it, something like respect. "Ain't you never felt the dark take you over, like whenever you're drinkin' beer or whenever you're with a woman? Ain't you never just been *took* unto sin?"

Manuel's gaze appeared troubled. "Maybe," he conceded.

"Well, that's whenever your bad twin's takin' over, and if your twin goes to hell, *you go too because you're attached.*"

"Where'd you hear all that?" Manuel's voice cracked, and within Glendon something swelled. The other man's eyes were troubled and, for the first time in his life, Glendon felt as though he had the power to influence someone else's mind: the Power of God Revealed.

The Prophet stood, feeling stronger than he ever had, carried his dishes to the sink, then strode to the door, calling over his shoulder, "Believe on the Lord."

"I do," he heard Manuel stammer. "Swear to God, I do."

If he did, J.R. didn't. "What's this religion deal ol' Manuel's tellin' me about?" he demanded at breakfast the following morning.

"Well, I'm fixin' to preach the gospel," Glendon stammered, not wanting to face the other man's disdainful eyes.

"You?"

"I been Called," Glendon mumbled.

"Oh, yeah," grinned J.R., and even Manuel smiled. It was clear that J.R.'s evil twin had took over.

For a moment, the table was silent except for the smack of meat being chewed, and Glendon felt their gaze heavy on his hot face. Finally he glanced up and, just as he did, J.R. stood with an odd expression on his face. He said nothing, but pointed at his gaping mouth, then dashed to the sink and tried without success to drink. He began hitting his own chest, his eyes all the while panning wildly around him.

"Hey, he's chokin'!" Manuel said, and he jumped up and began pounding the other man's back.

Mrs. Watson emerged from the pantry and asked, "What's wrong?"

J.R.'s face was darkening and he began swinging his arms like a man in a fight. Manuel ducked, calling, "Hey!"

Not knowing what else to do, the Prophet rose and, fearing that J.R. might accidentally hit Mrs. Watson, he moved behind the choking man and grabbed him, firmly pinning his arms. When he squeezed, J.R. made a coughing sound and a bullet of beef shot from his mouth. He collapsed in Glendon's grasp.

"Oh, God! Thanks, Glendon," J.R. finally gasped after being helped into a chair. "You saved my damn life! You saved my life!"

The Prophet stood there comforting the toughest guy he'd ever known, and through his head one message passed and passed again: His Ways Are Myster'ous.

"Don't thank me," he told the relieved man, "thank God. It was Him give me the Power." He had not only squeezed the chunk of beef from J.R., he had given the man's evil twin a good crushing too.

"I'll do it," J.R. assured him. "I'll surely do it."

Glendon noticed how the other man was looking at him, the obvious admiration, and he noticed that Manuel said nothing. He realized that he had brought into the Fold the two worst sinners he knew, maybe the two worst in Kern County. Why, the devil was easy to beat when you were Called; there was nothing to it. And he could tell that Mrs. Watson, a good Christian woman, now understood his Mission. She placed one hand on his arm and said, "That was a wonderful thing you done, honey. You'll have the highest seat in Heaven."

Well, maybe he *would*, Glendon realized, maybe he just would, but to earn it he would have to take his message to the World, show them his perfection as a kind of model deal. As he shoveled mud from rows that day, and patched up leaking ditches, he considered how he would begin spreading the Word. He had, of course, seen *Watchtower* sellers lining Arvin's corners on early mornings, all dressed up and grinning like street whores. They chose the right places, but they just *stood* there. Glendon would do them one better.

He dressed Sunday morning in his almost-new J. C. Penney suit. His boots were polished and he wore a necktie Mrs. Watson had given him for Christmas. He splashed on plenty of aftershave too. When he walked to the kitchen to fetch the key for the pickup, which he had permission to use, J.R. called, "This ol' boy smells like a French cathouse. Watch out, women!"

"You oughta be goin' to church with Manuel," the Prophet advised.

"Sure," grinned J.R.

No doubt about it, Glendon admitted, J.R.'s evil twin had took back over. He wouldn't be grinning if that meat was still stuck in his throat. Well, today the Prophet had other tasks, but he would save that sinner once and for all, and soon.

In town, Glendon stationed himself on the corner of Bear Mountain

Road and School Street, where most churchgoers would have to pass, as would the early-morning beer bar habitués. He stood quietly, hands clasped behind his back, waiting. Two small Mexican children, a boy and a girl holding hands, passed on their way to the Catholic church. "Do you believe on the Lord?" he asked with a smile. They glanced at him, then hurried on without replying.

Before the Prophet could become discouraged, a disheveled man approached walking in the opposite direction – heading, Glendon guessed, for that row of beer bars known locally as Tiger Town. Here was a sinner if ever he had seen one, the evil twin practically obliterating whatever remained of the good one. "Have you been washed in the Blood of the Lamb?" Glendon demanded. He could not mince words with sinners.

"Huh?" The thin man wore an old baseball cap at an askew angle with its bill pushed up so that he resembled in profile a duck with a broken neck.

"Have you been washed in the Blood of the Lamb?"

The man's rosy eyes seemed to throb as he examined the Prophet. "I ain't even had a shower. You can't loan a guy a buck for breakfast can you, pal?"

The old boy looked vaguely familiar; perhaps Glendon had once worked with him. In any case, he wasn't giving money away. In fact, he might just *collect* some like those TV preachers did, an idea he had been playing with. Feed the Hungry flashed into the Prophet's mind just as he started to say no. He realized that he was being Tested: His Ways Are Myster'ous. "You mean you haven't eat?"

"Not for days, pal."

"Well . . . here." He handed the man one of the trio of dollar bills he carried. "You *do* believe on the Lord, don't you?" he asked, but the man was already shuffling away.

"Sure thing," Glendon heard the unkempt man call over his shoulder, duck's bill bobbing toward Tiger Town.

Uncomfortably, the Prophet watched his dollar clutched in the man's hand disappear into the doorway of the Nogales Saloon. He wasn't certain they served breakfast there, unless the man favored pickled eggs and beer nuts, so Glendon continued staring at the distant doorway, half expecting the man to emerge in a halo of light and raise his hands toward Heaven

His Ways Are Myster'ous 169

in thanks for his meal. He knew this had to be a Sign, not one of those drunk-begging-money deals. All he saw, however, was two more men – one well dressed and wearing a vast white Stetson, the other bareheaded and tattered – slip inside the doorway. He was tempted to walk right down there and challenge those sinners, even if they were only eating breakfast, when he felt a tug at his sleeve.

He turned and faced a pale young woman – not much more than a girl – dressed in a green gown, who extended a rose wrapped in wax paper. "Peace, my brother," she murmured, smiling gently. "Won't you buy a flower for God's love?"

"A flower?" Maybe this was a Sign too.

"For God's love."

"Well, I been washed in the Blood of the Lamb."

"Won't you buy a flower?"

"How much?"

"God sets no price. Your love offering will suffice." She was a very pretty lady – her evil twin didn't show at all – and Glendon had not forgotten that he was to take wives unto hisself, so he withdrew a second dollar bill and handed it to her, then accepted the flower.

"Thank you, my brother." She touched his arm tenderly. "You are standing alone. Do you wish company and joy?"

"Well, I been washed . . ."

"Why don't you come with me to meet God on earth, the Bagwan Dawn Mahwa who has come to release life's love."

"Well, I been . . ."

Her grip on his arm tightened, and she pulled him. He noticed then other green gowns stalking the streets, several with people in tow. "Come my brother, to the earthly paradise where all is love and no needs go wanting."

Glendon jerked his arm free. "Hey," he said, "I don't think you believe on the Lord Jesus."

"He was a great teacher, like the Bagwan Dawn Mahwa who has succeeded him. Come to the new paradise. Join us. Join us." Again she gripped his arm.

"This ain't one a them *goo-roo* deals, is it?" he demanded.

Although the girl had given no visible signal, Glendon could see three other green gowns heading purposefully in his direction, and he sensed that they were reinforcements, so he hustled away after freeing himself from her grip, away toward Tiger Town where he thought she was not likely to follow. As he passed the Nogales Saloon, he heard harsh laughter and another girl in one of the green gowns fled, red-faced, out the door. "Where you goin', baby?" he heard a rough masculine voice call after her.

It's all different kind of sinners, he told himself as he stopped just beyond the saloon.

Glancing down the street, he noted that four green gowns were now heading in his direction, while one was scurrying the other way. Well, he knew a haven when he saw it, so he dashed into the Nogales's darkened interior and hurried to the bar's far end, then slid next to a guy – the same one with a crooked cap, the Prophet realized immediately – who was drinking his breakfast and, as it turned out, Glendon's dollar. Well, at least the old boy might keep them goo-roo deals away, the Prophet figured.

The red-eyed man turned and asked, "You ain't got a smoke, do you, pal?" He seemed unperturbed to find his benefactor seated next to him.

"I already *give* you a buck," Glendon pointed out indignantly. No doubt about it, he thought, this old boy is clean took over by his evil twin.

"No smokes, eh?" He sure looked like someone Glendon knew, but the Prophet couldn't name who.

Just as Glendon was about to snap a response that would shock this old sinner onto the Path of Righteousness, the thick-armed bartender said, "What'll it be?"

"Oh, gimme a beer," said the Prophet. He pulled his final dollar from his pocket.

"Comin' up."

"You wouldn't wanna buy me a refill, would you, pal?" asked the old drunk.

"I *already* give you a dollar," Glendon hissed.

No green gowns appeared, and the Prophet was drinking his draft with relief when he glanced at his image in the fancy mirror behind the cash register, a Man of God sitting next to a common drunk and slurping the devil's brew. His face warmed and reddened, his stomach suddenly churned, so he turned to the old boy and demanded: "How's come you to drink beer with that dollar I give you for breakfast, anyways?"

The red eyes faced him and he heard the man croak, "You *give* me the buck, so mind your own damn business!"

Glendon sensed that he had this sinner on the run. After he finished his beer – no sense wasting it – he really told him: "You got no business takin' folks' money that works hard for it. You're pullin' one a them beggar deals when you oughta be out workin' your ownself. Evil's flat took you is what's wrong and unless you wash in the Blood of the Lamb . . ."

For a second, Glendon didn't realize what had happened – the sudden shock – and by the time he did, the old boy had socked him a second time and was grappling with him, had him down in fact. He was strong for a skinny old weasel, or something was weakening Glendon, because the drunk – cap still firmly awry on his head – had the Prophet pinned to the floor while the saloon's other patrons laughed and shouted. Above him, Glendon registered only the flaring eyes and ghastly face of the man like sin itself.

It was humiliating because no matter how the Prophet bucked and surged, the old drunk stuck to him, and the laughter of those other drunkards burned his ears. Determined to teach this sinner a lesson, Glendon sucked in his breath for a decisive burst when, suddenly, he recognized the face snorting above his: it was the very one he had seen in his brass doorknob that first day, his own evil twin's, and that dark brother had him now as surely as Cain had Abel. Glendon Leroy Stone began to pray as he never had before.

THE GREAT NEW-AGE CAPER

Dunc he swaggered into the Tejon Club that afternoon a-wearin' this cap with "God, Guns, and Guts Made America Great" printed on the front.

Whenever I seen it, I said, "They give you the wrong hat there, Duncan."

"Wrong hat?" he said.

"Yeah, in your case, it oughta be 'God, Guns, and *Gut* . . .'"

That give the boys a laugh, but ol' Dunc he just grunted, "Eat shit."

The next thing you know, though, we was talkin' guns because Duncan claimed he'd bought him this fancy .30-06. He said he was gonna take it up to Greenhorn Mountain come huntin' season and bag him a buck. "I gotta get my deer, see," he said, quite the outdoorsman.

Well, he hadn't bagged nothin' but a six-pack at the Liquor Barn in years. I knew he wasn't no hunter, but he gets on these kicks and purty soon he takes to believin' his own bullshit. Around Oildale, ever' guy has to at least claim to be a deer hunter, seems like, or he ain't a real man.

Anyways, Big Dunc not only couldn't walk up a anthill without needin' oxygen, but he couldn't shoot worth a shit either, so I said, "I been out to the target range with you a time or two, Dunc, and the safest place to be is in front a the target. You couldn't hit a elephant with birdshot."

"Your ass!" he snorted. "Back in the Army I'uz a damn sharpshooter, see. The best in my damn outfit."

Bob Don that was slightly of the liberal persuasion like all your college types, he piped up, "What do you guys need with guns anyway? Insecure? Penis envy?"

"Huh?" said Dunc, a typical comeback. "What's that penis shit?"

"We need 'em because our forefathers told us to, Bundy," I responded. "It's in the Constitution, by the way!" I wasn't takin' no lip off of him.

"You need a musket, then, that's what our forefathers were talking about, not machine guns or automatic pistols or semiautomatic rifles. Those didn't even exist when they wrote the Bill of Rights."

"Oh, yeah," snapped Duncan. He was really on his toes.

"Why don't you guys knock it off?" urged Earl. He'd heard us on this subject before.

"They never said that, they said *firearms*," I pointed out.

"They said the right to bear arms, *period*, if you want to be technical, and arms in those days meant muzzle-loaders."

"Oh, balls!" I said. Your liberals won't talk reasonable.

"Well, I'm a-gonna get me my buck, see," groused Duncan into his beer. "And I'll carry all the damn guns I want."

Earl that run the joint, he slid out the pump .12-gauge shotgun he kept under the bar, then the .357 magnum he had in the slot by the cash drawer, and he said, "You guys shut the fuck up." He never did nothin' but show 'em to us, but he made his point. He was tryin' to watch the news on TV.

We shut up and Earl put his hardware away.

On the screen, some gal she was interviewin' this other gal that she was a ranger at this place where there was this big colony a barkin' seals – noisy as hell. Anyways, that ranger gal she grinned into the camera and said, "The bull elephant seals spend most of their waking hours trying to mate with the cows."

Big Dunc that was slurpin' a brew at the bar, he piped right up, "Just like me, see, them bulls, spend the whole damn day a-matin'."

Earl he couldn't resist: "Yeah, I seen some of the elephant seal cows you dated back in high school, Duncan. You and them bulls got more than double chins in common."

"Oh, yeah," snapped Dunc – his usual clever reply. Instead of arguin', he tried to divert attention away from his own pitiful teenage love life: "Oh, yeah! Well you shoulda seen the dogs ol' J.B. there usta take out, see."

He couldn't resist gettin' me into it, I guess, but I just ignored him. He's like talkin' to one a them elephant seals – all bark – so there ain't no point.

"Hey, Jerry Bill, guess who's back in town?" asked Bob Don Bundy, all pals again, and with this silly look on his face like a dog that found a fresh cat box.

I just shrugged. "Beats hell outta me," I answered. I mean, how do you answer a question like that?

"Earl?" asked Bob Don, tryin' to get somebody to give him a guess.

"How the hell do I know?" grunted Earl that runs the joint.

"Dunc?"

"Eat shit," grunted Big Dunc.

"Who?" I finally asked.

"Nedra Marie Dubarry Wilhite is who!"

"No lie!" I couldn't hardly believe it.

"Does Shoat know?" asked Earl. He was referrin' to ol' Nedra Marie's ex-husband that'd had her run outta town a few years back whenever he caught her and this young boyfriend dippin' into the till, among other things.

"She better hope not," I said. That's a fact because ol' Shoat's tough as a Mexican family – and that's *damn* tough.

Bob Don he's still grinnin'. "And guess what else I heard?"

Dunc cut the cheese.

"Is that your guess?" asked Bundy.

"That's the smartest thing you'll hear from him," I said.

"Eat shit, see," grunted Duncan.

"I heard she claims she's a *medium* now," said Bob Don with a grin.

"I'd a said she'uz a large," grunted Big Dunc. "'Specially her tits, see."

"Duncan," said Bob Don Bundy that graduated Bakersfield Junior College and worked in a office so he's a smart sucker, "you've got a mind like a racehorse. It runs best on a dirt track."

"Eat shit," come back that silver-tongued Dunc.

Earl he scratched his head and munched a handful a beer nuts. "What the hell kinda *medium* you talkin' about?"

"Well, I saw this ad in a little throwaway paper that had her picture in it and it said she was a 'New-Age Healer and Psychic' visiting from Texas."

"No shit?" I said. Me, I'd read in the newspaper about that New-Age deal.

"Yeah," he went on, "it said she's gonna give a free lecture at the Veterans' Memorial Hall tonight and she's a-gonna talk about fire walking. A tickler, I'd guess, to draw people in. You guys wanta go?"

"That ain't her favorite kinda tickler, see," snorted Dunc, that can come up with a goodun ever' once in a while. I had to laugh.

That encouraged Duncan, so he snapped that paper outta ol' Bob Don's hands, stared at it and chewed on the words a minute, then asked, "What the hell's a 'physic'?"

"It's what you need," answered Bob Don, grabbin' back his newspaper. "Any of you guys want to go hear Nedra Marie talk about fire walking?" he asked.

The Tejon Club it ain't but a short mile from the Vets' Hall, so I said, "Why not?"

"I don't get it. What it is she's supposed to do," said Earl.

Since I'd read about that New-Age scheme in the paper, I knew the answer to that one. "It's this latest deal to make money that they come up with, kinda like the old tent preachers but for rich folks."

"I still don't get it," admitted Earl.

"It's just that people are willing to pay for almost anything," Bob Don explained, "even the illusion that they're getting better or younger or stronger or some such when they know they aren't. In fact, that's when they pay the most."

"Those Yuppie deals got more money than good sense," I said.

"What I mean is what do they *do?*"

"Play with each other, see," Dunc grumped. I knew he didn't have a clue, but he wasn't too far off that time.

"All kinda silly stuff," I said. "Pretend they're someone else, do this Chinese shit, beat drums, play like they're babies . . ."

"Play doctor," interjected Dunc – one-track mind – but I ignored him and kept explainin' to Earl.

". . . mess with crystals, walk on fire, even take these high colonic deals."

"What's that, them 'high-colonic deals'?" asked Wylie Hillis that he'd just walked in. "It sounds rank to me," he added.

"That's an enema," said Bob Don.

"A *enema!* No shit?"

"Lotsa shit," grinned Dunc. He's on a damn roll, just full a cute remarks.

"It sounds crazy as hell to me," Earl grunted.

Just then the telephone rang and Earl he shuffled over and answered it. He got this grin on his face, then said, "Hey, Dunc, it's the war department."

Big tough Duncan flinched like someone'd hit him, and he whispered, "Tell her I just left, see."

"He just left," Earl said into the phone.

Still grinning, Earl held that phone away from his ear for what seemed like a long time and we could all hear this midget voice buzzin', then he hung up. "She says the insurance man's at the place and you was s'posed to be home to talk to him and get your big ass home."

"Oh, yeah!" said Dunc, real defiant. But he was slidin' off his stool and suckin' down the last dregs of his draft. A second later he scooted out the door.

"By damn," grinned Wylie Hillis, "ol' Dunc's sure got that woman under control," and we all had a laugh.

"Gettin' back to that Nedra Marie Dubarry Wilhite deal, we oughta at least go see what's up," I suggested.

"Let's do it," grinned Earl.

When me and Earl and Bob Don we seen her onstage, she looked younger than a few years back. I believe she'd had ever'thing lifted that'd go up. "Gol dang," said Earl, "that ol' hide's lookin' prime!"

Well, there was this funny music playin' and the hall it was dim whenever ol' Nedra Marie she walked out in a semi-see-through gauze gown into these blue and red lights. The first thing she done was announce that her "eternal name," as she called it, was "the Very Right Reverend Doctor Ramadama" and that she was this "Ascended Master" deal and that she'd had these six past lives: she'd been a princess and a king and a wizard and a priestess and a queen and a Aztec virgin. "I figgered it'uz about that far back since she'uz a virgin," I said.

Bob Don sneered, "I wonder if she was homecoming queen too?"

Ol' Earl he whispered, "She never mentioned that she'd been a crook and stole that money from Shoat Wilhite."

"Nobody ever seems to remember being a hooker or a gravedigger or a day laborer," hissed Bob Don. "They were all kings and queens and high powers."

"Me too," I grinned.

"You're still a queen," Earl grinned real evil when he said that and I had to laugh.

Anyways, ol' Very Right Reverend Doctor Ramadama she give a long talk all about this "empowerment" deal and how a new age it was comin' and everyone was gettin' stronger and spirits they was fixin' to talk to us. She got me to laughin' whenever she flashed this slide on the screen a her standin' out in the country and there was this streak on the picture like her camera leaked light. "That," she pointed out, "is a wood nymph that led me to the trees. She's the fairy that dwells in my clan's power spot there and gives me strength to share my enlightenment with you."

Earl he'uz was laughin' too. "That streak it looks like the time we turned the lights out at the club and lit one of Dunc's farts," he pointed out.

It really did, and ol' Bob Don he said, "That's Dunc's power spot."

"Besides, we brung our own fairy with us," I said to Earl and we both poked Bob Don.

"Screw you guys," he grinned. This was better'n a damn vaudeville show. We got a lotta dirty looks for laughin', but it seemed like nobody wanted to tangle with us 'cause nobody said nothin'.

Pretty soon the Very Right Reverend, she advised the folks there, "You must activate your kundalini."

"Do what?" asked Earl.

"Activate your wienie," said Bob Don.

Earl grinned. "Hell, I could go that."

"That's exactly what ol' Earl's wife wants him to do," I added.

What ol' Ramadama – I like that name – never said was that she was workin' on gettin' rich. Her folks was peddlin' all kindsa shit in the lobby: crystal rocks and these funny cards with pictures on 'em and calendars and tapes and books – you name it.

Best of all, though, she said that the very next afternoon this young guy that never had but one name, OmAr (no shit, he really spelled it that way with two capitals – I seen it on a sign in the lobby), he'uz fixin' to walk on fire and show other folks how to do it and that they'd get real brave and real successful if they just done like he done. But, of course, it was gonna cost some hard cash.

See, it'uz like them ol' deals at the carnival that they let you in the tent to see the good-lookin' dancin' gals for a quarter, but if you wanted to see 'em buck naked, you had to shell out another four bits and go behind the curtain. When you did, it was their mother or grandmother that stood there, naked and ugly and bored.

Anyways, the audience it was fulla young, kinda rich-lookin' folks and it seemed like they all had stars in their eyes and drool on their chins. It'uz like goin' to the Assembly of God for a revival, seein' them glazed eyes, hearin' them shouts of "Yes! Yes!"

Whenever ol' Ramadama introduced OmAr, this expensive-lookin' young guy next to me, he said to the gal next to him, "OmAr was a Druid priest who advised King Arthur!" That gal she blinked her eyes, all thrilled, and she said, "I heard he was born at Stonehedge."

"No," interrupted this other gal that she overheard 'em, "I heard he just appeared on the summit of Mount Shasta and Ramadama transported him down with psychic energy."

"Ohhh," cooed the first gal.

"Oh, bullshit," said Earl. Then he added, "I recollect that he usta be a tentmaker back when I'uz in high school – usta activate my wienie most mornin's." Me and Bob Don broke up.

"If he *is* OmAr the Tentmaker, then I got to know him real good back in high school too," I chuckled.

"Who didn't?" agreed Bob Don. "This really is a goofy bunch of people, isn't it? It looks like they'll believe anything Nedra Marie tells them."

Well, dopey or gullible or whatever they was, them folks had filled the parkin' lot with all these big fancy German and Japanese cars. It looked like to me they had more money than good sense, and wasn't no one in cowboy boots but us three from the club. I guess we looked strange to them, what with the way some of 'em stared at us, then real quick averted their eyes if we caught 'em. We musta been hard-lookin' to them.

The next day I'uz in the club after work talkin' to Wylie Hillis. I told him about that fire-walkin' deal and how it'uz supposed to give folks power.

"Far walkin'," he spit, then shook his head. "Some folks don't have brains enough to pour piss outta a boot." He looked real disgusted for a minute, then he said, "I'll tell ya, J.B., I recollect one time at a tent meetin' back in Fayetteville I seen these ol' boys that was dancin' with *snakes* in their mouths. They said God give 'em *par*. In fact, they thought they was real parful, but this one ol' boy he got bit and died deader'n a turd. I b'lieve he'uz a tad less parful than the snake. Is that what that far-walking deal does?"

"We'll see. I think maybe you hit it on the head, though. This's just a way those Yuppie deals can act like Pentecostals without feelin' guilty."

"Ya reckon?" grinned Wylie.

That next evenin', there was another crowd at the auditorium for the fire walkin' and I couldn't resist. There'uz a goofy mix a folks wanderin' from the parkin' lot – heavy gals in mu-mus and skinny guys in them designer jeans, thin gals in these pants suits and fat guys in what looked like robes. Before I ever even got inside, though, I seen this one ol' boy maybe my age – no spring chicken – and he'uz dressed like one a them San Francisco hippies. Wellsir, he'uz a standing right in front a the door in one a them funny colored T-shirts and a bandana on his long hair; his eyes they looked like pinwheels and he'uz a-preachin' to whoever's dumb enough to listen, and I was. But just for a minute.

"Free the Oakland Five! We have to like legalize our sacramental LSD," he said. "LSD is like derived from living plants and it is like our brothers in the vegetable kingdom talking to us humans. It *must* be legalized! It like *must* be! All power to the people! Free the Oakland Five!"

He looked crazier'n a three-peckered goat to me, what with his little pointy beard and all. "Hey, pal," I said to him.

"What, man?"

"Free the Indianapolis Five Hundred!" I said, then I winked, made one a them V-for-victory deals with my fingers, and walked away.

"Right on!" he called after me.

Anyways, at the box office, I found out you could watch the fire walkin' for twenty bucks, but it cost another century note if'n you wanted to trot the coals. I said no thanks on that hundred-bucks part, and I damned near give up and went home before they got to the hot stuff because for a good two hours the Very Reverend Doctor Boobs and ol' OmAr they just talked and preached and cajoled a few more bills from the faithful, but finally ever'one paraded outside to the lawn behind the hall and there was this shallow pit, maybe ten or twelve foot long, and it was filled with what looked like charcoal briquettes. They looked damn hot to me. At the far end, somebody'd filled a kid's plastic wadin' pool with water.

First let me tell you that ol' OmAr, he had one a them A-rab towel deals wrapped around his head, and he was wearin' this gown that it looked like my wife Heddy's housecoat. When he had apprentice fire walkers all assembled at one end of the pit and was givin' 'em a pep talk, he swished his arms all around in that housecoat like a damn butterfly.

Me, I'uz with the spectators lined up along the side to watch folks hike them coals. And guess who I all of a sudden noticed in the big crowd with me: Shoat Wilhite. He seen me too, so we made our ways to each other, shook hands and exchanged howdies. He's a good ol' boy, Shoat, and I'uz really glad to see him. He had this other young guy in a suit and tie with him and he introduced him as Jim Fishman, his attorney.

"Jim and I intend to have a word or two with my ex-wife," he told me, and his eyes they went all hard and cold. "I warned her way back when never to come back here, but I guess she thought I was kiddin'. I wasn't." Me, I was glad I wasn't the one he'uz pissed at.

Just then all them apprentices they commenced chantin': "Cool, wet grass! Cool, wet grass!" and who should appear but the Very P*ight Reverend Ramadama herownself. She exchanged a few inspirational words with the suckers, then turned and announced to all of us, "I shall defy the great flames!"

There wasn't no flames but, like I said, them coals looked hot enough.

Ramadama she swirled around and begun callin', "Cool, wet grass! Cool, wet grass!" and she d'rectly stepped right onto the coals just as she noticed Shoat a-glarin' at her. She forgot the cool grass and hesitated on them hot coals, almost stumbled, then she said, "Ouuu! Owww! Eeee!" and hopped into that wadin' pool as quick as she could, her face suddenly lookin' old, like the one on that naked lady at the carnival all them years ago. Shoat and Jim they buttonholed her right now and marched her – she'uz limpin' some – back toward the hall.

A lotta the spectators they was laughin', and them apprentices they never looked quite so confident all of a sudden. In fact, maybe half of 'em commenced marchin' away despite ol' OmAr's protests: "Find your center! Don't surrender to fear. Empower yourself! Find your cool center!"

Apparently a bunch of 'em thought they'd find their centers somewheres else, because they departed.

OmAr he done the best he could to talk folks into crossin' them coals, walkin' across a couple a times real fast hisownself, but only a few turned their faces to stone and hurried across, sayin' "Cool, wet grass," then jumpin' into that wadin' pool. The others just drifted away into darkness. The edge had went from the evenin' and the big show it petered out d'rectly. Ol' OmAr he looked like he could use a tentmaker of his own.

Shoat come in the club that next long, hot afternoon and announced, "My ex-wife's gone and her fancy man's packin' up this afternoon. She won't be back . . . unless she wants to see the inside of the jailhouse."

"Have a brew, pard'," I said, and he accepted.

Not fifteen minutes later here come my boy Craig and his pal Junior and they'uz and laughin' to beat hell. "Hey, Dad," Craig called. "Me and

Junior went over to the auditorium after school to watch them close up that fire-walking pit and pack up." (I'd told him what I'd seen the night before and he'uz disappointed he never got to see the fire walkin'.) "Anyway, that Arab guy took his shoes off for some reason, so we took them and put them on the hood of a car in middle of that big parking lot. We wanted to see if he could walk barefoot across the hot blacktop like we do all the time." He grinned. "He couldn't."

Him and Junior commenced hoppin' on one foot then the other, callin', "Ouch! Eeek! Ohhh!" gigglin' and pokin' each other. Then ol' Craig he said, "Maybe he forgot to say, 'Cool, wet grass.' You know what? Me and Junior ought to start a pavement-walking class, sort of empower people to walk barefooted in Oildale during the summer the way all the kids do."

"You got it, son," I grinned, real proud. That boy was gonna be rich some day.

"Hey," said Bob Don real serious. "You guys shouldn't make fun of psychics like that. Look what they taught me," and he real quick showed us a crystal and popped it into his mouth and begun crunchin' it. Hell, I thought he'd went nuts – he was gonna break his damn teeth – then he grinned and showed us a plastic bag labeled Rock Candy. "Care for some?" he asked the boys.

While we'uz helpin' ourselves, Earl he got this real serious look on his puss and he turned to Craig and Junior. "Listen, you young bucks," he told 'em, "you better hope you never pissed off that A-rab. If there's anyone kids your age don't wanta piss off it's Omar the Tentmaker. Without him, your whole day might be ruined. Am I right, fellers?" he asked us old poops.

"Oh, yeah," we agreed.

Then I added, "All but 'cept Duncan. He might've had guns, God, and guts, but he only had him a little pup tent and the pup was usually asleep."

While ever'one else was laughin', that silver-tongued Big Dunc grunted, "Eat shit."

HOME TO AMERICA

Hideko hid. She had heard her brothers, Warren and Charles, talking the night before, heard them discuss the big policeman who was coming to get them, and the torture chamber to which they were being taken. She heard that little girls would be roasted and eaten, so Hideko hid, burying herself deep in the dirty clothes bin under soiled garments they could not take with them.

When the U.S. marshal arrived, Mother and Father searched frantically for her, their own sadness and rage rendering their efforts frenzied and random. "I think I know where she is," Charles finally volunteered, then he led them to the bin. Through the muffling laundry Hideko heard people approach, knowing only that it was the man who roasted little girls, and that he was near, near.

"What's wrong with her, Miz Takeda?" the marshal asked. He was a large, pale man with graying blond hair, who seemed vaguely uncertain about Hideko's closed-eyed terror. "I ain't gonna hurt you, honey," he soothed, trying to touch her, but she cringed.

Mother's own voice was tight and angry. "You're taking her, us, away from home, and you ask what's the matter. She's scared, that's what!" Then, to Hideko: "Poor baby. Poor, poor baby. Momma's with you. Momma's with you." Mother picked her up.

The pale-eyed man turned to Father. "Mr. Takeda, I don't like this either. I don't believe you folks're spies like they say, but I got my job to do. I really do."

Father, who was not much given to talk, nodded. "Yeah," he said.

The truck honked, causing the marshal to jump. "Sorry to rush you folks, but we got to get to town. Can I help you carry your things?"

"The order said we can take only what we can carry," Mother snapped, "so we'll carry it." Each of the boys lifted two bundles, and Warren wore his old Boy Scouts of America knapsack filled with sports magazines and books. Father carried four large bags – his and Mother's – and Mother carried Hideko and Hideko's own small bundle. Hideko, her eyes tightly shut, clasped only Raggedy Anne to her small breast.

Outside, in the yard, Mr. and Mrs. Epp, who owned the farm across the road, stood with Reverend Meyer, who'd just driven up. "Let me help," Mr. Epp volunteered, taking two of the bags from Father. Mrs. Epp put her arm around Mother, and both women immediately began weeping.

As they tossed the bags into the military truck, seeing two other families huddled in the darkness of the covered bed, Mr. Epp heard the pimply driver mutter something about "lousy Japs." He rushed to the cab and thrust his meaty arm through the window. "Son," he said with a low, quivering voice, his face flushed, "you use that word again and I'll break your goddamn neck!"

The marshal hurried to the cab, told the driver to keep his mouth shut, then eased Mr. Epp away.

They climbed into the truck, and Mr. Epp reached up to shake Father's hand. "Mas," he said, "we'll look after your place for you. Don't worry. Just take care of yourself and Lucy and the kids." Reverend Meyer advised them to have faith during these difficult times; "God hasn't forgotten you." Then they were bouncing out the country road toward town, sitting near the open, sunny end of the truck's bed.

"I wouldn't sit there," said a man from the depths of the truck. Father recognized him without knowing his name because the man displayed sheep every year at the county fair.

"Why not?" Father asked.

"They're throwing things in the truck. You wait, they'll do it again."

Father and Mother moved into the back with the other families, next to the cab. Warren and Charles stayed at the open end until Father spoke sharply to them, then they reluctantly joined everyone else. Hideko, curled on Mother's lap, clasped Raggedy and kept her eyes shut; she was trembling.

"Lucy?" It was Emily Kozasa. She had been crying, her eyes red and swollen. Next to her sat her aging, blind aunt who spoke no English, so Mother answered in Japanese. The men began talking too, speculating on where they were going, their voices quiet, yet harsh. Ed Kozasa said it looked like this was going to be a great growing year, but . . . The sheep man shrugged. "Or a great dying year," he muttered, and his wife poked him, nodding toward the children.

They could tell they were nearing town, for the farms they could see out the truck's back were smaller, and a few billboards sprouted along the road. The truck jolted to a halt at a crossroad, and there was a sudden hollow thunk! thunk! on its canvas sides; a clod flew through the open back and exploded on the floor. Warren and Charles sprinted to the open end just as high-pitched voices shouted: "Dirty Japs! Dirty shittin' Japs!"

"I see you, Arnie Presley!" Warren shouted. "I'll beat hell out of you when we get home!"

The truck jerked away from the stop sign, and Mother, her voice shocked, said, "Warren Ken Takeda! Who taught you to talk that way?"

"Do you know who that was?" Warren answered tightly. "It was that dumb Arnie Presley and his brothers. I'll kick his butt."

"Sit down," Father said, and the boys sat.

"I'll talk to you about this tonight, Warren," Mother continued, but Warren seemed not to hear her. He kept repeating to himself: "That stupid Arnie Presley."

"It really was Presley, Mom," Charles piped in. "I saw him too."

"That'll be enough from you, Charles. We'll talk about it at ho . . . we'll talk about it tonight." Mother bit her lip, and squeezed her silent, shut-eyed daughter.

Downtown, everyone climbed from the truck with their baggage. There were nearly twenty families, their belongings piled on the sidewalk next to a worn-looking bus. Around them crowded townspeople, neighbors, and a line of soldiers holding rifles with bayonets. The spectators were quiet mostly, talking among themselves: farmers, business people, many children among them. Seeing Hideko clinging to Mother, one older woman remarked to her husband, "You have to admit, they're cute when they're little."

A few younger men, cigarette packs rolled into the short sleeves of their T-shirts, explained to an older marshal why they should be allowed to hang "just one Jap" as an example. The marshal responded loudly, "I understand how you boys feel, but the rule of law has to be observed." With that, the leader of the young men flung a tattooed arm past the marshal and struck an old man who stood with his back to him. The old man's glasses and hat were knocked to the ground, his bundle bounced away, but he remained on his feet, while his tattooed assailant was restrained and led away by his friends, several of them shouting, "Remember Pearl Harbor!"

Another marshal, afraid of more incidents, quickly read the roster and urged people into the old bus.

Just as Warren tossed his bundles into the bus's baggage compartment, he felt a tap on his shoulder and, for a moment, expected a fist to smack his jaw. He turned and faced Coach Nizibian from the high school. "We're really gonna miss you this year, Scooter," the coach told him. "There goes our championship."

"Tell the guys I said so long," Warren rasped, his voice turning soft. "And tell that punk Arnie Presley I'm gonna pound the pud out of him when I get back."

"We're really gonna miss you," Coach said again, his handshake lingering, his own voice softening.

"Charley," Coach smiled, rumpling Charles's hair, "you let Scooter teach you a few moves. I'm gonna count on you in three or four years.

Mr. Takeda, these're fine boys." He shook Father's hand. "And I want you to know how sorry I am, and ashamed." Both men's eyes glistened.

Mother and Hideko were already in the bus when Father and the boys joined them. Just as they found seats and settled, they heard a rumpus outside. A large man in a business suit was arguing with the U.S. marshals. "I just wanta say a few words . . ." he urged, but the marshals said no. A man sitting behind the Takedas – Father recognized him as Mr. Takeuchi, who owned a small market in town – growled that the loud man was Harry Livingstone, president of the local chapter of the Native Sons of the Golden West. "He's a big windbag," Mr. Takeuchi added.

The bus was started and two soldiers who looked very young and frightened carried their rifles in and sat in front seats next to two marshals. From outside the bus, just as it began to move, Livingstone shouted: "We don't want you Nips back ever!" And many of the spectators who had seemed merely curious before were suddenly screaming and shouting, even throwing a few rocks and clods, their faces unrecognizable as the bus picked up speed. "Here we go," Mother sighed. Hideko, trembling on Mother's lap, did not open her eyes.

They arrived at the relocation camp late and were told they'd be processed the next day. It was dark, but they could clearly see the racetrack and the maze of stables behind it and the high wire fence around it, and they could smell the somehow comforting aroma of horse manure. Everyone stood as though stunned – eyes furtive and frightened – until soldiers marched them into a smaller, penned yard and building – "Holding Area One" the sergeant called it.

Mother carried Hideko, whose eyes remained tightly shut, into the barracks. It was empty and echoing, containing only metal cots without mattresses. Everyone was tired and hungry, but they bustled about, trying to make the best of things. One old man suddenly began shouting over and over that they were going to be shot, but he calmed quickly when friends comforted him. A soldier stood at the door of the building and announced that one member of each family could come to the mess to collect rations. For a moment no one moved. Was this the firing squad? Then slowly people began wandering toward the open door which framed the barbed-wire fence outside.

Sitting on the bare springs of a cot, Mother rocked Hideko, purred to her: "It's all right now, baby. It's all right," until finally Hideko stirred, sitting up though still leaning on Mother's chest and clasping Raggedy. She opened her bright brown eyes and looked down the hollow building and out the open doorway.

"Mommy," she asked quietly, "when are we going home . . . to America?"

Mother jolted, and her eyes at first seemed blank, then she focused on their surroundings. "Home," she said. "I'm not sure where that is anymore."

Charles glanced at his older brother, made a face, then grinned, but Warren poked him. He understood the gravity in his mother's voice, and it frightened him.

Father reached out and touched Mother's arm, saying only, "Hon' . . ."

Her chin was suddenly quivering, and she gazed stonily ahead. "No, I mean it! I wonder if we've ever *really* been home in America!"

Father's voice was certain when he replied, "This is our land, hon'. *Ours*. We were born here. Our folks helped make it what it is. We've got as much claim to it as anyone. Don't let those damned racists ruin it for you."

Her expression did not change. "Our land," she said, as she gazed down the long barracks toward barbs clustered like thorns on the wire enclosing them.

RISING ACTION

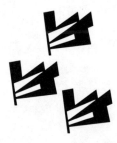

      I am pushing a shopping cart through Safeway behind my mother when another, younger woman wearing white slacks strolls up the aisle ahead of us. Gazing at her slim flanks, I note VPL – the beguiling Visible Panty Line – and, while I am far from certain exactly what nestles within that outlined territory, my own Levi's are suddenly the scene of rising action. My pace slows and soon I cease walking at all.

Ahead, the VPL has stopped to inspect a product, so I can keep her flanks in view. Beneath those slacks, she wears white panties, and I can see her clad only in them, beckoning. Except for an occasional sloppy sitter at school, I've never seen any occupied underwear, although the silken empties at a women's lingerie display can send me breathless in search of a lockable door. My imagination, unlimited by knowledge, veers toward unspeakable realms.

I begin a slow friction-strut, tasting my own breath. My mother has continued her own measured stroll, unaware of the momentous event within my Levi's. "Ernest, will you *please* catch up!" Her voice sears me. I manage to ease beside her and she demands, "Why are you *walking* so funny and why were you *looking* so funny at that lady? Do you know her?"

My mouth opens, but no sound emerges. I try again, croaking, "Ahhh . . . no . . . I guess."

"Why are you *talking* so funny? I don't know what's wrong with you. Look how you're standing! I'm going to take you to Doctor Marconcini," she admonishes, and immediately I see my meager artillery lying limp and bloody on one table, me singing countertenor on another, while our family doctor stands nearby holding a red scalpel.

Mom turns to the VPL woman, who is passing, smiles, and shakes her head, "Boys!"

The white panties nod and smile back, then glance at me. Despite the scalpel scene, I am certain that I see interest in those knowing eyes, and I think of the bathroom and the lock on its door as I see her hips slide around the corner into another aisle. I am taking her there, rolling in the bathtub with her, wrestling in the clothes hamper, romping on the commode.

"Will you come *on*. And *stop* walking so funny. Did you hurt yourself at school?"

I struggle to keep up, prancing slowly like a crane on the hunt, a rapturous dance.

The next day after junior varsity football practice, Buzzer Gaona – proprietor of the ninth grade's only mustache – announces to Bobby Silva and me, "Hey, ladies that use those Kotex deals, they do it, man."

I have seen a Kotex box in our bathroom, so I demand, "Who told *you?*"

"Everybody knows that, don't they, Silva?"

Bobby is not certain. "I . . . guess," he stammers.

"I sneaked in the girls' bathroom at school and found some, man." Buzzer nods knowingly. "Some of the girls at school, they done it. If your mother uses 'em, she done it too, man."

"You better watch it," I warn.

"Everybody's mother done it at least once."

Silva looks troubled. "Maybe it was a mistake," he pleads. "Maybe mine didn't *know*."

"Some of 'em *like* it, man."

"You better watch it, Gaona," I growl, outrage pushing me toward recklessness.

He ignores me. "Mrs. Calloway done it, man. She gots two babies, don't she?" Mrs. Calloway is the women's P.E. teacher at the high school. Her tan legs have entwined me in dreams. Despite my lingering anger, there is rising action.

"Does she like it, do you think?" asks Silva.

"Heck, yeah, man. She gots them big jugs. They get those from doin' it all the time."

"No lie? You mean all the girls with big boobs do it?" asks Silva.

"Heck, yeah, man. They *like* it."

My mother is flat-chested, so I breathe more easily in spite of the rising action. I will not have to fight the formidable Gaona.

"Anyway, I was just kiddin' about your mothers, man," he adds with a tight laugh. "I got you guys pissed, huh?"

"No way," I insist.

A week later, I am leaning against the wall of the gym during lunch hour with Silva and Gaona. After a dull silence, Buzzer announces, "Brandy done it, man."

"Brandy did it?" I ask, a little stunned. Bedelia "Brandy" Vigil, a busty classmate, has been dating varsity football players. She is cute and the very chance that she might be doing it . . . well, action rises. In my mind I can suddenly see her soft brown body involved with mine. My breathing quickens. "I gotta go," I announce.

"This guy on the varsity, he told me he felt her up, man."

Action continues rising because, although I'm not exactly certain *how* it's done, I can see her doing it with the team, all of them, with the team manager, even with the bald-headed coach, and with me, rolling around the locker room among the towels. "See you guys," I choke.

These images are sinful, so next day I must go to confession. Guilt has lately burdened me. Brother Mario, our religion teacher, has been stressing what he calls evil thoughts, sins of self-abuse and inevitable damnation. "You are being tested," he warns, and his eyes always seem to meet mine. "Those who abuse their flesh in this world will have it *stripped* from them *eternally* in the next, *burned* and *twisted* and *torn*." He seems to relish each word like rare beef.

"When evil thoughts invade and you find yourself in the near occasion of sin," he advises, his eyes boring into me as though he can see the scene of Brandy and me that I am even then imagining, "a sincere Hail Mary will ease temptation."

But when evil thoughts encroach, I become the Shakespeare of eroticism and forget his advice entirely, then end up uttering a remorseful Act of Contrition instead of a prophylactic Hail Mary. As a result, each week I have been entering the confessional to cleanse myself – if only temporarily – of sin.

It is roulette with eternity, since I often manage only a few hours of sanctity before rising action sweeps me back toward flesh eternally burned and twisted and torn. I walk in fear of lightning bolts and runaway cars, of rabid dogs and wayward bullets, those dangers that might pluck me unconfessed at some capricious moment, full of sin and doomed. And that means I must regularly close a dark confessional door to earn a few minutes or hours of safety from Hell, then begin the cycle again – literally a spiritual rat on a treadmill to eternity.

This sacrament is vital, but there are necessary strategies. First of all, avoid certain priests: Father Riley, Father Perdue, Father Garcia, and Father Duggan – they are lecturers and they will expose you to a half-hour of purgatory at every opportunity. Seek priests reputed to be gentle, even somnolent, confessors – old Father Flaherty or Father Cronin or Father Dominguez; those three are famous among adolescent males because they rarely bother to admonish, only grunt, assign three Hail Marys, and offer absolution. Second, try not to engage any one priest too frequently so that he doesn't become familiar and recognize your habitual sins. Travel from parish to parish if necessary, even across town to St. Joseph's or Guadalupe or Perpetual Help in order to evade detection. Third, *never never never* confess to a missionary priest.

In search of Father Dominguez, I take a city bus all the way to Our Lady of Guadalupe Church for confession. The line of those waiting to unburden themselves is long and after nearly half an hour I realize that each individual seems to be spending considerable time in the booth. More ominous still, as I move closer I am hearing the dangerous rumbling of an unfamiliar voice from within those three darkened doors. I debate whether to leave and catch a bus to St. Joseph's in the hope of finding Father Cronin, but time is short; I could never make it. Well, I can leave – except that everyone else would notice my belated departure and someone would surely recognize me, perhaps tell my mother.

Quickly, I hatch a plan: I'll groan softly a few times, then more loudly, and grab my stomach. I'll double over slightly, then limp toward the bathroom in the vestibule. From there I can sprint to freedom. I have not avoided exposure for so long without resourcefulness, and this plan ranks with the best. I begin with a few short, soft moans, hurrying because I am only two people away from the now ominous confessional door. Immediately, I feel a strong tap on my shoulder and hear a familiar voice: "What's wrong, Ernest? Are you ill?" It is Dr. Marconcini who has, unnoticed, been in line behind me.

"No . . . no, sir," I improvise, "just gas."

"Do you want an antacid?"

"No, sir."

"You eat too fast," he adds, then returns to his place.

I am stuck now. I cannot flee. There is nothing left to do but quickly devise a plan for the confession itself, but just as my mind begins to churn, ashen-faced Billy Castro, an eighth grader I know slightly, emerges from the booth, rolls haggard eyes, and whispers the dreaded words, "A *missionary*, man!" He looks as though he has been burned and twisted and torn. Suddenly I really do feel sick, but it is too late. I am next and I must enter.

Kneeling in the darkness, I carefully plan my confession. I have become expert at hiding my most heinous offense. Employ unspecific terms to describe it and slip the explanations quickly into the midst of small sins. I line up the venial infractions, and decide where and how to obscure my great and repeated crime.

I am nervous but growing increasingly confident in my tested strategy – it has rarely failed me – when the small window slides open and finally I can get it over with. To begin, I acknowledge that I've had a nasty dream (the priest only grunts), that I've told a white lie to a friend (he grunts again), then I whisper quickly, slurring my words, "I have committed the sin of self-abuse, and I . . ."

"You have committed what?"

"I have committed the sin of self-abuse."

"What is this, this 'sin of self-abuse'? What sin is this?"

"Against the Sixth Commandment," I breathe.

"With yourself or others?" His tone has hardened.

Uh-oh! "Myself." I want to move on, so I add, "and I was late for mass once."

"What did you do?"

"I was just late."

"What did you do with *yourself?*" He is louder now, and I am afraid that those waiting outside can hear him, maybe even Dr. Marconcini.

"I played with myself," I gasp in a voice so faint that I am not certain that I hear it myself.

"Speak up!"

"Played with myself."

"Played with yourself? What does this mean?"

"Touched myself for pleasure," I mutter, using a term I learned in religion class.

"*Speak up!*"

I repeat so quickly that it sounds like one word. "Touchedmyselffor-pleasure."

"Touched yourself where?"

I gulp. "In the bathroom, mostly."

"Where on your *body?* And *speak up!*" I cringe at the sharpness of his tone.

I cannot immediately reply, so he adds, "Others are waiting."

"My private parts," I choke, wanting to flee, tensed for a sprint.

"Your *what?* You touch yourself *there* for pleasure, where God allows *only* procreation. Those are not *your* private parts, they are *God's* and you are abusing them! Do you spill your seed?"

Spill my seed? Oh, God . . .

"*Do you spill your seed?*" he demands.

"I guess."

"You *guess?*" His tone strips my flesh.

"Yes . . . I . . . do . . . spill . . . my . . . seed." My words are dead as clay.

"*How old are you?*" His voice has risen to a muted shout. Everyone is hearing this. Dr. Marconcini, I am certain, is scribbling notes.

"Fifteen," I whisper.

"*Speak up!*"

"Fifteen."

"And how often did you do this *terrible* thing?"

"Two times."

"*Speak up!*" His voice seems to echo through the church.

I have been in the confessional at least an hour – a world record – and I am despairing of ever escaping it. I will grow old here, that missionary shouting, "*Speak up!*" in my bruised ear, a great hoary beard caressing my knees, filling this small room until I suffocate. This is the anatomy of Hell. "Two times," I gasp.

"You did this *terrible* thing two times in just one week?"

"A day," I add as softly as human breath can escape.

"A *day! A day! A DAY!* You are a *ROTTEN* boy and you will *ROAST* in hell for your perversion!" People a block away are listening, I know, they are rushing from all directions to hear this, clustering in front of the church, a great grinning hoard, but I am so battered that by now I want only to accept what follows and escape.

I am willing to be castrated, to become a Trappist monk and to never speak again, to do *anything*. I will never again sin. I will never touch myself. I will never so much as *look* at a female, but please God, let me leave this booth. "I will give you absolution this time," fumes the priest, "but you had *better* turn your *rotten* life over to Our Lady or you will be cast into the flames where there is much moaning and gnashing of teeth!"

I am already moaning and gnashing my teeth, so when he assigns my penance and absolves me, I slink from the confessional, feeling the weight of eyes on my miserable, my doomed and utterly exposed form. I refuse to look up, for I am certain that spectators have now come in from the street to stare at me, that programs listing my various abuses are being sold at the door.

Eyes down, I slip into a pew and begin to say the rosary, my penance. I will not look up or around and, in the back of my mind, I have decided to remain in this pew until everyone else in the church has departed: I cannot face them, their sneers or their snickers.

"Hail Mary full of grace the Lord is with thee . . ." I am halfway through my third decade of prayers and beginning to calm somewhat when someone slips into the pew ahead of me. For a moment, I do not look up, then I do and realize that it is Brandy Vigil. She kneels and quietly prays. I lower my eyes, then lift them, my vision stopping just below her belt line where her sweet bottom lurks, an upside-down valentine in a tight red skirt, the near-occasion of sin placed there to tempt me, to ascertain whether this confession, this final chance at salvation, has been wasted, so I look down again, but in doing so I notice her slim brown ankles, one encircled by a golden chain. Something seems to pulse beneath that gold, and, just above it, the satin swelling of her calf twitches. Rising action.

I say three more rapid Hail Marys, but the passion does not abate. I add a Glory Be, yet the denim titillates and my breath shortens. I struggle through three more desperate Hail Marys. Then my eyes notice Brandy's VPL and I am seized by images of her lovely brown body with mine in a hammock, spinning, struggling together, slick with sweat.

When she stands and leaves, I remain kneeling, glazed with the knowledge that I am committing the gravest of all sins here in the gravest of all places, and that I must somehow return to that confessional if I am to avoid perdition. I squeeze my eyes closed, but all I can see is her anklet, her VPL. Finally, I stand and turn. The church is almost vacant. Near the entry loom those confessionals, three small doors, dark and apparently bare except for the middle one above which a small light is ignited, warning that the missionary lies in wait. Next to them, I behold the orange and red of an early sunset framed by the church's open front portal.

"ROTTEN!" still rings in my ears – that relentless judgment, that overwhelming force from which nothing is hidden, awaits my sin in the confessional, marshaling its prodigious power to finally refuse me absolution. I fear damnation, but I cannot this day return to that small dark box.

After a moment I swallow hard, then plunge out the door into the flaming world. I hesitate on the church's steps. It's not too late to return to the missionary, then I spy curvaceous Brandy Vigil standing across the street, perhaps waiting for a ride. She notices me and smiles, waves slightly. My breath catches and there is . . . there is gentle but undeniable rising action. I hesitate only a moment, then lift one hand and wave to her. "Hey, Brandy," I call with sudden abandon, "can I buy you a Coke?"

She smiles and nods, and without looking back I move from the church's portal toward the ruddy light of a larger world.

Driving with Gerry

I have never ridden in a pickup truck with Gerald W. Haslam while the busted speedometer glowed o and the radio twanged country music from a cracked speaker. But I can picture such a homely ride. The backdrop is a wheat-colored sun dipping down in the San Joaquin Valley. Road kills dot the littered highway, the paws of dogs and rabbits pointing toward heaven – a good sign. There are tumbleweeds snagged on fences, and in the furrowed fields, a tractor with its plume of black smoke. It's a good day for my spiffed-up friend, who is wearing a plaid cowboy shirt with imitation pearl snaps. A red kerchief around his neck flaps in the wind, and an ornate belt buckle with a silver dollar pressed in place winks in the sunlight. He smiles through his cologne – Brut or Aqua Velva – nothing fancy, but its sweetness enchants the valley. He turns to me and says, "*Amigo*, this is a hot-ass valley, and I love it!" He may or may not be sucking on a fresh piece of alfalfa. He will be nursing, though, a Pepsi, the sugary drink of all happy-go-lucky Okies.

Unfortunately, I haven't had the fortune of driving the San Joaquin Valley with Gerry. If I had, I might have heard a story – one completely fiction, or hearsay, or pulled from his childhood with his large bare feet planted in work and play. Perhaps we can soon drive south, down U.S. 99 with Bakersfield to our left and Taft and Oildale to the right, towns busting at their seams.

At a barbecue I once heard Gerry tell a story about playing football for Sacramento State, that is, warming the bench through a leafless fall. It was the late 1950s, and what better sight than young people crushing each other at the beginning of fall? The coach could have slapped his clipboard against his leg and shouted, "Haslam, get in there and do something! We're down by a hundred." But he didn't. Instead he asked for Gerry's jersey when a running back – a regular – tore his. So under the glare of stadium lights and ten thousand spectators, Gerry had to strip his jersey, his green and gold school pride, and hand it over to the coach.

Gerry Haslam is an essayist, regional historian, short story writer, and novelist. He is also a professor of English, a mystery to the local boys who grew up with him. Luckily we don't need a pickup truck on a valley highway to hear Gerry out. We have these pages, and the pages of his earlier books, to hear his stories of the valley. Gerry knows this place, in both its humanity and its geography, as he illustrated in his essays in *The Great Central Valley* – a book that at first appears to be coffee-table material but on closer reading is both thoughtful and scholarly. Better yet, he has explored this sun-brutal terrain first as a boy in Oildale and later as a man who has moved around the state of California and beyond. He has lived the valley through its people, from Mexican to Okie to Armenian to Portuguese to Yokut Indian – the wily crop of inhabitants who have assembled their lives and families in this valley. He knows the place, of this much I'm convinced, and his appreciation of valley life has deepened.

Haslam is a fine stylist and for many years I thought his prose had a literary kinship with that of Sherwood Anderson, a writer who lived what he wrote, with no qualms about being American – not European – in his stories. Both writers have scratched at new surfaces – Anderson at the flatness of Ohio and Haslam at the walled-in valley of central California. Both started humbly. Both served in the army, married, fathered children, and eked out a living first by labor and later by their wits. Finally, both felt tender about the experiences of everyday life. But while Anderson was primarily interested in the subliminal nature of his small-town characters, the understated and "grotesque" nature of manners, Haslam is drawn to portrayal of characters set in drama. Haslam is less interested in commentary than he is in a plain good story in which action precedes meaning. If we look at *Winesburg, Ohio*, we can see that Anderson was given over to large passages where the narrator describes the inner actions of his characters. He explained, truthfully, but seldom allowed the characters to speak for themselves. In turn, Haslam lets them speak in their valley drawl, even if what is mustered up by the characters, all poor and working class, some even drunk beyond memory, is outrageous gibberish. Haslam uses dialogue to his benefit. He lets them spit out their love, anger, craziness, and loneliness. This is the excitement of this new collection: talk that goes on and on while the characters with names like Haig, Flaco, Shorty, and Cleve tear up the world with life.

Haslam's voice can be reflective, wise, and delicately instructive. The opening story, "Condor Dreams," is a quiet tale of a father and son in an agricultural valley, the disappearance of nature, and a condor that serves as metaphor. It's about the passage of time: The father dies, pulled away by an unexpected flood in an arroyo. Years pass. The son becomes a boyish man who can't handle his father's farm. He still lives under the rule of memory and the prodding of his father's worker, Don Felipe, a half-Mexican, half-Yokuts Indian. The son is confused and full of vengeance that no weeping can resolve because the bank is taking over his farm. It's a telling reversal: A son finds self-knowledge and redemption through a sagacious worker, dusty with age.

In turn, Haslam can be whimsical and so funny that we may wonder whether what we are reading is from the same author. This is true of "Mal de Ojo," in which a boy sits at the feet of two Armenian brothers jabbing each other with offhand memories. The boy is mostly curious about Haig, the brother with an eye patch and crusty pronouncements of wisdom. Haig tells a story of one of the longest fistfights in small-town history: "We fought all the way up Van Ness Avenue to Blackstone, and then we fought for a mile down Blackstone. . . . The police stood back in awe to watch such a battle. Businesses closed. . . ." It's a confirmed yarn, though. The boy later realizes that Haig has been switching his patch from eye to eye, and that it's *he* – the boy – who is blind to trickery.

Haslam's stories are primarily the stories of men, some of them bright and courageous and some of them dim as twenty-watt bulbs. They drink a lot of beer and drive around, seldom getting anywhere. They sit in taverns, nursing beers, their lives used up in high school or early marriages. They hunker down on riverbanks where the cottonwoods hang over the water and muse over their lost youth. They speak about the ground-level advice that worked in the 1950s. Haslam has caught the pitch of these men – Okie or Mexican, farmer or farmworker, veteran or rowdy citizen – without parody. These are characters we know or have seen in passing, characters we make room for when they start to fight. In all their humor and craziness, in all their unexpected trials into manhood, there is a sadness that shadows our own lives, even if we're not from the valley and can't spit in a shallow river that pushes along on its own.

Gerry and I could jump into the cab of that pickup truck and take a wild ride through the valley. It would be early September, the almond trees letting loose their leaves and grape trays heavy with drying raisins. The sun is flush against the coastal mountains. A blackbird, big as a boot, sits on a wire and the Johnson grass has flattened from wind and the lack of rain. I look at the gauges: The speedometer won't flicker or the odometer roll to add up our miles. I turn to my friend and teasingly ask, "Gerry, what's this 'W' in your name mean when you write books?" He turns to me, imitation pearl snaps and all, and jokes, "Wily. Gerald 'Wily' Haslam."

Gary Soto
August 1993

ACKNOWLEDGMENTS

The author wishes to thank the editors of the following publications, where some of the stories originally appeared. All of the stories were copyrighted by the author in the year of original publication and are used here with his permission.

"The Killing Pen." *Tawte: A Journal of Texas Culture*. Summer 1975.
"Widder Maker." *Drilling*. December 1975.
"Home to America." *Sonoma Mandala*. Spring 1976.
"Medicine." *Scree*. Fall 1976.
"Return, Prodigal." *The Wages of Sin*. Duck Down Press, 1980.
"The Last Roundup." *Toward the Twenty-first Century*. Red Earth
    Press, 1981.
"Madstone." *Hawk Flights*. Seven Buffaloes Press, 1983.
"The Souvenir." *Cross Timbers Review*. Autumn 1984.
"Sojourner." *Unknown California*. Macmillan, 1985.
"The Condor." *Amapola*. 1986.
"Road Kill." *AKA Magazine*. Winter 1988.
"Rising Action." In *Eroticism: From Sublime to Grotesque*. California
    State University, Long Beach, 1989.
"It's Over." *Chiron Review*. Summer 1991.
"Romain Pettibone's Revenge." In *Contemporary American Satire II*.
    Exile Press, 1992.

WESTERN LITERATURE SERIES

Western Trails:
A Collection of Short Stories by Mary Austin
selected and edited by Melody Graulich

Cactus Thorn
by Mary Austin

Dan De Quille, the Washoe Giant:
A Biography and Anthology
prepared by Richard A. Dwyer & Richard E. Lingenfelter

Desert Wood: An Anthology of Nevada Poets
edited by Shaun T. Griffin

The City of Trembling Leaves
by Walter Van Tilburg Clark

Many Californias: Literature from the Golden State
edited by Gerald W. Haslam

The Authentic Death of Hendry Jones
by Charles Neider

First Horses: Stories of the New West
by Robert Franklin Gish

Torn by Light: Selected Poems
by Joanne de Longchamps
edited by Shaun T. Griffin

Swimming Man Burning
by Terrence A. Kilpatrick

The Temptations of St. Ed and Brother S
by Frank Bergon

The Other California:
The Great Central Valley in Life and Letters
by Gerald W. Haslam

The Track of the Cat
by Walter Van Tilburg Clark

Condor Dreams and Other Fictions
by Gerald W. Haslam